Angela Thirkell

Angela Thirkell, granddaughter of Edward Burne Jones, was born in London in 1890. At the age of twenty-eight she moved to Melbourne, Australia where she became involved in broadcasting and was a frequent contributor to the British periodicals. Mrs. Thirkell did not begin writing novels until her return to Britain in 1930; then, for the rest of her life, she produced a new book almost every year. Her stylish prose and deft portrayal of the human comedy in the imaginary county of Barsetshire have amused readers for decades. She died in 1961 just before her seventy-first birthday.

"Mrs. Thirkell's novel is very funny indeed."
—Graham Green, *London Times Literary Suppliment*

"Satirical, ironic, frankly farcical though it is at times, through all the books there glows the steady beacon light of courage."
—*The New York Times*

"These are novels full of what might be called applied literature, whole lifetimes of shared reading welling up allusively in conversation. The reader hears the constant sound of familiar authors passing back and forth behind the scenes, like servants heading from the kitchen to the dining room in great English houses. And yet the talk is wonderful because it is simply neighborhood gossip. The war encroaches on Barsetshire, but the gossip continues, against a broader, grimmer backdrop."
—Verlyn Klinkenborg, *The New York Times*

Table of Explanation

Roads..............	
Railways..........	+++++++++
Rivers.............	
Towns.............	HOGGLESTOCK
Parish Villages...	Puddingdale
Small Villages....	Little Misfit
Mansions..........	*Pomfret Towers*

0 1 2 3 4 5

Scale of Miles

artletop Priory

N

Lufton Park

WEST

BARSETSHIR

Silverbridge

GREAT WESTERN R

rleybridge

Hallbury

River Rising

River Rising

Framley

Framley

Harefield

Gatherum
Castle

Crabtree
Parva

BARCHESTER

Rushmere Brook

Uffley

Chaldicotes

Brandon
Abbey

Rushwater

Courcy

Northbridge

Plumstead E

Rushwater House

Marling

ington
tation

to Allington

Marling
Hall

River Rising

The River

School

Southbridge

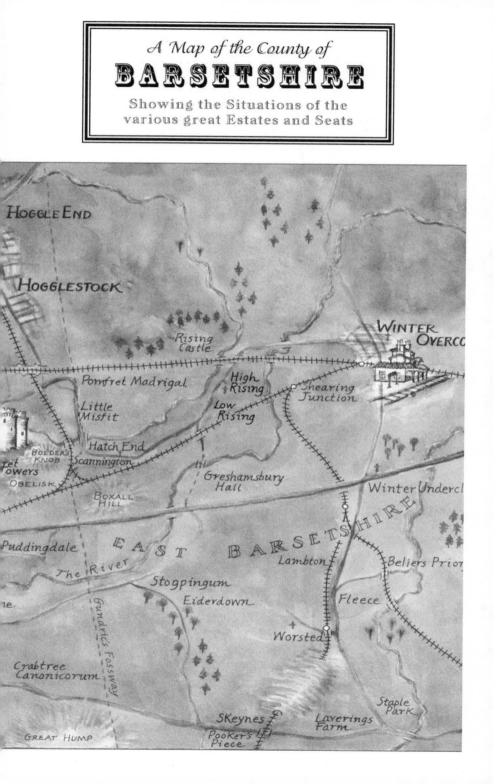

A Map of the County of
BARSETSHIRE
Showing the Situations of the various great Estates and Seats

HOGGLE END

HOGGLESTOCK

Rising Castle

WINTER OVERCO

Pomfret Madrigal

High Rising

Shearing Junction

Little Misfit

Low Rising

Hatch End

BOLDERS KNOB

Scannington

et owers

OBELISK

Greshamsbury Hall

Winter Undercl

BOXALL HILL

Puddingdale

EAST BARSETSHIRE

Lambton

Beliers Prior

The River

Stogpingum

Fleece

Eiderdown

Gundric's Fossway

Crabtree Canonicorum

Worsted

Staple Park

GREAT HUMP

Skeynes

Pooker's Piece

Laverings Farm

Three Houses (1931)
Ankle Deep (1933)
High Rising (1933)
Demon in the House, The (1934)
O, These Men, These Men (1935)
August Folly (1936)
Coronation Summer (1937)
Summer Half (1937)
Pomfret Towers (1938)
Before Lunch (1939)
The Brandons (1939)
Cheerfulness Breaks In (1940)
Northbridge Rectory (1941)
Marling Hall (1942)
Growing Up (1943)
Headmistress, The (1944)
Miss Bunting (1945)
Peace Breaks Out (1946)
Private Enterprise (1947)
Love Among the Ruins (1948)
Old Bank House, The (1949)
County Chronicle (1950)
Duke's Daughter, The (1951)
Happy Return (1952)
Jutland Cottage (1953)
What Did It Mean? (1954)
Enter Sir Robert (1955)
Never Too Late (1956)
Double Affair, A (1957)
Close Quarters (1958)
Love At All Ages (1959)
Three Score and Ten (1961)

WILD STRAWBERRIES

A Novel by

Angela Thirkell

 MOYER BELL

Kingston, Rhode Island & Lancaster, England

Published by Moyer Bell
This Edition 2008
Copyright © 1934, 1992, 2008 by the Executors of
Angela Thirkell

Published by arrangement with Hamish I Hamilton, Ltd. All
rights reserved. No part of this publication may be reproduced
or transmitted in any form or by any means, electronic or
mechanical, including photocopying, recording or any information retrieval system, without permission in writing from
Moyer Bell, 549 Old North Road, Kingston, Rhode Island
02881 or Moyer Bell, c/o Gazelle Book Services Ltd., White
Cross Mills, High Town, Lancaster LA1 1RN England

LIBRARY OF CONGRESS
CATALOGING-IN-PUBLICATION DATA

Thirkell, Angela Mackail, 1890-1961.
Wild Strawberries: a novel by Angela Thirkell
        —1st ed.
240 p. 21.5 cm.
1. Barsetshire (England: Imaginary place)—Fiction.
2. French--England--Fiction. 3. Country homes--Fiction.
4 Royalists--Fiction. 5. Royalists--Fiction.
I. Title.
PZ3.T3486 Wi PR6039.H43   2008
ISBN 978-1-55921-324-0   34020931
                                 CIP

Cover Illustration by Childe Hassam, *Geraniums*

Printed in the United States of America.

Distributed in North America by
Moyer Bell, 549 Old North Road, Kingston, Rhode Island 02881,
401–783–5480, www.moyerbellbooks.com
and in the United Kingdom, Eire, and Europe by
Gazelle Book Services Ltd., White Cross Mills, High Town,
Lancaster LA1 1RN England,
1–44–1524–68765, www.gazellebooks.co.uk

TO
My Father and Mother

CONTENTS

WILD STRAWBERRIES

CHAPTER I
MORNING SERVICE

THE VICAR of St. Mary's, Rushwater, looked anxiously through the vestry window which commanded a view of the little gate in the churchyard wall. Through this gate the Leslie family had come to church with varying degrees of unpunctuality ever since the vicar had been at Rushwater, nor did it seem probable that they had been more punctual before his presentation to the living. It was a tribute to the personality of Lady Emily Leslie, the vicar reflected, that everyone who lived with her became a sharer in her unpunctuality, even to the week-end guests. When first the vicar came to St. Mary's, the four Leslie children were still in the nursery. Every Sunday had been a nervous exasperation for him as the whole family poured in, halfway through the General Confession, Lady Emily dropping prayer books and scarves and planning in loud, loving whispers where everyone was to sit. During the War the eldest boy had been in France, John, the second boy, at sea, and Rushwater House was a convalescent home. But Lady Emily's vitality was unabated and her attendance at morning service more annoying than ever to the harassed vicar, as she shepherded her convalescent patients into her pew, giving unnecessary help with crutches, changing the position of hassocks, putting shawls round grateful embarrassed men to protect them from imaginary draughts, talking in a penetrating whisper which distracted the vicar from his service, behaving altogether as if church was a friend's house. There came a moment at which he felt it to be his duty for the sake of other worshippers to beg her to be a little more punctual and a little less managing. But before he had summoned up enough courage to speak, the news came that the eldest son had been killed. When the vicar saw, on the following Sunday, Lady Emily's handsome face, white and ravaged, he vowed as he prayed that he would never let himself criticize her again. And although on that very Sunday she had so bestirred herself with cushions and hassocks for the comfort of her wounded soldiers that they heartily wished they were back in hospital, and though she had invented a system of silent communication with Holden, the sexton, about shutting a window, thus. absorbing the attention of the entire congregation, the vicar had not then, nor ever since, faltered from his vow.

At her daughter Agnes's wedding to Colonel Graham she had for once been on time, but her attempts to rearrange the order of the bridesmaids during the actual ceremony and her insistence on leaving her pew to provide the bridegroom's mother with an unwanted hymnbook had been a spectacular part of the wedding. As for the confirmation of David, the youngest, the vicar still woke trembling in the small hours at the thought of the reception which Lady Emily had seen fit to hold in the chancel afterwards, though apparently without in the least offending the bishop.

Rushwater adored her. The vicar knew perfectly well that Holden deliberately prolonged his final bell-ringing to give Lady Emily every chance, but had never had the courage to charge him with it. Just then the gate clicked and the Leslie family entered the churchyard. The vicar, much relieved, turned from the window and made ready to go into the church.

It was a large family party that had come over from Rushwater House. Lady Emily, slightly crippled of late with arthritis, walked with a black crutch stick, holding her second son, John's, arm. Her husband walked on her other side. Agnes Graham followed with two nannies and three children. Then came David with Martin, the Leslies' eldest grandson, a schoolboy of about sixteen. It was his father who had been killed in the War.

Lady Emily halted her cavalcade in the porch.

"Now, Nannie," she said, "wait a minute and we will see where everyone is to go. Now, who is having communion?"

Both the nurses looked away with refined expressions. "Not you, Nannie, and not Ivy, I suppose," said Lady Emily.

"Ivy can go to early communion any morning she wishes, my lady," said Nannie, icily broadminded. "I'm chapel myself."

Lady Emily's face became distraught.

"Agnes," she cried, laying her gloved hand on her daughter's arm, "what have I done? I didn't know Nannie was chapel. Could we arrange for one of the men to run her down to the village if it isn't too late? I'm afraid it's Weston's day off, but I dare say one of the other men could drive the Ford. Or won't it matter?"

Agnes Graham turned her lovely placid eyes on her mother.

"It's quite all right, mamma," she said in her soft, comfortable voice. "Nannie likes coming to church with the children, don't you, Nannie? She doesn't count it as religion."

"I was always brought up to the saying Thy will not Mine, my lady," said Nannie, suddenly importing a controversial tone into the conversation, and know where my duty lies. Baby, don't pull those gloves off, or granny won't take you to the nice service."

"For Heaven's sake, Emily," interrupted Mr. Leslie advancing, tall, fresh-faced, heavily built, used to getting his own way except where his wife was concerned. "For Heaven's sake don't dawdle there talking. Poor old Banister is dancing in the pulpit and Holden has stopped ringing his passing bell. Come along."

No one knew whether Mr. Leslie was as ignorant of ecclesiastical matters as he pretended to be, but he had taken up from his earliest years the attitude that one word was as good as another.

"But, Henry, the question of communion is truly important," said Lady Emily earnestly. "The ones that wish to escape must sit on the outside edge of the pew and the ones that are staying must sit inside, to make less fuss. Only I must sit on the outside, because my knee gets so stiff if I sit inside, but if I go in the second pew with Nannie and Ivy and the children, they can all get past me quite well, can't they, Nannie?"

"Yes, my lady."

"Very well, then; you go in the front pew, Henry, with Agnes and David and Martin, and the rest of us will go behind. Only mind you put Agnes right inside against the wall, because she is staying for communion, and if she is outside you will have to walk over her and the boys too."

"But Martin and I aren't staying for communion," said David.

"No, darling? Well, just as you like. It is disappointing, in a way, because the vicar does dearly love a good house—but what I meant was that if Agnes were outside, you and your father and Martin would all have to walk over her, not that he would have to walk over her and you."

By this time Nannie, a young woman of strong character who was kind enough to tolerate her employers for the sake of the babies they provided, had taken her charges into the second pew and distributed Ivy and herself among them so that no two children should sit together. The rest of the party followed between the rows of the already kneeling congregation. Just as they came to the nursery pew, Lady Emily uttered a loud exclamation.

"John! I had forgotten about John. John, if you don't want any communion you had better go in front with David and

Martin and the others, only let your father have the corner seat."

John helped his mother to settle into her pew, and then slipped into the pew behind. Lady Emily dropped her stick with a clatter into the aisle. John got up and handed it to his mother, who flashed a brilliant smile at him and said in an audible aside:

"I can't kneel, you know, because of my stiff leg, but my spirit is on its knees."

But before her spirit could settle to its devotions she leant forward and tapped her husband's shoulder.

"Henry, are you reading the lessons?" she inquired. "What's that?" asked Mr. Leslie, through the *Venite*.

Lady Emily poked at Agnes with her stick.

"Darling," she whispered loudly, "is your father reading the lessons?"

"Of course I am," said Mr. Leslie. "Always read the lessons."

"Then, what are they?" asked Lady Emily. "I want to find them in the Bible for the children."

"I don't know," said Mr. Leslie, crossly. "Not my business."

"But, Henry, you must know."

Mr. Leslie turned his body round and glared at his wife.

"I don't know," he insisted, red in the face with his efforts to whisper gently, but angrily and audibly. "Holden marks the places for me. Look in your prayer book, Emily, you'll find it all in the beginning—number of the Beast or something."

With which piece of misinformation he turned round again and went on with his singing. As he announced the first lesson from the lectern, his wife repeated the book, chapter and verse aloud after him, adding, "Remember that, everyone." She then began to hunt through the Bible. Agnes's eldest child, James, who was just seven, looked at her efforts with some impatience.

"Just open it anywhere, granny," he whispered.

But his grandmother insisted not only on finding the place, but on pointing it out to all the occupants of both pews. By the time the second lesson was reached she had mislaid her spectacles, so James undertook to find the place for her. While he was doing this she leaned over to Nannie and said:

"Do you have the lessons in chapel?"

But Nannie, knowing her place, pretended not to hear.

When the vicar began his good and uninteresting sermon, James snuggled up to his grandmother. She put an arm round him and they sat comfortably together, thinking their very different thoughts. Never did Emily Leslie sit in her pew without thinking of the beloved dead: her first-born buried in France, and John's wife, Gay, who after one year of happiness had left him wifeless and childless. John had left the navy after the War, gone into business, and was doing well, but his mother often wondered if anyone or anything would ever have power to stir his heart again. Whenever he was off his guard his mother's heart was torn by the hard, set lines of his face. Otherwise he seemed happy enough, prospered, was thinking of Parliament, helped his father with the estate, was a kind uncle to Martin and to Agnes's children, went to dances, plays and concerts in London, rode and shot in the country. But Lady Emily sometimes felt that if she came up behind him quietly and suddenly she might see that he was nothing but a hollow mask.

Then there was Martin, so ridiculously like his dead father, and as happy as anyone of sixteen who knows he is really grown-up can expect to be. His mother had remarried, and though Martin was on excellent terms with his American stepfather, he made Rushwater his home, much to the secret joy of his grandparents. Inheritance and death duties were not words which troubled Martin much. He knew Rushwater would be his some day, but had the happy confidence of the young that their elders will live for ever. His most pressing thoughts at the moment were about the possible purchase of a motor bicycle on his seventeenth birthday, and his hopes that his mother would forget her plan of sending him to France for part of the summer holidays, It would be intolerable to have to go to that ghastly abroad when one might be at Rushwater and play for the village against neighbouring elevens. Also he wanted to be in England if David pulled off that job with the B.B.C.

David should by rights have been Uncle David, but though Martin dutifully gave his title to his Uncle John, he and David were on equal terms. David was only ten years older than he was, and not the sort of chap you could look on as an uncle. David was like an elder brother, only he didn't sit on you as much as some chaps' elder brothers did. David was the most perfect person one could imagine, and when one was older one would, with luck, be exactly like David. Like David one would dance divinely, play and sing all the latest jazz hits, be president of one's university dramatic society, write a play which was once acted on a Sunday, produce a novel which only really understanding people read, and perhaps, though here Martin's mind rather shied off the subject, have heaps of girls in love with one. But not for a long time.

It need hardly be said that the qualities which filled Martin with the pangs of hero-worship were not altogether those which David's parents would have most desired. If he had had to earn his living, David would have been a serious problem. But, owing to the ill-judged partiality of an aunt, he had been independent for some years. So he lived in town and had hankerings for the stage and the cinema and broadcasting, and every now and then his looks and his easy manners and his independent income landed him in a job, though not for long. And, as Martin had dimly surmised, heaps of girls had been in love with him. When the Leslies wished that David would settle down to a job and stick to it, they never failed to remind each other that the house would not be the same if David were not there so often.

Mr. Leslie was thinking partly how well he had dodged a difficult name in the first lesson, coughing and turning the page noisily as he came to it, and partly about a young bull whom he proposed to visit after lunch; and occasionally, why Emily couldn't be like other people.

As for John, he looked at his mother with her arm round James in the pew in front of him and wished, with the ache that was never far from his heart, that there were anyone whom he could hold close to him, even for a moment, even in the coolest way, with no disloyalty to Gay, only not to feel that emptiness at one's side, day and night.

"But I suppose one couldn't do it in church," he thought, and then, being his mother's son, nearly laughed out loud at his own thoughts and had to pretend it was a cold. Luckily the sermon came to an end at that moment, and among the shuffling of feet his voice was not conspicuous.

Just then his mother, loosening her hold of James, said in an anxious voice:

"This seems a good moment to escape."

John leant over.

"We can't yet, mother," he whispered; "we must stay for the collection, you know."

His mother nodded her head violently and asked James to find her bag. After a prolonged scuffle it was found under the hassock, just as the collecting-bag came round. Mr. Leslie stuffed some paper into it and passed it along the pew to Agnes, who handed it over the back of the pew to Nannie. The two younger children put their sixpence in, but James only smiled and showed empty hands.

"Here you are," said John, passing sixpence over.

"Thank you, Uncle John," said James, taking it, "but grandfather subscribes to the church, so we needn't give anything."

Short of wrenching the sixpence away from James by main force there was nothing to be done. The nursery party filed past Mrs. Leslie and left the church, followed by the men. Only Agnes remained with her mother.

John and his father strolled up and down in the sun, under the low churchyard wall, discussing the young bull.

"What have you called him, sir?" John asked.

The naming of Mr. Leslie's bulls was a matter of great moment. All had the pr[ae]nomen Rushwater, and each had a second name which had to begin with an R. Their owner, who bred them himself, attached great importance to this, trying to find names which would come easily to the tongues of the Argentine ranchers, by whom they were usually bought. But the supply of names which, in Mr. Leslie's opinion, could be easily attuned to a Spanish tongue, was nearly exhausted, and a good deal of his time and conversation had been devoted to the subject of late.

"I had thought of Rackstraw, or Richmond," said Mr. Leslie doubtfully. "But they don't sound Spanish enough to me."

"What does Macpherson say?"

Mr. Leslie made an angry noise.

"Macpherson may have been agent here for thirty years," he said, `but he hasn't any more sense than to suggest Rannoch. How does he think an Argentine is going to say Rushwater Rannoch?"

John admitted the difficulty, while mildly wondering why Argentines should be even less intelligent than other people.

"And now there's this business of letting the vicarage," said Mr. Leslie. "Banister will be away for August and wants to let. It's a confounded nuisance."

"But Banister's tenants needn't worry you, sir."

"He said something about Foreigners," said Mr. Leslie. "People he picked up somewhere abroad. One never seems to have any peace. Your mother will ask them all up to dinner here twice a week. I shall go abroad for August."

"Lots of foreigners there," said John.

"Yes, but they're all right in their place. It's here we don't want them. Buy British, you know. If it weren't for the foreigners we should be much better off."

"Then you wouldn't have any Argentines to buy your prize bulls."

"Foreigners, I said. Germans and French and that lot," said Mr. Leslie, who appeared to make a subtle distinction between the various branches of the non-English-speaking races.

"Aren't Argentines foreigners, too?" asked John, rather unkindly.

"When I was a boy, foreigners meant French and Germans and Italians," said Mr. Leslie with dignity.

At this moment Lady Emily came out of the church with Agnes. Her husband and son went to meet her.

She sat down on a bench in the porch and began to wind herself up in a long lavender-coloured scarf, talking all the while.

"Henry, I was thinking in church that if Agnes's niece, at least she is really her husband's niece, but Agnes is devoted to her, is coming to us for the summer, we might have a little dance for Martin's birthday in August. Perhaps a cricket match first and then a dance. Agnes, dear, see if you can find the other end of my scarf and give it to me—no, not that end, I know about that one, the other one, darling. That's right. It is so inconvenient having to take one's gloves off for communion, because I nearly always forget and it keeps Mr. Banister waiting."

By this time she had wound her head into an elaborate turban, very becoming to her handsome haggard face with its delicate aquiline nose, thin carved lips and bright dark eyes. With the help of John's arm she got up.

"Now my stick, Henry, and you might put that shawl over my shoulders and I don't think I shall put on my gloves just to walk home with. What have you and your father been talking about, John?"

"Bulls, mamma, and foreigners. Father says he will go abroad if Banister lets the vicarage to unsuitable tenants."

"No, Henry," exclaimed Lady Emily, stopping short and dropping her bag, "not really. Mr. Banister would feel it."

"Well, my dear," said her husband, picking up her bag, "he's going abroad himself and I don't see that it is any business of his where I go."

"We must have a good talk about it," said Lady Emily, continuing her progress through the churchyard gate and across her own rose garden, "thresh it out all together at lunch-time. It came to me, while we were having that awkward interval which happens while the people who don't stay for communion are escaping, that if we can get the roof of the pavilion mended, before the cricket really begins, it would be such a good thing. Henry, will you speak to Macpherson about it?"

"I did speak to him, Emily, last October, and it has been mended for the last six months."

"Of course it has," said Lady Emily, stopping to adjust her shawl, which was dragging on the ground. "I must have been thinking of that little shed away by the saw-mill, where David sometimes used to put his bicycle. Or was it something quite different? One's thoughts get so confused in church."

As no one seemed equal to discovering what she had really been thinking about, she resumed her way, leaving a trail of belongings behind her for her family to collect, and disappeared into the house.

CHAPTER II
THE LESLIES AT LUNCH

RUSHWATER HOUSE WAS A LARGE, rather Gothic house built by Mr. Leslie's grandfather. Its only outward merit was that it might have been worse than it was. Its inner merits were a certain comfortable spaciousness and a wide corridor running the whole length of the top story where children could be kept out of sight and hearing and rampage to their hearts' content. All the main rooms opened on to a gravelled terrace from which one descended to gardens bounded by a little stream and bordered by woods and fields.

Gudgeon, the butler, was giving the finishing touch to the lunch-table when a short, middle-aged worn, in a dark-grey striped dress came in.

"Good morning, Mr. Gudgeon," she said, with a foreign accent. "'Er ladyship's bag as usual."

"Mr. Leslie was carrying a bag when they return from church, Miss Conk," said Mr. Gudgeon. "It is probably on the library table. Walter, see if her ladyship's bag is in the library."

The footman went on his errand. Mr. Gudgeon cc drilled his supererogatory finishing touches while M Conk looked out of the window. Lady Emily's maid h come to her many years ago as Am[e]lie Conque, but t assimilative genius of the English language, Mr. Leslie's determination not to truckle to foreigners in the matter of. pronunciation, and Mr. Gudgeon's deep-rooted conviction of the purity of his own French accent had all united to form the name Conk. By this name she had been known with terror and dislike by Lady Emily's children, with love and disrespect by her grand-children. Whether Conk had softened with years or the new generation were more confident than the old, we cannot say. Probably both.

Conk had, as far as was known, no home, no relations, no interests beyond Rushwater and the family. For her holiday she always went to a retired housekeeper of the Leslies' , an ill-tempered old lady called Mrs. Baker who lived at Folkestone. Hence it was her habit, after her annual quarrel with Mrs. Baker, to make a day excursion to Boulogne, from which glimpse of her native land she always returned in tears because she had been so homesick for England.

Walter returned with the bag, which he attempted to give to Conk. Conk, ignoring his very existence, waited with an air of spiritual suffering till Gudgeon took it from Walter's hand and gave it to her.

'We shall be late for lunch," said Conk, who was apt to use the royal and editorial "we" in speaking of her mistress.

"That's nothing new, is it, Mr. Gudgeon?" said Walter, as Conk left the room.

Gudgeon gave Walter a look which made him retreat hastily to the service-room, and rearranged everything which Walter had happened to touch. Then he went to sound the gong.

To sound the gong was, though he would have died rather than confess it, one of the great joys of Gudgeon's life. The soul of the artist, the poet, the soldier, the explorer, the mystic, which slumbered somewhere inside his tall and dignified presence, was released four times a day to empyrean heights unknown and unsuspected by his employers, his equals— these being but two, Conk and Mrs. Siddon, the present housekeeper—and his underlings. There had been a black time the previous autumn when Mr. Leslie, solicitous for his wife's nerves after a long illness, had ordered Gudgeon to announce meals by word of mouth. Only his devotion to his mistress had sustained him under this trial. It was no pleasure to him to enter the drawing-room, bringing with him a presence which put the most distinguished guests to shame; no pleasure to him to announce in the voice which might have led him, except for a slight uncertainty in the matter of initial aspirates, to the highest preferment the Church can bestow, that dinner was served. His inner being was mute and starved. One day, in the course of a conversation with Conk, he threw out a feeler, suggesting that her ladyship had been a little less punctual for meals since Mr. Leslie had abolished the use of the gong.

"'Er ladyship is just ze same," said Conk. "She never 'ear ze gong. If she was in 'er bedroom she often say to me, "Conque, 'as ze gong gone?' "

Gudgeon pondered these remarks. One day he ventured to sound the gong, gently and for a short space, for lunch. After a day or two, finding that no one checked him, he sounded it for tea, then for dinner, but always with brevity and restraint. Finally, taking advantage of the absence of Mr. Leslie in town, he liberated his soul in tocsins, alarms, fanfares of booming sound. At the end of the week when Mr. Leslie returned, Lady Emily remarked at dinner:

"Gudgeon, did you sound the gong to-night? I never heard it."

"Yes, my lady," said Gudgeon, "but I can sound it a little longer in future if your ladyship wishes."

"Yes, do," said Lady Emily.

Mr. Leslie, occupied with Mr. Macpherson about the matter of mending the cricket pavilion roof, did not hear this conversation, and being at the time absorbed in a cattle show at which Rushwater Robert was like to do well, he never noticed that the gong had begun again.

To see Gudgeon sounding the gong for dinner was to see

an artist at work. Taking the gong-stick, its round end well
padded with wash-leather, which it was his pride to replace
with his own hands from time to time, he would execute one
or two preliminary flourishes in the manner of a drum-major,
or a lion lashing itself to a frenzy with the fabled claw in its
tail. Then he let the padded end fall upon the exact centre of
the gong, drawing out a low ringing note. With increasing
force he sounded it, the end of his stick moving in ever-
widening circles upon the dark, pitted surface of the gong, till
the sound filled the whole house, booming through corridors,
vibrating in every beam, thrilling and pleasantly alarming
Agnes's children in bed upstairs, making David in his bath
say, "Damn that gong; I thought I had five minutes more,"
making Mr. Leslie, in the drawing-room, say, "Everybody late
again as usual, I suppose," making Lady Emily say as Conk
pinned up her hair, "Has the gong gone yet, Conque?"

To-day the last ripples of its booming had hardly died
away when Mr. Leslie came in with Mr. Macpherson, the
agent, and Mr. Banister. Agnes, with James, who came down
to Sunday lunch, David and Martin followed close behind.

'We shan't wait, Gudgeon," said Mr. Leslie. "Her ladyship
will be late."

"Very good, sir," said Gudgeon pityingly. There was very
little about the family that Gudgeon did not know before they
knew it themselves.

"When are you expecting your niece, Mrs. Graham?"
asked Mr. Macpherson.

"To-morrow for lunch. She was seeing her mother off to-
day."

"Let me see," said Mr. Macpherson, who prided himself
upon knowing every ramification of the Leslie family, "she
will be the daughter of Colonel Graham's eldest sister, I'm
thinking, the one that married Colonel Preston that was
killed in the War."

"Yes; that's it. My eldest brother was in his regiment, ,you remember, as a subaltern. They were killed about the same time, poor darlings. Mrs. Preston has never been very well since then."

"I mind it now," said Mr. Macpherson, "and there was but the one child, this Miss Mary. I saw her the once, here, when she was only a lassie."

"She is such a darling, we all adore her. It is so sad for her that her mother has to go abroad, so mother and I thought she had better come here for the summer."

'What does Mrs. Preston want to go abroad for?" asked Mr. Leslie.

"I think her doctor wanted her to, father," said Agnes.

"Doctors!" said Mr. Leslie, wiping the whole of the Royal College of Physicians off the face of the world with this withering remark.

"And when do you expect your husband back, Mrs. Graham?" continued Mr. Macpherson, bent on bringing his family knowledge up-to-date.

"I don't quite know. It is so annoying," said Agnes in a gently plaintive voice. "The War Office said three months, but you never know. And it really takes quite some time to get back from South America, you know. But what is very nice is that he has seen father's bull out there."

"Not Rushwater Robert?" asked Mr. Macpherson.

"Yes, he was champion at Buenos Aires and Robert, I mean my Robert, not the bull, saw Robert at the show. But he didn't know him."

"Then how did he know it was Robert?" asked Mr. Leslie.

"He didn't, father, that was the sad part. Darling Robert looked at him with his lovely great eyes, but he had forgotten him. And when you think that he was called after him!"

Agnes sighed comfortably.

"There was something to be said for the Romans having more than one kind of personal pronoun," said John, to no one in particular. Mr. Leslie grappled mentally with the difference between his prize bull and his son-in-law, but Agnes's next remark drove it out of his head.

"Can Weston meet Mary to-morrow, father?" she asked.

"Meet who? Oh, Mary; yes, of course, Mary Preston. Bless me, I remember her mother quite well at your wedding, Agnes. Why does she take any notice of the doctors? Why doesn't she come here? She might take the vicarage, Banister, if you really want to let it

"But my dear Leslie, I have already let the vicarage as I told Lady Emily last week."

At this moment Lady Emily came in with her hear mobled in fine lace and a large silk shawl clutched round her.

"What did you tell me last week, Mr. Banister?" she asked as she arranged herself in her chair. "Gudgeon, take my stick and put it there; no, just there in the corner. And have I got a footstool? Yes, here it is; I can feel it with my foot. Was it about your tenants, Vicar? I know you did tell me something about them and must call on them, only I can't go till Tuesday, because Sunday is Sunday, and then," she continued with the air of one who has brought to birth a profound thought "Monday is Monday, and, Henry, we must see about having Mary Preston met at the station. Do you remember her father, Colonel Preston, Mr. Macpherson He was here once before the War. Well, about your tenants, Mr. Banister, Tuesday is Tuesday, and then I hope to be able to go. What is that?" she inquired o Walter, who was handing her a dish.

"Eggs in mushroom sauce, my lady."

"Oh, I see, you have all got on to the second course No, not egg. Give me some—what is it you are all having? Chicken? Give me some chicken. Mr. Macpherson, I was thinking in church this morning about the cricket pavilion roof, but Henry tells me you mended it last October. Oh, Walter, that is too much chicken. I'll put some on the vicar's salad plate as he has finished his salad, and then you can bring back the eggs and I'll have some of everything all together. Do you think Tuesday will do?"

"My tenants," said Mr. Banister, who had been vainly endeavouring to get a word in, "don't come till August, Lady Emily, but if you will be kind enough to call upon them.' when they do come, it will be very good of you."

"Oh, August," said Lady Emily, rather dashed. "Then I had better not call on them on Tuesday. Henry," she called to her husband at the other end of the table, "who do you think I have had a letter from?"

"Can't say, my dear."

"Wait a minute, I had it somewhere," said Lady Emily, turning out the contents of a large bag on the table. "No, it isn't here. Gudgeon, tell Walter to ask Conque for a large flat basket in my bedroom with some letters in it. Not the small round basket with the green edge, because that has only answered letters in it. I can't think why I keep answered letters," she said to the company generally, flashing a self-deprecating look on them, "but some day I must really go through them and burn some. David, you shall help me and we will have great fun reading them before we burn them. But it is not that basket, Gudgeon, but the other basket which has my painting things and a dead thrush in it. Martin, did I tell you I found a dead thrush on my window-sill this morning, and I don't know what to do with it?"

"Oh, the poor darling," said Agnes.

"Can I have it for a funeral?" asked James, raising his head from his chocolate pudding.

"Yes, darling, of course. Well, then, Gudgeon, I want the dead thrush and a letter with a coronet on the back of it. And who are your tenants, Mr. Banister?" said her ladyship, who however far she divagated always returned to her subject in the long run.

"Very delightful people. I am sure you will like them. I met them in Touraine last year, where I went to see my old friend, Somers, who keeps a coaching establishment."

"Will he bring Mrs. Somers too?" asked Lady Emily, who had minced her chicken up into small pieces and was eating it and tepid egg with a spoon, with apparent relish.

"No, it isn't Somers who is taking the vicarage. It is some friends of Somers's called Boulle."

"Funny thing," said Mr. Leslie, "I have never met anyone called Bull in France. Plenty of people called Bull in England, of course."

"Not Bull, Leslie, Boulle. They are French."

"Like something out of the Wallace Collection, father," said David helpfully.

"Good name for your young champion," said John. "Rushwater Boulle."

"First time I ever heard Bull was a French name," said Mr. Leslie, sticking manfully to his guns.

"I believe the family is Alsatian," said Mr. Banister. "You might make a joke about Alsatians and Boulledogs," said Martin.

"No, you mightn't," said David.

Here Gudgeon came back with a silver tray on which were the dead thrush and a letter.

"Oh, thanks," said Lady Emily. "Gudgeon, put the poor bird in a box and Master James can have it as soon as he has finished lunch."

"Can I get down now?" said James, rapidly spooning the last of his second helping into his mouth. Permission being given, he pushed his chair back, took possession of the corpse, and left the room.

"Has anyone seen my spectacles?" inquired Lady Emily. "Gudgeon, tell Conque I want some spectacles and I must manage somehow till she finds them."

"Let me read the letter for you, mother," said David, coming round and pulling a chair between his mother and Mr. Macpherson. "It's from a person called Holt, Yours sincerely

C.W. Holt. He wants to come to lunch to-morrow and see the garden, and he is staying with Lord Capes at Capes Castle, and he wants you to send the car to fetch him as Lord Capes's is not available. He seems to have considerable aplomb, mamma, whoever he is."

"Well, he's really a very nice little man," began Lady Emily, but Mr. Leslie interrupted her.

"He's an infernal bore, Emily. Last time he came here he invited himself for a night and stayed for three, and treated the car as if it were his own. He talks about nothing but gardens and his titled friends. I can't stand the fellow, no more can anyone else. He invites himself to people's houses and they are too good-natured to say they don't want him. I shouldn't wonder if he is keeping a diary about us all and means to publish it when he is dead, like that Weevle fellow or whatever his name was."

"Creevey," said David.

"Greville," said Mr. Banister at the same moment. "Jobling," said John, under his breath, for his own satisfaction.

"I said Weevle," said Mr. Leslie angrily. "Emily, must you have him?"

"Not if you'd rather not, Henry. Thanks, Gudgeon. Oh, it's the wrong pair, but I dare say I can manage. You see, he says Lord Capes is going to town and he will be all alone, and as he is going on to the Nortons we are really on his way, and I can't help feeling sorry for him."

'Well, mamma," said David, "the Nortons are thirty miles away on the other side of the county, but I dare say in the eye of the Almighty—sorry, Mr. Banister—it's the same thing."

"Look here, Emily," said the exasperated Mr. Leslie, "the car can't fetch Holt from Lord Capes's and meet the train for Mary Preston, that's all."

"But, Henry, if Weston went early to fetch Mr. Holt, and got him here about twelve, he would have plenty of time to go on and meet Mary. She is coming to Southbridge because there aren't any good trains to Rush-water on Whit Monday."

"Gran," said Martin, "couldn't I take the Ford over to Southbridge?"

"Certainly not," said his grandfather.

"But I could run the Ford over, father," said David, "and Martin can come with me. So that's all right."

"Then, Gudgeon," said her ladyship, "tell Weston he will be wanted to-morrow to fetch Mr. Holt from Lord Capes's in time for lunch. I suppose he had better leave here about eleven o'clock, at least, I don't really know how long it takes to get there, because last time we went, you remember, Martin, we were coming from London, so of course it took several hours, but I dare say Weston knows. And then, David, you and Martin had better leave with the Ford at— Oh, what time does Mary's train get there, Agnes?"

"Gudgeon will see about it, mamma," said Agnes. "He always knows everything. Let's come in the drawing-room now, because the children will be coming down for their afternoon walk."

"Oh, but one moment," said Lady Emily, rewinding her shawl round her. "My stick, Gudgeon. What about Mr. Banister's tenants? Am I to call on Madame Boulle this week? And is she a widow?"

"My dear Lady Emily, I don't know what I can have said to lead you to think that she is a widow—" began the vicar.

"Frenchwomen are all widows," said Mr. Leslie. "Look at them."

"But Alsatians are different," added David, with great presence of mind.

"No, no, she has a husband and two or three young people. They are in some way connected with a French university. In fact, both M. Boulle and his eldest son are, I believe, professors. They just want a month's holiday in England. They take

in paying-guests in France, young men and women who want
to study French for business, or for a degree. Delightful and
cultivated people."

"I shall certainly call on them," said Lady Emily, "but not
before Tuesday. Now we must go and see James's funeral."

The vicar excused himself on the grounds of a children's
service. Mr. Leslie and his agent went off to look at the young
bull, while the rest of the party rejoiced James's heart by fol-

CHAPTER III
ARRIVAL OF A TOADY

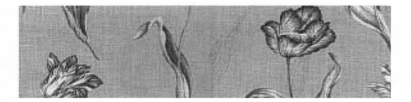

lowing the thrush to its wormy home.

IT WAS THE HABIT of Lady Emily's children and grandchildren to make her bedroom a kind of family council chamber. She herself believed, and told all her friends, that she used the hour between nine and ten for writing her letters and getting through any business connected with the house. But as this was the only time of day when her family could be sure of finding her in a given place, her room was usually a melting-pot for the day's plans.

On Whit Monday morning at half-past nine Lady Emily was still in bed, wrapped in two large Shetland shawls, her head swathed in folds of soft cashmere pinned with diamond brooches. On her bed were a breakfast tray, the large flat basket of letters, the small round basket with the green edge which contained answered correspondence, a large piece of embroidery, several books, another basket of combs and pins, and some newspapers. On a table by her side were a paintbox, a glass of water, and a white paper fan, which she was decorating with a dashing design of fishes and seaweed. The large bedroom was crammed to overflowing with family relics, and examples of the various arts in which Lady Emily had brilliantly dabbled at one time or another. Part of one wall was decorated with a romantic landscape painted on the plaster, the fourpost bed was hung with her own skilful embroidery, watercolour drawings in which a touch of genius fought and worsted an entire want of technique hung on the walls. Pottery, wood carving, enamels, all bore witness to their owner's insatiable desire to create.

From their earliest days the Leslie children had thought of their mother as doing or making something, handling brush, pencil, needle, with equal enthusiasm, coming in late to lunch with clay in her hair, devastating the drawing-room with her far-flung painting materials, taking cumbersome pieces of embroidery on picnics, disgracing everyone by a determination to paint the village cricket pavilion with scenes from the life of St. Francis for which she made the gardeners pose. What Mr. Leslie thought no one actually knew, for Mr. Leslie had his own ways of life and rarely interfered. Once only had he been known to make a protest. In the fever of an enamelling craze, Lady Emily had a furnace put up in the service-room, thus making it extremely difficult for Gudgeon and the footman to get past, and moreover pressing the footman as her assistant when he should have been laying lunch. On this occasion Mr. Leslie had got up from the lunch-table, ordered the car, had himself driven straight to London, and gone on a cruise to the Northern Capitals of Europe, which were not so essentially foreign as more southern parts. When he returned, the enamelling phase had abated and the furnace had been moved to the cellar.

Agnes Graham was sitting in the window, looking over the gardens, with Clarissa, her youngest, on her lap. Agnes was not so tall as her mother, whose dark hair and eyes she had inherited. She had an appealing smile and a very gentle voice, which she never took the trouble to raise. Her marriage had been settled for her, to her entire satisfaction, by her mother, who, despairing of ever marrying a daughter who had gone through two seasons without appearing capable of showing any preference of any kind, had told Colonel Graham to declare himself. When Robert Graham had disentangled from his future mother-in-law's very discursive remarks what it was she wanted to say, he had at once proposed to Agnes, who said she daresaid it would be very nice to marry dear Robert, and the affair was concluded. She now lived in a state of perfectly contented subjection to her adoring husband and children. Her intelligence was bounded by her house and her exquisite needlework, and to any further demands made by life she always murmured, "I shall ask Robert." When Robert's sister, Mrs. Preston, had been ordered abroad for the summer, it was Robert who offered to pay for her stay at a Swiss clinic, while Agnes so far exerted herself as to write to her mother and say how nice it would be if darling Mary could go to Rushwater for the summer, especially as she and the children were to be there while Robert went on a mission to South America, and Mary was always so good with the children. She was the special favourite of her elder brother, John, who often wondered lovingly how anyone could be quite such a divine idiot as Agnes.

On the floor James and his other sister, Emmy, were doing a large jig-saw puzzle, assisted by John. Emmy was a stout and determined young woman of five of whom her elder brother was rather in awe.

"All the same, John," said Agnes, in her comfortable, placid voice, "you might let the children have their fair share. You have got more green and blue bits than anyone could possibly want over on your side."

"I am concentrating on the trees and the sky," said John. "James is doing the dark bits which are either somebody's clothes or a railway engine, we aren't quite sure which yet. This is called division of labour. Emmy has been trying for ten minutes to fit two bits together that anyone can see with half an eye bear no relation to each other. This is called determination, or imbecility."

"Imbecility, I expect," said Agnes fondly. "She is the silliest of a clever family, just like me. Darling Emmy."

"It is spiritual pride to run yourself down like that, Agnes," said Lady Emily from her. bed. "How old is Robert's niece now?"

"Mary? About twenty-three, I think. You will like her so much, mamma, and she sings so nicely, and she can help you with your village mothers and things. She will love to help."

"But isn't the poor girl coming here to rest?" asked John. "Someone said something about a breakdown."

"No, not a breakdown. But Robert's sister is really rather selfish and she makes poor Mary quite a slave, so Mary got quite run down, and when her mother had to go abroad, Robert said he thought it would be a good thing for Mary to come here. Running down is quite different from breaking down."

There was a knock at the door and David came in.

"Good morning, mamma," he said. "May I just finish my cigarette, or shall I chuck it out of the window? Here's a telegram for you, Agnes. I know what you are thinking. Your offspring are all here under your eyes, so they can't have fallen into the fire or broken their legs. Therefore it must be Robert. Shall I open it for you and tell you the worst?"

"Yes, do," said Agnes plaintively, but without any signs of emotion. "Telegrams are always so alarming."

'Well, I can tell you it isn't Robert without opening it," said David, "because he would break his leg in a cable, not in a telegram. It's from Mary, to say she arrives at Southbridge at twelve-thirty."

'Well, that's very nice," said Lady Emily, who was absent-mindedly trying on a pair of long suede gloves. "She can help us with Mr. Holt at lunch. Your father gets so angry, and though Mr. Holt is really a great trouble and so terribly dull and nobody wants him, still, when someone takes the trouble to invite themselves one feels one ought at least to be civil. David, you and John must help your father."

"Darling," said David, "if this Holt is such a crashing bore as you suggest, I think I'd better be out to lunch. Martin and I are going to fetch this Mary Preston, and we could all have lunch somewhere and not come back till he has gone."

Just then Martin came in.

"Good morning, gran," he said. "David, I've been looking for you. Macpherson asked me to tell you he wants the Ford the minute you come back, as he and John have got to go out on estate business."

'What a selfish man Macpherson is," remarked David without heat. "I wanted to take sandwiches and hear the lark so high about me in the sky. Why do people never take sandwiches when they go poetizing on hills? Does one have to poetize on an empty stomach?"

'Well, I couldn't go sandwiching, anyway," said Martin. "I have to be back for something."

'What have you got important enough to come back for?" asked David.

"I've got to see the vicar."

By the way in which his whole family there assembled repeated "The vicar!" one would have thought that Mr. Banister was some loathsome speckled disease rather than an old family friend.

"Are you going to run the Boy Scouts?" asked David, not quite kindly.

"No, I'm not."

"Or become a Cathedral Alto?"

"Oh, shut up, David. It's something private," said Martin, casting an appealing look on his young uncle.

"David, dear, Martin must of course see the vicar if he wants to," said Lady Emily. "Mr. Banister is always most helpful and Martin couldn't do better than go to him, whatever it is."

The implications which Lady Emily put into her last words were so appalling that everyone began to laugh. Agnes said that Mr. Banister had read the marriage service quite beautifully at her wedding. A yell from James then drew attention to the fact that Emmy had broken the two recalcitrant pieces of jig-saw. John, getting up in a hurry, dislocated the already-finished section. James hit Emmy and Emmy wept aloud.

"Ring the bell for Nannie, Martin," said Agnes, making no kind of attempt to cope with her offspring. "They are so tiresome when they don't agree."

After a short interval of pandemonium Nannie and Ivy arrived and removed the two elder children. John set himself to repair the damage on the floor, while Mar- tin collected the fragments of Emmy's pieces.

"Have you any seccotine, gran?" he asked.

"Yes, darling, in that red bowl on the bookcase near the fire. Don't squeeze it too hard, because the end is broken and you never know where it is going to come out."

'Well, I must go," said David, a little bored by this super-domestic atmosphere. "Good-bye, mother. Twelve o'clock, Martin."

"Thank you so much, Martin, for mending James's jig-saw," said Agnes. "Emmy is so very silly. Mamma, I must take Clarissa to Nannie now. John, will you be in to lunch?"

"I expect so. I've got to go round with Macpherson at two o'clock. Give Clarissa to me. I'll take her to Nannie."

Uncle and niece went off hand in hand.

"If you'll ring for Conque, I'll get up now," said Lady Emily to her daughter. "But why," she added, looking with great surprise at her own hands, "why on earth did I put my gloves on?"

"I can't think, mamma," said Agnes, ringing the bell.

At twelve o'clock David was heard shouting for Martin. At five minutes past twelve Martin was heard shouting for David. By ten minutes past twelve the two shouters had found each other, got into the Ford and driven off.

"Can't I drive?" asked Martin, as soon as they were out of

sight of the house.

"You can not. We shall have to step on it if we aren't to keep this Preston affair waiting. Why weren't you ready at twelve?"

"I was, but I couldn't find you anywhere, so I went all round the stables to look for you."

"It's an impossible house to find people in. They ought to block up a few doors and staircases and then there'd be a chance of cornering people. You can drive part of the way back."

"David, you are mean."

"Not mean, dear nephew, only sensible. If anyone sees you driving in Southbridge they'll see you aren't old enough for a licence and haul you up before the beak.'

After this the Ford made so much noise going up hill that conversation became impossible. The road across the hills from Rushwater mounted steadily for three miles, first among beech trees, then through cornland, and at last onto the bare green heights. David put his foot down on the accelerator and thumped the side of the car after the manner of a jockey encouraging his horse with the whip. Martin sang at the top of his voice, conducting himself with both arms. On the lonely heights the horn went mad and emitted a long blast which nothing could stop.

"Haven't got time to mend it," yelled David.

"All right," yelled Martin, and incorporated the horn into his imaginary orchestra.

At the brow of the hill above Southbridge David pulled up.

"We can't go through the town like the Last Judgment," he said, poking about among the wiring. "The Preston will just have to wait. Blast, I can't find the

thing. I'll have to cut it and Weston can mend it. Find the pliers, they are somewhere under your seat."

Having cut the wire, they proceeded more soberly on their journey and were not unduly late at the station. The crowded bank-holiday train had only just pulled in. David parked the car on the far side of the station yard and looked with distaste at the crowd of hikers which the London train had just disgorged.

"The Esk was swollen sae red and deep, but shoulder to shoulder the brave lads keep," he announced to Martin. "Tackle them low, my boy, and come on."

In any other place the sight of two stalwart young men advancing with a gliding step, arms linked like skaters, uttering what they fondly hoped was a college yell, might have attracted attention, but the hikers, many of whom had already struck up folk-songs of whose doubtful meaning they were luckily unaware, took David and Martin for some of themselves. A few gave the Fascist salute, to which David politely made reply, "Good morrow, good my lieges," while Martin more simply responded "Ave. By this means they reached the station entrance in safety and there found Miss Preston and her suit-cases.

"Miss Preston, I presume," said David.

"Yes, I'm Mary Preston. I am so glad you both came through safely. I was afraid you might both be knocked down and trampled on."

"I would have been, only my good father Tiber bore bravely up my chin. This," he added, introducing Martin, "is my father Tiber, Martin Leslie."

"How do you do?" said Miss Preston. "And you," she said to David, "are another Leslie, I suppose."

"I am David. Do you mind if we get into the car at once, as my father's agent is waiting to snatch it the moment we get back."

Mary's suit-cases were put in the back with Martin and Mary sat in front with David.

"You do horn, Martin," shouted David over his shoulder.

Martin obligingly made a number of hideous noises, supposed to be a warning to passengers and other vehicles, and presently the town was left behind them and the car breasted the hill. At the top Martin hit his uncle on the back.

"You said I could drive, David."

"All right. Do you mind if we practise the change over, Miss Preston?"

The changeover was an elaborate system of changing drivers without slowing down to which David and his nephew had devoted much thought.. It was designed as a time-saving device in the event of being pursued by Red Indians, Touaregs and other motor bandits. Martin climbed over the back of the front seat and slipped down with a leg on each side of David. He then gripped the wheel with his right hand, while David slithered over his nephew's left leg and squashed himself into the space between Martin and Mary, keeping his foot on the accelerator. A substitution of Martin's foot for David's was effected without mishap, and David removed himself into the back seat.

'What do you think of it, Miss Preston?" he inquirerd.

"Splendid," said Mary. "Did you have much trouble in getting it right?"

"Rather," said Martin. "We nearly smashed the Ford up twice before we got the technique right. Next holidays we are going to try it on David's sports car."

'Was it you or your brother who invented it?"

'Who? Oh, David isn't my brother; he's my uncle. You can't judge uncles by appearances."

"Then you are Aunt Agnes's brother," said Mary, turning round, "and my Uncle David, I suppose."

"Good Lord, no," said David, much alarmed. "At least I'm Agnes's brother all right, but not an uncle, please. Hi, Martin, horn!"

Martin executed his fantasia on horn noises, which made a couple of women walking along with baskets giggle pityingly at the eccentricities of the gentry.

"Excuse us, Miss Preston, but we can't help it. We're all mad, you know, and Martin *is* mad."

"So am I," said Mary; not wishing to be left out of it, "but not Miss Preston, please. After all, we are a sort of in-laws."

"Bricks without straw, bricks without straw, a man may not marry his mother-in-law," sang Martin.

"All right, my boy," said David. "Change-over again. Macpherson or father are bound to spot you driving."

"Oh, please, not change-over," pleaded Mary. "My nerves couldn't bear it. Please stop, Martin, and let David come round in the ordinary way."

Martin pulled up by a bluebell wood and both young men got out.

"Bluebells," said David, introducing them with a wave of the hand. He leaned over the side of the car looking at Mary.

"Do you like walking?" he asked.

"Love it."

"Then we'll do some walks when I come down for week-ends."

"Don't you live here?"

"No, I live in town mostly, but I'm often down here. Come on, Martin, we'll be late."

Martin made his horn noise, doors were slammed and they drove on. After a quarter of a mile they came to the gates of Rushwater House. The drive wound through a large meadow where the hay was not yet cut. Rushwater House came into sight behind the trees in all its complacent ugliness. David drew up under the portico and Gudgeon opened the door.

"Lunch over, Gudgeon?" said David.

"No, sir, luncheon has not yet begun. The car with Mr. Holt is not yet here, so her ladyship is waiting."

"Right-oh. Oh, Gudgeon, you might let Weston know that the horn died on us this morning, so he'd better fix it up for Mr. Macpherson. Come along, Mary, and see mamma."

He took Mary's arm and propelled her into the drawing room where his mother was sitting at a large table, busily painting her fan.

"Dear child," she exclaimed, opening her arms to Mary in a warm embrace. "I am so glad to see you again. Did the boys take care of you?"

"Yes, thank you, Aunt Emily."

"Luckily you have come in time for me to warn you about Mr. Holt," said Lady Emily. "Henry and the children are always so unkind about him, but really he is quite a nice little man and always invites himself."

Mary was not a little bewildered by the sudden introduction of Mr. Holt, and was hoping for more information about him, but her Aunt Agnes took her off to her room and left her to get ready for lunch. When Mary had tidied herself and unpacked a few things she went to the window and kneeling on the window-seat looked out into the park. Her bedroom was at the front of the house, overlooking the great meadow which lay bathed in warmth and peace. After a long London winter it felt like Paradise. Much as she loved her mother, that lady's half-imaginary maladies were rather wearing. Mary had found some work in a library, more to have a pretext to get away for regular hours than because she actually needed the money, but when Colonel Graham had offered to pay for his sister's treatment and after-cure at a Swiss clinic, and Providence had provided a friend to go with her, Mary was thoroughly glad to give up her so-called work and go to Rushwater for the summer.

Agnes, whose soft silliness was only equalled by her strong family affections, had not been thinking entirely of her niece when she agreed with her husband that it would be a good thing for Mary to go to Rushwater. She wanted her mother to have a nice girl with her who could help with letters and possibly snatch a little order from the large-hearted chaos which was Lady Emily's normal life. She also had a mild hope that John might be induced to take an interest in her niece. As Agnes had been happily married for ten years to a man who was worthy of her affection and inordinately proud of her gentle foolishness, she could wish no other good than matrimony to her elder brother. So far her efforts at finding suitable wives for John had met with no success, but all the more did she exert herself. David, she considered, could well look after himself, and was obviously doomed to marry an heiress, but dear John would be a difficulty. If she had realized how very far John was from thinking of a second marriage, she might have given up in despair, if there were room for so definite an emotion in her placid breast. When Gay died after a year of perfect happiness John had tried to make a grave for every memory of that year. But he could not find for them the eternal rest which her spirit had found. It was an unquiet grave where those memories lay. They stirred unbidden and rose sometimes at midnight or at noonday to wring his heart. No ninefold Styx could bind them, no prayers for forgetfulness move them. At every hour he was defenceless against the bitter waters of memory which rose to his lips and chilled his heart. But Agnes, happily ignorant of this, thought that darling John must marry again, some really nice girl, and why not Mary. Robert would be pleased.

Meanwhile Mary, all unconscious of her aunt's plans and almost of John's existence, went on looking out of the window and thinking of those two very nice silly Leslie boys. Martin, still at school, was of course really a boy, and David one thought of as a boy to show one's own womanly superiority. But one also thoughts of him as a boy rather deliberately, to hide one's own consciousness of his disturbing presence. He was certainly a person one would like to see a good deal. Not because he was amusing and could drive a car so well, for Mary's world contained several young men who were excellent amusers and first-rate drivers. Probably just because he was David, which was an exciting, a delicious thought.

The noise of a motor woke her from this unmaidenly reverie, and she became conscious of the Leslies' car coming across the green meadow, containing what was presumably

Mr. Holt. So she plunged downstairs, getting safely to the drawing-room before Gudgeon announced Mr. Holt, my lady.

There emerged from behind Gudgeon's pontifical form a stout little man in a grey suit, walking delicately on rather pointed brown shoes. His round red face had an air of being imperfectly shaved, or of having some light fungoid growth upon it, his short hair and moustache were grey, he clasped his plump hands across him as he moved. Mr. Leslie's nebulous idea of Mr. Holt as a Greville or Creevey was not so far out, though Creevey was really what he would have meant if he had the faintest idea what his own meaning was. Mr. Holt was an astounding survival of the hanger-on, although he did not keep a diary. Bred to the law, he had been placed by his father, a county town solicitor in a small way, in the estate office of a noble lord on whom he had some slight claim. Here young Holt had assiduously studied the art of pleasing his superiors. Realizing that he could not get a footing in great houses unless he could prove himself useful or amusing, better to be both, he had early formed his plan of life. To be witty was not in him, but he had a magnetic attraction for gossip. Small talk of every kind flew to him, followed him, came in at his window almost unsought. All that he heard he retained in his excellent and well-trained memory and was able to pour out in the right quarters. At the houses which he sometimes had to visit on business he made himself very entertaining to the magnates, who enjoyed hearing malicious stories about their friends and unwittingly themselves furnished material for Holt's next visit. Thus he obtained a reputation as an amusing fellow whom you could ask to dinner at a pinch. To get a footing among the wives was more difficult in those late Victorian and Edwardian days. After some thought he decided to enter the charmed world of his ambition by the garden gate. Great ladies were taking up gardening. Mr. Holt applied himself to the science, read copiously, neglected no opportunity of picking up information, and in a few years made himself a first-rate authority on shrubs and flowers, from the wild flowers of a particular county of England to the rarest bulbs or slips from the Himalayas or the Andes. By the time his father died, Mr. Holt had so well established himself as tame cat, or up-to-date toady, that he was able to give up his legal work and take a modest room in town on what his father left him, counting on his friends for holidays and for fruit and game in season.

To do him justice it must be said that the pursuit which he had taken up as a means to social improvement had finished by winning what heart he had. In spite of his snobbery, his pedantism, his insufferable egotism, a new blossom, a rare bulb would thrill him with a lover's emotion. As he had no garden of his own there was no fear of his competition. Great ladies rivalled each other in their efforts to get him week-ends, for summer and Easter visits, for Christmas house-parties. Here he moved in complete happiness, amusing such guests as he did not irritate to madness, and making himself really useful in the garden, to the ill-concealed fury of the good Scotch head-gardeners.

But it is doubtful whether any toady's prosperity has lasted as long as his life. These glories had diminished.

The War broke up the happy life of county England. Many of the houses where he used to visit were shut or sold. Old friends and patrons were dead, dividends had fallen, game no longer reached him. Life was becoming a skimpy business for Mr. Holt, but unable to put a good face on it he was becoming more exacting, more jealous, more querulous with every passing year. A severe illness left him a little deaf, not able to walk about gardens by the hour as he used to do, assuming an almost insane proprietorship in what friends he had left. In the few houses where he still visited, he became less and less welcome. Younger men combined garden lore with good figures and pretty manners, or even more endearing rudeness. They laughed at Mr. Holt and made the new chatelaines laugh too. The little man, cross and on his dignity, began to press for invitations, for which in the past a hint had sufficed. Some hostesses cut him, others continued to invite him, or rather to tolerate his forced visits, from sheer kindness. Among the last of these was Lady Capes, who allowed him to come whenever he liked, as she lived mostly in the south of France. At Capes Castle he could browse in the library on herbals, or superintend an addition to the rock-garden in which the earl took an interest. His lordship was no ruder to him than he was to anyone else, and the servants were fairly kind.

Mr. Holt had planned to be sent on from Capes Castle in the belted motor of his lordship to stay with Lady Norton, another of his autocratic old friends. Lady Norton, however, had forbidden him to come before dinner because she had friends staying with her who might have picked his gardening brains, and he dared not offend her. Lord Capes, without inquiring his humble guest's movements, had gone off to Bath for the week-end in the car, leaving word that he didn't expect to see Mr. Holt when he got back on Monday. At his wits' end how to spend Whit Monday at the least personal expense, the unfortunate hanger-on had written to Lady Emily the letter which David has read aloud to us. It would be easy to be sorry for Mr. Holt in his old unhonoured age; but he is so conceited and irritating that compassion melts to bored anger.

To reproduce his first remark as he followed Gudgeon into the room would be difficult, consisting as it did of the word "Oh"; to which, however, he gave a vowel sound, or rather a combination of vowel sounds, at whose peculiar affectedness phonetics boggles.

"Eu-ah-oo," he began in a high voice, so unexpected that Mary nearly giggled.

"Eu-ah-oo, dear Lady Emily, you must forgive this unpar-

donable lateness. I trust you have all lunched—you have not
kept luncheon waiting for me, I trust."

It was unfortunate that Mr. Leslie should have chosen this
precise moment to inquire from Gudgeon in the hall, in a
loud angry voice. distinctly audible to everyone in the drawing-room, whether her ladyship wanted them all to starve.
Gudgeon sounded the gong.

"Ah," said Mr. Holt, beaming, "I hear the voice of my good
friend Mr. Leslie, who has so kindly allowed his chariot of
fire, his fiery Pegasus, to convey me hither from Capes Castle.
I must explain to him, and to you, dear lady, exactly how it
occurred that this regrettable delay took place.

"You must tell me all about it at lunch," said Lady Emily,
rising and coming forward on her stick. "You know my
daughter, Mrs. Graham, and this is her niece, Miss Preston,
and you know David and Martin. Come into lunch and tell us
all about Lord Capes. I haven't seen him or Alice for ages. I
was ill, you know, last summer, and then they were away for
most of the winter. Indeed Alice is really always away, so you
must give me all her news."

"May I trespass on your kindness, dear lady, for a
moment," said Mr. Holt, as they entered the dining-room,
where Mr. Leslie was already sitting waiting, "so far as to-
entreat that your fairy carpet may of its goodness transport
me to Norton Manor during the afternoon, where I am to
spend the night with my dear old friend, Lady Norton.
Indeed she makes no demand on my time until the hour of
dinner so if you will let me wander a little in your garden I
could leave you, though with so many regrets, after tea."

David and Martin made hideous faces at their grandmother, expressive of a desire to stop Mr. Holt having the car.

"There's a jolly good train from Rushwater to Norton at
three-fifteen, Mr. Holt," said Martin kindly. "Gets you there
in no time."

"How kind of our young friend," said Mr. Holt, who had

defeated too many schemers in his time to take any account of a schoolboy, "but I fear that I should hardly have time to give attention to the garden if I made so early a departure. Also, we know that the railway system is *taut soit peu* disorganized at Whitsuntide, and I should fear to spend a lonely hour at some far-off junction if I ventured the attempt. Perhaps your kind chauffeur might be at liberty later, Mr. Leslie."

Thus appealed to, Mr. Leslie had no choice but to say grudgingly that the car was at Mr. Holt's disposal.

"Martin and I had meant to take Mary to see the Rushmere Abbey ruins if Weston was free," said David in an unnecessarily loud voice to his father.

"Oh, darling," cried Lady Emily, cutting short the opening stage of Mr. Holt's account of why he was late in starting, "couldn't you have the Ford?"

"Macpherson has the Ford," said Mr. Leslie. "He and John will be out on business all afternoon. John couldn't wait any longer for lunch."

Having shot this bolt at his wife and her ill-judged hospitality, he continued his lunch. Martin exploded into a schoolboy laugh, while David made such a deliciously sympathetic face at Mary that her heart contracted.

"Then," continued Mr. Holt, whose deafness enabled him to ignore his rude young hosts, "may I beseech your kind butler, Lady Emily, to ring up Lady Norton and say that I shall be with her by dinner-time, that is if your patience can bear with me so long."

"Yes, please telephone, Gudgeon," said Lady Emily, "and see if I left my spectacles and a little grey silk shawl in the drawing-room, and tell Conque I want my other stick, the one with the rubber tip. And now, tell me all about Lady Capes, Mr. Holt."

Mr. Holt was just beginning to explain that neither his host nor his hostess had been in residence for the week-end, but had sent for him to give his invaluable advice about replanting the water garden, when his hostess called to the footman:

"Tell Gudgeon I mean the spectacles in the green case, not the ones in the black case that he brought me at lunch yesterday, because those aren't my reading ones. It was Conque's fault really, because though she has been with me all these years she never knows one pair of spectacles from another, and when I put them into their wrong cases, as I often do, it is even worse, though I suppose somehow that ought to even the odds, if that is what one says."

"Yes, my lady," said Walter, who, not sure how much of this confidence was addressed to him, or required transmitting to Gudgeon, had been waiting in respectful embarrassment.

"And now," continued her ladyship, smiling entrancingly on Mr. Holt, "you must tell me all about Alice Capes."

Mr. Holt, accustomed for so many years to be listened to with attention, if not with deference, stiffened. Three times he had tried to explain about Lady Capes, and three times had he been interrupted. Thoroughly annoyed, :which happened so easily nowadays, he entered into the fit of sulks with which he was formerly wont to subdue hostesses. But Lady Emily was so unresponsive to these fine shades as to embark on a deeply interesting conversation with Martin on her other side about the possibilities of the cricket match and dance on his birthday. Agnes, with her usual sweetness, soothed Mr. Holt's ruffled feelings till he began to feel important again. When Mr. Leslie had finished his lunch he went to the sideboard, helped himself to a cigar and left the room, saying as he went, "I'm sure to see you again, Mr. Wood."

"I can't think why Henry called you Mr. Wood," said Lady Emily. "He must have been thinking of that horrid little clergyman who came here for a fortnight last year while Mr. Banister was away. You remember, David, the one that had such an extraordinary affected voice."

Seeing the younger members of the party inexplicably amused, Lady Emily flashed her brilliant vague smile over them and got up.

"It has been too delicious to hear all about the Capes'," she said. "And now I've got to lie down and be quiet, Mr. Holt, but Agnes and the others will look after you, and then we must have a nice cosy chat at teatime, and Weston shall be here at five to take you to Norton."

"Suppose the rest of us go to the morning-room," said Agnes. "The children are coming down for half an hour and we can look at picture-books with them."

But curiously enough, as they crossed the hall, Mary, David and Martin lagged behind.

"Quick, into the drawing-room," said David, grabbing Mary's arm. "Agnes must take on that job. Let s all go for a walk till after tea."

"I can't," said Martin. "Got to go and see Mr. Banister."

"All right, my young catechumen," said David.

"Oh, shut up, David, don't be a fool," said Martin, attacking his uncle.

"Queensberry rules," said David, "no scrapping in the drawing-room. Come on the terrace, Mary, and see fair play."

Uncle and nephew wrestled for a few minutes till Martin jumped onto the balustrade, threw his arms above his head, uttered a loud shriek, and jumping down into the garden, strolled off to the vicarage.

"That's the chivalry of young England," said David; smoothing his hair, "leaving us in the lurch like that. I say, do you really feel like a walk?"

"I'd love to."

"Then get ready at once, before we are discovered, and meet me here."

CHAPTER IV
AN ABBEY AND A NURSERY

WHEN MARY came back David made mysterious signs of secrecy and beckoned her to follow him. He tiptoed along the terrace to where a large magnolia grew between two windows.

"Look in," he whispered, "but don't let them see you."

Mary peered cautiously round the magnolia into the room. Mr. Holt was sitting in an armchair, his hands clasped on his stomach, an expression of angry misery on his face. Agnes's gentle voice could be heard reading an incredibly silly storybook aloud to Emmy. James was painting, deeply absorbed. Clarissa was pushing a small perambulator round and round the room, staggering as she went.

"I am greatly looking forward to my visit to Lady Norton," said Mr. Holt, interrupting the reading rather rudely. "She is a very old friend and a cousin of my good friend Lord Capes. I go to her every year to help her with her garden. I understand that your mother is an excellent gardener, Mrs. Graham. I trust I may be privileged to add her garden to my collection."

"Yes, you must see the garden, of course, it is too delicious," said Agnes. "We will all go there when Nannie is ready, won't we, darlings? Look, Emmy, there is a picture of naughty Hobo-Gobo trying to snatch the poor little fairy Joybell's golden doll away. Wasn't he a naughty Hobo-Gobo?"

David and Mary retreated from the window. "I do love Aunt Agnes," said Mary.

"No one could have a nicer elder sister. I simply adore that kind of woman. Come on, we'll go to Rushmere Abbey."

"But I thought you wanted the car for that."

"Oh, that was only to annoy old Holt and show my father I was on his side."

The way to Rushmere Abbey lay at first by a shaded lane, then a footpath led through fields.

"It isn't a good country for cowslips," said David, "but we have everything else. Fritillaries are an absolute pest hereabouts. Look there."

Not far from the stream which bordered the meadow, a number of the snake-headed flowers, white and purple, rose among the grass. Mary knelt down to look at them, fingering one or two, but not plucking them.

"Do you know what I'd like, David?" she said. "I'd like a lot of shoes, exactly like these lovely snake-skin creatures. White shoes and purple shoes."

David's mocking spirit lay mute for the moment. At any other time he would have greeted so unromantic a suggestion with ribaldry, but this afternoon he had escaped for an hour or two from his familiar.

"I would like to give them to you," he said.

"Thank you very much," said Mary, rising, and they went on.

"I'm not much good at flowers, really," said David. "You should get John on them."

"Is that another brother?"

"Yes, another of your uncles. He's a dear old fellow and jolly good to young Martin. John puts his back into helping father with the place, but the kid gets it. His father was my eldest brother, you know, who was killed in the War."

"No, I didn't know that. You see, I'm not really Aunt

Agnes's niece, only her husband's, so I don't know all about the family."

"You soon will. We cling together a good deal and if you are to be here all summer you'll have unlimited opportunities. Here's the abbey entrance. We used to go in and out as we liked, but now it is a National Trust or something and costs sixpence. I say, I haven't any money. Have you?"

"I'm afraid not."

'Well, it won't matter. Old Sutton will let us in on tick."

He rang a bell at the gate and an old man came out of a cottage.

"Afternoon, Sutton. We haven't any money. Can we come in?"

Sutton touched his cap and let them in.

Rushmere Abbey was the meagre remains of a great Cistercian foundation. Little of it was left but the broken arches of part of the cloisters and a fragment of the dormitories. Since a public body had taken it over, the outline of the great abbey church and such other buildings as could be traced had been marked in the ground with white stones and the grass was kept neatly mown.

"Let's sit down and bask," said David. "I can't feel happy till I get the sun in my bones, can you? What would one do without the Riviera?"

"Do without it, I suppose," said Mary, sitting down on a stone where the sun shone upon a sheltered corner of the cloister wall. "I've never been there, but I'm still alive."

"Never been to the Riviera?" said David, looking at her with interest.

"No, nor the Lido, nor Algiers, nor winter sports."

"Good Lord, we must go there some time. I know heaps of people who are always making up parties and going," he added vaguely.

Mary felt that to go to the Riviera with David would be

the most perfect, but at the same time the most improbable, thing that could happen. She realized that to him an existence which did not imply at least a couple of thousand pounds a year of one's own was fantastic. She was tempted to say, "I have two hundred a year of my own and mummie has about six with her pension for daddy, and we pig along somehow," but felt this would not be ladylike. So instead she asked him what he did in town. David needed very little invitation to talk about himself, an art which he had brought to a high degree of polish, and conversed for some time about his various activities. Mary gathered that he might at any moment write a novel, which would be a best-seller without having anything second-rate about it, then be dramatized, then filmed, and probably be translated into several European languages.

"My first novel was only a try-out," said David carelessly. "The sort of thing every undergraduate has to write, but now I know much more clearly what I ought to do. I don't suppose you read my first book?"

"I don't think so. What was it called?"

"*Why Name.*"

"Why?" asked Mary.

"Exactly. Why? It is so cretinous to give a book a name. A book exists freely in itself and a name pins it down horribly. When you are in town you must meet some of my friends who are doing advanced writing and plays."

"Are they all great successes?"

"Of course not. None of them could write successes if they tried and luckily they don't need to. But they are full of delicious ideas. But I shall double-cross them all and write a howling success with no ideas at all."

"What will it be about?"

"A simple love-story," said David piously, "about a girl that loves a man frightfully and he is married, so she goes and lives with him, and then his wife is very ill and going to die, so the girl and the man both offer themselves for blood transfusion in a very noble way without each other knowing. But only of them has the right kind of blood and I can't decide which. Do you think it would be more pathetic if the girl gave her blood and died, and then the man went off into the desert to be a monk, or if the man died and the wife and the girl made friends over his corpse and both became nuns? One might do good business with that, because in films no one much cares if the hero lives or dies so long as there are plenty of lovely heroines."

"How lovely. I shall come and see it."

"I'll give you a part, if you like. A friend of mine is thinking of starting a studio of his own. You can be the wife. She hasn't much to do but look lovely and deeply wronged. You have just the hands for a wronged wife," he said, taking one of her hands in his, "absolutely perfect."

'What is a wronged hand like?" asked Mary, too conscious of the warmth of David's hand on hers.

"Quite perfect."

He pulled a large yellow silk handkerchief out of his pocket and folded it round Mary's hand. "So perfect that I shall do it up in a parcel and give it back to you." So saying, he laid her hand, neatly enfolded in his handkerchief, back on her knee.

Mary hardly knew whether she was more afraid of the silence or of the sound of her own voice, but David spared her any further embarrassment by resuming possession of his handkerchief and getting up.

"Four o'clock," he said. "A little walk among the ruins and then we will go home. I simply must get back before Holt goes, to see how he survived an afternoon with Agnes and the children. Agnes looks so lovely and fragile, but she has no nerves and the resistance of an ox, bless her. An hour of James and Emmy leaves me limp, but Agnes is quite happy to spend six weeks at the sea with them, on the beach all day. When James hits Emmy, or Clarissa breaks a teacup, she just says,

'Wicked one, wicked one,' in her delicious, cooing voice, and does nothing about it. Come up here. This is the only staircase left. It went to the monks' dormitory, and you can see the plan of the abbey better from the top."

Mary followed him up a narrow winding stair into a long roofless chamber from which the whole extent of the abbey could be seen. Behind them rose a steep wooded hanger and before them lay the rich meadow land.

"They were frightfully well off," said David. "They had twenty or thirty farms, and mills and a river. The old fish-pond is still over there, just below the woods. We can look at it as we go home. I'm going up to the next floor; you'd better not come."

"But there isn't any next floor."

"I know, but you can walk round the walls on the remains of a gallery. I expect the head monk used to sneak round it to watch if the monks said their prayers before going to bed. You'll see me again in a minute."

He disappeared under an archway and Mary sat in the embrasure of a window. Presently he reappeared, twelve feet or so above her, walking on a ledge that ran round the building.

"Don't look if it makes you feel sick," called David obligingly. Mary did feel rather sick, so she looked away through the window into the cloisters. Had David really thought her hands were perfect, or was it just his amusing way? It was difficult to know whether he meant anything he said or not. Mary was not sure whether she liked him better ragging with Martin or sentimentalizing over her hand.

On the whole, she thought the ragging was better fun. She was not going to admit to herself how difficult it had been when David took her hand to let it lie in his, not to let it close a little over his, not to let a little pressure of her fingers ask for an answering pressure from his. That was the kind of thing people did in cinemas on Saturday nights and not to be thought of. Delicious anger flooded her, and she was lost for a moment, sitting between heaven and earth with a blue sky beyond. At the sound of footsteps she said, without turning round:

"So you haven't broken your neck, David?"

There was no answer. She looked up and saw a stranger standing beside her. In his face she saw reflections of David, as if David's face were seen in an old mirror which dimmed its lustre and darkened its smile. David's voice above them cried out:

"The ledge has gone since last time. Look out, I'm going to jump. "

There was a little noise of falling mortar, and then David landed suddenly on toes and fingertips beside them. Mary, startled, drew back quickly into the window and nearly fell. The newcomer caught her and held her steady.

"Jolly good jump," said David dispassionately. "Hallo, John, where did you come from?"

"I've just finished up with Macpherson. I thought I heard your voice gabbling away up here and came to see. This is Miss Preston, I suppose. You nearly made her fall out of the window with your gymnastic tricks."

"Here's your other uncle, Mary," said David. "Uncle John. Though what he is doing with his arm round you, I don't know."

John retreated.

"I ought to have explained who I was," he said to Mary. "I saw you in the window and guessed who you were, and then that ass David had to show off, as usual. I hope you weren't frightened."

"Of course she wasn't," said David indignantly. "Steel true, blade straight, the great artificer made Miss Preston. And as for showing off, John, that's just sour grapes. I bet you couldn't do that jump as neatly as I did."

"I wouldn't do it at all if I was going to make my guests fall out of the window. Shall I take you two back in the car? Macpherson has gone home."

"Right," said David. "We'll be home just in time to do a little Holt-baiting. Oh, John, we had a splendid time at lunch. Mamma was at her vaguest and little Holt was bounding like anything, and papa just got up and left him to our mercies. He has been with Agnes and the children all afternoon. Mary and I escaped for a walk. She is going to act in my film when it gets going."

By this time Mary and John had got into the front of the Ford and David was sitting behind, his elbows on the back of the front seat.

"You'll be glad to hear," said John, "that father has at last named the bull."

"Poor darling, I thought that was going to last him at least another week. However, something accomplished, something done. What is it to be?"

"Roderick. He says the Argentines can call it Roderigo if they want to."

"And what has Macpherson to say?"

"He is quite pleased. He says doubtless Roderick is a very good Scots name and he is going to call his new terrier Rannoch, so that the name shan't be wasted. My father's bulls are nearly all bred for export," added John, turning to Mary, and obviously struggling to find conversation for a guest. "Most of them go to South America."

"Oh," said Mary, deeply conscious of David's elbow almost touching her shoulder.

When they came in they found Lady Emily, Agnes and Mr. Holt sitting at tea in what used to be Agnes's sitting-room, but was now used for sit-down tea at a round table. Mr. Holt was in a state of sulks which he hardly endeavoured to control. He had come, ruffled by Lord Capes's treatment, expecting to be honoured, taken round the garden by his hostess, his opinion sought, and deferred to. Instead of that he had spent the whole afternoon with Mrs. Graham and her children, first being an unwilling audience of the adventures of Hobo-Gobo and the fairy Joybell, and then being taken round such parts of the garden as the children preferred. These included the potting-shed, the furnace for the hot-houses, the compost bed, a small plantation of larches in which only those of tender years could walk with any comfort, and finally a pond in the kitchen-garden. Here Agnes, look-ing cool and lovely, had sat on the stone edge under a parasol while her offspring tried to catch goldfish in their hands, and Nannie and Ivy walked up and down with Clarissa in her perambulator. Mr. Holt had not at all enjoyed the sun on his back, nor was his plump figure adapted to sitting on a low stone edging. James had reached over too far, soaked his tunic, and been removed yelling by Ivy. Emmy had succeeded in fishing out a small piece of duckweed, which she kindly laid in tribute on Mr. Holes knee.

"Oh wicked one, wicked one," said her mother in tones of besotted tenderness, while the unhappy guest gingerly laid the duckweed on the stone edge. "Mr. Holt, you must wipe it off at once. Duckweed always stains."

"Emmy, you are a bad girl," said Nannie coming up. "Shall I get a cloth and wipe the gentleman's trousers, madam?"

"Yes, do, Nannie. You can leave the perambulator here."

"Fish," said Emmy, pointing to the duckweed. "Yes, dar-ling, fish," said her mother, "green fish." "Green fish," said Emmy.

"Yes, darling, lovely green fish."

"Lovely green. fish," said Emmy.

Conversation maundered along on these lines till Nannie returned with a jug of boiling water and a cloth, with which she rubbed Mr. Holt's knee, making a large damp patch.

"It's better to wet a large surface," she explained, "other-wise the stain is more likely to show."

"Thanks, thanks," said Mr. Holt testily, getting up and

walking about in the hopes of assisting the drying process.

"Has Lady Norton a lovely garden?" asked Agnes, dimly feeling that some kind of reparation was necessary. "I hear it is too lovely."

"It is quite the best in the county," said Mr. Holt, still offended.

"Tell me all about it," said Agnes, throwing into her voice a warmth which would have deceived none of her family.

"That might be a little egotistic as I help Lady Norton in the planning," said Mr. Holt, slightly mollified. He sat down beside Agnes. Emmy began to cry.

"Fish, fish," she wailed.

"Oh, Mr. Holt," said Agnes, her wits sharpened by mother-love, "I am afraid you are sitting on Emmy 's fish."

Mr. Holt got up violently. The piece of duckweed, well flattened, was where he had been sitting.

"There now," said Nannie, returning, "if the gentleman hasn't got all over that green stuff again. Emmy, you *are* bad girl."

"Oh, wicked one," said Agnes lovingly. "Take her in to tea, Nannie."

"Shall I get the cloth again, madam?" asked Nannie.

"Certainly not," said Mr. Holt. "If tea is really ready I had better go in, as I have to leave shortly."

If Agnes had not been an earl's granddaughter he `would certainly have killed her.

This accounts for the state of simmering fury in which he was discovered by the party from the abbey.

"Come and sit by me, Mary," said Lady Emily. "I have had a really restful afternoon on my sofa, thinking about all sorts of things. Where did you go?"

"David took me to the abbey and we explored the ruins."

"David," said his mother, raising her voice across the table. "Did you see Sutton?"

"Yes, mother."

"Did he tell you how Lottie was?"

"No, darling. Is she a cow?"

"David! She is that nice girl of his, the one that used to be scullery maid here till she went mad."

"I saw Sutton, mother," said John. "He visited Lottie last week and she is very happy."

"Poor Lottie," said Lady Emily, turning to Mary again. "She was a very nice girl, but peculiar, and has to be in the county asylum. All her mother's family are queer. I always think it was such a pity the abbey was put down at the Reformation. The monks might have been able to do something for her, as her people have always lived on this land."

"I expect they'd have burnt her, mother," said David, "or put her in a cell with straw in her hair. You never know your luck with monks."

"Talking of the abbey," Mr. Holt began, "Lady Norton told me—"

"Oh, we all know her people are mad, but we don't talk about it," said David cheerfully. "Have you any lunatic ancestors, Mr. Holt? We have heaps."

Gudgeon came into the room to announce the car just in time to save Mr. Holt from exploding. His adieux were brief and cold except to Lady Emily, to whom he expressed his intention of inviting himself again during the summer, hoping to see the garden with her. His emphasis on the word "her" was accompanied by a venomous look at the unconscious Agnes.

"That will be too delicious," said Lady Emily, "though I'm afraid Henry isn't a very good host, but he never troubles to be nice to people unless he likes them, and he likes hardly anybody. Next time you come you must tell me all about Lady Capes, Mr. Holt, and I shall read you some of David's book aloud. You must tell all your friends to buy it. It is perfectly delicious and none of us can understand a word of it, but I always think reading aloud is the greatest help, don't you?"

Mary was rather glad to escape to her own room before
dinner, from the overpowering personalities of so many
Leslies. First she explored her drawers and cupboards to discover in what unlikely places the housemaid had hidden her
belongings, then she began to write to her mother. But before
she had got very far her Aunt Agnes came in to invite her to
see Clarissa have her bath.

"Just in case you felt homesick, darling," said Agnes, who
was convinced that her children were a panacea for every ill.

Mary, who knew her young cousins well in their London
home and was very fond of them, was glad to go with Agnes.

"I am not homesick in the least," she explained, "but I'd
adore to see Clarissa bathed."

"I thought you would be missing your mother," said
Agnes, with mild reproach.

She led Mary along the corridor, through a green baize
door, and up some stairs to the nursery quarters, which
opened off the long passage before mentioned. The nursery,
which had been the home of Lady Emily's four children, was
a large, sunny room made from several half-attic rooms
thrown into one, with sloping ceilings in odd corners. It was
filled with the accumulation of many years of children. A
large dappled rocking-horse with fiery nostrils stood in one
corner. One eye was gone, and its tail was little more than a
wisp. The pommel had long since been lost, and down its
socket, which communicated darkly with the horse's inside, a
good deal of property had been lost, with or without intent, in
the last forty years. Part of a doll's tea-set and two nursery
teaspoons were known to be in Dobbin's stomach, and no
power on earth had ever been able to get them out. Mr. Leslie
had once made an ominous utterance about having a piece
sawn out of Dobbin underneath, but Agnes had cried so bitterly that he had given up his plan. Scarcely had David out-
grown the horse, when Martin was old enough to be held
upon it for a short ride. It was later David's avuncular pride to

rock his nephew upon it, a treat which always began for
Martin with tremulous anticipation, continued in hysterical
shrieks of joy, and usually ended in tears. By rocking at full tilt
it was possible to make Dobbin move bumpily round the
room, and at times Martin in his turn did not disdain to dazzle Agnes's children on their frequent visits by showing off his
prowess in this way.

Just inside the door was an enormous upright mechanical
organ, product of the Fatherland in its milder days. Into this
you inserted a large metal disc covered with perforations, and
then turned a handle. A huge metal roller, studded with
spikes like some engine of the Inquisition, could then be
observed in motion through the glass front of the upper part,
and crashing melody poured forth. The discs, also from the
Fatherland, were for the most part extracts from such master-
pieces as *William Tell* or *La Sonnambula*, varied by such well-
known English airs as *Oft in the Stilly Night*. This triumph of
Euterpe's art, known as a Polyphone, was still in good working order, and the delight of James, Emmy, Clarissa, Nannie
and Ivy.

A large doll's house stood over by the window, its once elegant contents a mere jumble of wreckage. This regrettable
mishap had taken place when David was the spoilt baby. He
had decided that his friend the kitchen cat wanted to be
introduced to the joys of domestic life on a small scale. He
therefore formed the habit of fetching George, all unwilling,
from the kitchen, carrying him upstairs with his arms tightly
clasped under George's front legs, while George's furious
hind legs clawed the air in vain for support. He would then
push George in at the front door and shut it behind him.
George, much agitated, would worm his way up the staircase
and squeeze his body into each room in turn, vainly seeking
some mode of exit. Then David discovered that if he opened
the windows George, who was just too large to get through
them, would in his frenzy paw all the smaller articles of fur-

niture out of the window and then sit, crossly regarding his kind young benefactor, his large sullen face far larger than the window at which it appeared. The doll's house had also at various times been used as a home for mice and silkworms, and was rapidly qualifying for demolition under a slum clearance scheme.

The usual pictures adorned the walls. Coloured supplements from old *Graphics*, an engraving of a little girl in a long frilly frock standing on the lowest step of the staircase, entitled "All turn here and see me dump," other engravings of more little girls in crinoline hats and empire frocks with large collies or small puppies, and a coloured representation of Queen Victoria receiving the news of her accession. These, with quantities of old family photographs, heads of Lord Kitchener, Lord Roberts and General Buller, represented art, as did the large fourfold screen pasted all over with pictures cut from story-books, or newspapers, or coloured catalogues. A canary in a cage in the window made a deafening clamour.

A slight concession to more modern methods was visible in the shape of a small blackboard fastened to the wall, but all three children preferred to use the distempered surface of the nursery walls as a medium for their urge to mural decoration. There was, however, nothing modern about the nursery tablecloth of dark red and blue checks, nor in the large old-fashioned grate with a hob on each side, nor in the high nursery fender with its brass airing-rail. On a rug in front of the fire was an oval bath of japanned tin. In it sat Clarissa, trying to catch the soap.

"Good afternoon, Nannie," said Mary.

"Good afternoon, miss. Baby is ever so pleased to see you, aren't you, baby?"

But Clarissa very properly took no notice of this rhetorical question, concentrating her whole attention on the soap, which had an annoying way of slipping through her fingers just as she thought she had grasped it.

"Could I speak to you for a moment, madam?" said
.Nannie to Agnes.

It was at moments of crisis like this that Mary chiefly
envied her Aunt Agnes's imperturbable disposition. Most
mothers feel a hideous sinking at the heart when these fatal
words are pronounced, but Agnes only showed a kindly and
inactive interest. In anyone else Mary might have suspected
unusual powers of bluff, hiding trembling knees, a feeling of
helpless nausea, flashes of light behind the eyes, storm in the
brain, and a general desire to say "Take double your present
wages,. but don't tell me what it is you want to speak to me
about." But Agnes, placidly confident in the perfection of her
own family and the unassailable security of her own existence,
was only capable of feeling a mild curiosity and barely capable of showing. it.

"Yes, Nannie, what is it?" she asked, settling herself comfortably in the nursery rocking-chair.

"It is about the children's breakfasts, madam," Nannie
began. "Come out now, baby, and get dried."

"Oh, do let me dry her," interrupted Mary, feeling that the
situation would be less acutely unbearable if she had something
to occupy her. Nannie rose with a superior smile and taking off
her flannel apron handed it and the bath towel to Mary.

"I don't wish to complain, madam," she continued, "but as
I was saying to Ivy only this morning, if this state of affairs
goes on continuing I must speak to Mrs. Graham. Come out,
baby, like a good girl when Auntie Mary tells you."

"Yes, Nannie," said Agnes, her mind obviously occupied
with Clarissa's enchanting form as, leaning gracefully on
Mary's arm, she stepped uncertainly out of the bath.

"It's the cereals, madam. You know Dr. Horne said Emmy
and baby were to continue with the puffed wheat for the present. I made a point of mentioning it to Mrs. Siddon myself
when we arrived, not wishing to trouble you nor her ladyship,
but this is the third morning that barley kernels have been

sent up. I am sure for my own part I am not at all particular, and would really never feel like more than a cup of tea and a piece of toast for my own breakfast, but I thought you ought to know, madam."

"Oh, Nannie, how annoying," said Agnes, with such complete absence of conviction that Nannie spoke again.

"I am sure, madam, I wouldn't have mentioned it at all, only Dr. Horne did say that Emmy and baby were to have the puffed wheat. I am sure Mrs. Siddon doesn't mean anything, but I always like to carry out a doctor's instructions, otherwise I say it is waste of money. Mrs. Dashwood's nannie never lets her children have barley kernels, they are so heating to the blood. Don't wriggle like that, baby, when auntie is putting your nice bedroom slippers on. So I thought you would wish to know."

"Oh, Nannie, how annoying," said Agnes again. "I must see about it, mustn't I, my own precious Clarissa?"

Clarissa, dried and robed, slid off Mary's lap and made her way cautiously to her mother, who took her up and hugged her, regardless of the havoc it made with her delicate dress.

"And there is one other thing, madam," continued Nannie. "Is Ivy to go down for the children's fruit every morning? I am sure she doesn't mind, for she is a nice obliging girl, but I don't see how I am to get the children out by . eleven as you wish, madam, if Ivy has to be downstairs getting their fruit. Last time we were here one of the under-housemaids always brought it up, but she has gone and the new girl, Bessie, doesn't seem to understand, and I have been obliged to send Ivy down for the last two mornings, so we couldn't get out till nearly twelve and baby is quite losing her roses."

"Darling Clarissa," said Agnes,. whose younger daughter looked as pink and flourishing as could be expected under the horrifying circumstances. "I must see Mrs. Siddon about it, Nannie. It is so annoying, isn't it?"

John then came in.

"Here is Uncle John come to say good night to baby," said Nannie, who appeared to regard her employers and their relations as well-disposed half-wits who needed encouragement. "Can I leave baby with you, madam, while I fetch the elder ones? Ivy has gone down to the village on her bike to see about a canary for James."

"Isn't one enough?" said John.

"Oh, no, sir," said Nannie pityingly. "Canaries pine unless they have a little husband or a little wife, and ever since our little lady died this poor little fellow has been quite mopy."

"I wish he would keep his grief to himself," said John, looking unsympathetically at the sorrowing widower, whose feathers were standing straight out all over him with the vehemence of his song.

"He is only saying 'Good night,' sir," said Nannie, rather shocked. "We heard of a little wife in the village, so Ivy is going to get her for James. Then we shall have some nice music again, shan't we, baby?"

Nannie went off to fetch James and Emmy. 'Well, darling John," said Agnes, "have you had a nice day?"

"I got a lot of business settled with Macpherson and made Mary's acquaintance," said John, smiling kindly at Mary, who looked very pleasant, sitting in her flannel apron by the fire. "And father made up his mind what to call the bull, so we are getting on. Agnes, what I really wanted to talk to you about is Martin. You know his mother wants him to go to a French family for part of the summer holidays. I'm not sure that it is a good plan. Mother and father are very keen to have him here, and the more he learns about the place the better. It isn't as if he had a father of his own to carry on. If father died, and he isn't as young as he was Martin would have to walk straight into his responsibilities. His mother and his stepfather will be in America all the summer, and it was quite settled that Martin was to be here till his mother got this idea of his learning French. I don't see why he couldn't do French

next year. Macpherson is always talking of retiring, and
Martin ought to be as much with him as he can. Besides
school holidays aren't very long. When he is at Oxford he will
have plenty of time to put in a month in France if he wants
to. What do you think?"

"I'd better write and ask Robert. He will know exactly
what Martin ought to do. Daddy will know, won't he, darling
Clarissa?"

John restrained an impulse to shake his sister.

"Yes," he said, "Robert will undoubtedly know exactly
what would be best, but it will take about six weeks to get an
answer. Meanwhile, will you back me up? I have to go back to
town to-morrow morning and Martin goes up with me on his
way back to school. If I tackle the parents about it, will you be
on my side? Martin's mother won't mind either way, so long
as he is provided for."

"Of course you are quite right," said Agnes decidedly.
"Martin ought to be here. I am sure Robert would think he
ought to stay here. We do want Martin to stay with us, don't
we, darling Clarissa?"

Nannie's return with James and Emmy put an end to the
discussion. Clarissa was taken off to bed in the night nursery.
Agnes and Mary went downstairs while John stayed behind to
give the elder children a riotous ride on Dobbin.

"Let us go and find mamma," said Agnes to her niece.
"She likes to see me before dinner so that I can do the name
cards."

They found Lady Emily in the morning-room, writing
letters.

"I was just writing to your mother, Mary," she explained,
"to say how we love having you, and how useful you are going
to be. Is it twopence halfpenny to Germany?"

"It's Switzerland, Aunt Emily, but it will be twopence
halfpenny all the same. Mummie will love to have a letter
from you."

"I thought Switzerland was cheaper," said Lady Emily, "because of the League of Nations which seems to make it so English. I am sure when I was at Geneva, when I took David to that delightful professor he was with in one of his long vacations, I met *quantities* of English friends there. Agnes, do you think Mr. Holt was annoyed? Your father was not very kind to him and I feel when anyone is as trying as Mr. Holt one should make a special effort to be nice. He didn't seem pleased at tea-time, but perhaps it is my imagination. We must have him again, and I must ask his friend, Lady Norton. He seemed to want me to ask her. She is a most tiresome woman, and I don't want her here at all, but perhaps it would be civil. Who is it? Oh, come in, Siddon."

"I beg pardon, my lady," said the housekeeper. "I didn't see Miss Agnes and the young lady was here."

Mrs. Siddon—Mrs. only by courtesy—was a spare, middle-aged woman, who had been stillroom maid in more spacious days, and now ruled Rushwater House with a firm hand. She was devoted to Agnes and her children, but usually in a state of simmering feud with Nannie, not holding, she said, with those girls from institutions. This was aimed at the highly respectable training-school for children's nurses, from which Nannie had originally come and whose uniform she wore.

"I beg pardon, my lady, if I am interrupting, but could I speak to you for a moment?"

Mary looked at Agnes, but her aunt's face betrayed no emotion.

"It's about the children's breakfasts, my lady. I am sure I would wish to study nurse's fancies in every way, but to send down her breakfast untouched for two mornings and then say it is because the children don't like their cereals is hardly reasonable. And as for the fruit, I am sure I have no wish for Ivy to come down for it, and I would be glad, Miss Agnes, if you would speak to Ivy, because skylarking in the pantry with

Walter is what she does. The fruit is put out every morning for Bessie to take up to the nursery, but when Mr. David and Mr. Martin are here they get up so late that she gets behind-hand with her work."

'Well, Siddon, that is all too dreadful," said Lady Emily, "and we must see about it. Couldn't Bessie just run up with the fruit a little earlier?"

"Of course, my lady, if you wish Mr. David and Mr. Martin's beds to be left, she could," said Mrs. Siddon, resolutely thrusting away responsibility.

"Mamma darling, I am afraid Nannie is being a little difficult, and I am quite worried," said Agnes with a serene countenance.

"It was just the same when you were all little," said Lady Emily to Agnes. "You remember old Baker, Siddon, when she was housekeeper, how she always quarrelled with the children's nurses all about nothing."

"Mrs. Baker, my lady, was of a difficult temper, as well I know, having been under her. It wasn't only Miss Agnes and the young gentlemen's nurses, but the maddermazells and the frawlines. We never had peace, as we used to remark in the Hall. But I am sure I am the last to take offence, and I am only too wishful to meet nurse half-way sooner than have any difficulty, or worry your ladyship or Miss Agnes."

Having so far perjured herself, Mrs. Siddon waited with an expressionless face.

"Well, Siddy," said Agnes taking up her embroidery, "I am sure it is all most annoying, and if the children don't like their cereals they are bad little things. Mamma, did you take my green wool?"

"Yes, Agnes. I wanted some this afternoon, though I can't think what for. I thought I put it back in your bag."

"Perhaps it has gone on the floor," said Agnes.

"Is this it?" asked Mary, picking up a ball of green wool which was lying in a pot of carnations.

"Thank you, dear," said Lady Emily. "I know now! I wanted to tie up those carnations and then tea was ready. Well, Siddon, we must see about it and Mrs. Graham must speak to Ivy."

"Aunt Emily," said Mary, "excuse me interfering, but Nannie did say she wanted puffed wheat instead of barley kernels, because the doctor said so."

After a good deal of talk, to which Agnes's only contribution was that darling Clarissa looked so sweet eating her cereals, Mrs. Siddon agreed to provide puffed wheat for the nursery and see that the children's fruit went up with their breakfast.

"I am much obliged to you for mentioning it, miss," she said to Mary. "If nurse had demeaned herself to explain what was wrong, I should have ordered puffed wheat at once. But eggs and bacon coming down all cold on a plate are no explanation at all. Thank you, my lady."

"Now, mamma," said Agnes, "we can do the name cards."

CHAPTER V
SOME ASPECTS OF MILTON

AT DINNER Mary found herself between Mr. Leslie and John. She wished it had been David, as she had an uneasy feeling that John found her rather young and rather a bore. But with Mr. Leslie she got on excellently. She listened to his stories about his cattle and was placed in his mind as a thoroughly sensible kind of girl. Pity David couldn't find some nice girl like that, he thought, instead of the queer young women he brought down from time to time. Encouraged by her interest he gave her a detailed account of the trouble they had had in getting someone to play the organ in church since the old schoolmaster died.

"We really ought to ask the education people to let us have someone musical next time," said John, who had overheard his father's remarks. "This young woman means well, but her idea of an organ is the electric organ at a cinema, all vox humana and tremolo."

"Lovely things those organs," said David. "The keyboard always reminds me of a gigantic set of false teeth."

"Do you play the organ, Mr. Leslie?" said Mary to John, trying to make conversation.

"A bit. I hope you aren't going to call me Mr. Leslie though. I shan't know if I am myself or my father."

"Thank you," said Mary, wondering whether she was to say John or Uncle John. He was older than Aunt Agnes, so she supposed Uncle John would be more suitable, but it seemed a little ridiculous. After all, Aunt Agnes was married to Uncle Robert and had three children, so she was a real aunt. But this Mr. Leslie with no wives or children didn't seem to have the status of an uncle. To call him John, on the other hand, was a familiarity from which she rather shrank. She didn't know how old he was, but he must be quite middle-aged, though he wasn't at all fat or bald. From which we may gather that Mary's ideas of middle-age were not very sound.

"Does David play?" she asked, bringing out his name with a little difficulty and wondering if this Mr. Leslie would think her impertinent. But to her relief he took it all quite calmly.

"Not the organ," he said, "but he plays the piano very well. If you want any jazz, put David at the piano and he will do the rest."

"Oh, I adore jazz."

"So do I," said John, "but I can't play it—haven't got the gift. I only play highbrow stuff. What about you?"

"Oh, I don't do anything in particular. I like listening."

When pudding had subsided, Martin, who had been strangely quiet all through dinner, suddenly said in a loud and ill-assured voice:

"I say grandfather."

Though Martin's voice had broken some years ago, it still had an uncomfortable tendency to betray him in moments of emotion, and detaching itself from his control, emerge as a squeak or a bellow. At this moment it was a deep bass which startled him as much as it did the rest of the company. The silence that followed was so complete that Martin blushed to the roots of his dark hair.

"Owbridge's lung tonic for you tonight, my boy," said David.

"Well, Martin?" said his grandfather.

"I say, grandfather, it's about this plan of me going abroad in the summer. I've got an awfully good idea if you and gran don't mind. You know Mr. Banister is letting his house to those French professor people. Why couldn't I be a P.G. there for August? I could learn a lot of French and then I wouldn't have to be away all the summer."

"This requires a little consideration," said his grandfather, secretly not displeased at the idea of having Martin near him for the holidays. "Your mother was arranging for you to go to France and she may not wish to alter her plans."

"Oh, mother will be all right, sir. I say, grandfather," he repeated, his eager face looking younger than ever by the candlelight which was now the only light in the room, "don't you think we could work it? It would be a ripping plan. I've had a jaw with Mr. Banister about it, and he says these Boulles always take pupils in France and he doesn't see why they wouldn't in England. And then there are two sons, one is a professor and awfully good at French and the other is about my age, so I could learn a lot."

At any other time the prospect of spending a month in the company of a French boy of his own age would have filled Martin with terror and disgust, but in the light of his new plan young Master Boulle was assuming sterling qualities.

"I know exactly what young Boulle will be like," said David. "If he is your age he will have knickerbockers and short socks and a sailor blouse, and a fluffy moustache and beard that his fond mamma won't let him shave, and lots of spots on his face."

"Oh, shut up, David."

"And you will have to learn La Fontaine by heart," continued David, "and recite your piece to show your kind grandparents what progress you have made.

"I once knew a very nice French boy," said Mary, feeling sorry for Martin. "He played tennis awfully well and looked just like anyone else and hadn't any spots at all. And he was just about Martin's age."

Having said this, she subsided into embarrassment, thinking her remark stupid and unhelpful. But Martin clutched at it with enthusiasm.

"I dare say this chap plays quite well, too," he said. "Gran, don't you think I could?"

"I think it is such a good plan," said Lady Emily. "If they haven't enough beds at the vicarage we could easily send one down for you, and some sheets, because I don't suppose Mr. Banister has enough. And of course they'll get their milk from us, because Gooch's milk in the village really can't be trusted. I do hope, Henry, the vicarage drains are all right if Martin is to go there, because the French are rather vague about drains."

"Yes, but darling, they aren't bringing their drains with them," said David.

"No, of course not, David, don't be so unreasonable. You know perfectly well what I mean. When you were all little I would never take you to any lodgings at the sea till all the drains had been tested. Well, it's a delicious plan and we must have a long talk about it and see what Mr. Banister says."

"If the vicarage drains are out of order it's Banister's fault," said Mr. Leslie angrily. "Macpherson had them overhauled only the year before last and it cost me a matter of fifty-five pounds. Why he had to let the vicarage to foreigners, I don't know. Have an outbreak of typhoid as likely as not."

Martin was going to expostulate, but a look from John warned him that it was not the moment. While Lady Emily collected her spectacles, which had got into a banana skin, and readjusted her shawl, John said to Martin:

"I'm delighted with your plan, Martin. Don't bother grandfather about it again just now. I'll see him before I go and it will be all right."

"Oh, thanks awfully, Uncle John."

Mary heard this conversation and her heart warmed to John for his kindness to Martin.

"Now, mamma, where will you sit?" asked Agnes when the

ladies reached the drawing-room.

"I'm going to be very selfish and have this long comfortable chair by the fire," said Lady Emily, letting herself down into it. "Now, I shall put my feet up. Put my red shawl over them, Agnes; it is on the table with my painting things."

"It isn't here, mamma."

"Then I know where it is," said Lady Emily triumphantly. "It is on the chest of drawers, not the walnut one, the other one, in my room. I told Conque I would want it."

"Can I get it for you, Aunt Emily?" asked Mary.

"Yes, dear, do. And you will find too a very large bag of embroidery on a chair."

"Mamma, you have got your red shawl under you," said Agnes reproachfully, and the embroidery is on your worktable. Don't you remember you left it here last night, and that was why you hadn't got any green wool and took some of mine to tie the carnations up."

"Then that's all right," said Lady Emily. "And now, Mary, just put that little blue silk cushion off the sofa in behind my back and ring for Conque."

Mary rang. Gudgeon appeared.

"Oh, Gudgeon," said Lady Emily, untwisting the chiffon veil she had round her head at dinner, "tell Conque to bring my hot-water bottle."

"The bottle was placed here, my lady, just before you came in from dinner," said Gudgeon, extracting it from among the rugs at Lady Emily's feet.

"Oh, thank you so much. And Mr. John and Mr. David and Mr. Martin are all going to-morrow, but I don't know when. I suppose they will be going by train as Mr. John and Mr. David haven't brought their cars and Mr. Martin, of course, hasn't got one. You had better find out what time Weston will be wanted to take them to the station and if it is Rushwater or Southbridge. Mary, dear, give me a little screen that you will find on the mantelpiece, just to keep the fire off my face—no, the other side of the mantelpiece—thank you, darling. Wait a moment, Gudgeon, because I know I had something else to say. Oh, yes, if they go by the twelve-forty they will want sandwiches, I expect, as it would mean lunch at twelve if they wanted lunch, and that is so early. Or if there is a dining-car they will want to lunch on the train, because Mr. John hates sandwiches, but I don't remember if that train has a dining-car; but if they go by another train of course that won't matter. But you had better tell Mrs. Siddon, just in case. And, Gudgeon, does Walter skylark with Ivy in the pantry?"

"I couldn't say, my lady. Not in my presence."

"No, I thought not. Well, then, that's all right; only Mrs. Siddon seems worried, so I said I'd speak about it, but of course if you say so it's all right. And tell Walter if he is packing for Mr. Martin not to put in any books because last time he packed two library books and Mr. Leslie was annoyed."

"Very good, my lady."

"Then that's all settled," said Lady Emily with a sigh of relief. "Thanks, Gudgeon. Oh, I expect the trains will be different to-morrow, as it is Whit Tuesday, or are they the same again? You could telephone to the stationmaster at Southbridge and make sure, only you had better do it to-night, in case the gentlemen want to know which train they can have."

"Gudgeon will see to-it all, mamma," said Agnes. "Now, Mary, darling, do sing to me," said Lady Emily. "Agnes says you have a delicious voice."

"If you really want me to, Aunt Emily."

"It will be delicious. But you can't see in the dark over there. I can't think why there isn't a light for the piano. Agnes, where are those candlesticks we used in the winter?"

"I will ring and ask Gudgeon, mamma."

"I know," said Lady Emily, getting painfully up, scattering shawls, hot bottles, embroidery in confusion around her. "They are on the top of the bookcase. Yes, here they are. And,

Agnes, put out all the other lights except just my little lamp for my table and then we can have a delicious cosy time."

Lady Emily went back to the long chair, recovered her hot-water bottle, red shawl, blue silk cushion, embroidery, spectacles and screen, and composed herself to at least a temporary attention, while Mary, shy and unhappy, sat down at the piano. But finding that Lady Emily and Agnes kept up a low murmuring conversation in which the words "cereals," "bath water not nearly hot enough," "darling Clarissa" might have been distinguished, she gained courage and went on singing quite happily in the half-light at the end of the long drawing-room.

So it happened that John, coming in before the others, heard a small clear voice and paused to listen.

"'Bist du bei mir,' " it sang, very sweetly and without effort, " `geh' ich mit Freuden zum Sterben and zu meiner Ruh. '"

There seemed to be no reason why the linked sweetness of the air should ever come to an end. John standing unseen in the dim room felt that time was still for the space of that song. Quiet waters flowed into his heart, a rose blossomed and bloomed; the waters ebbed, the rose petals fell. Without disturbing Mary, he trod

softly to the hearth and sat down with his mother and sister. Whatever else Mary may have sung, the three did not hear it. John was following a vision, while his mother offered silent thanks for the look of peace in his face. Agnes, who liked music with all her gentle uncritical nature, thought how nice it would be if dear John did marry Mary, because then they could have some music in the evenings and perhaps the children would be musical.

Therefore Mr. Leslie coming in with David and Martin was surprised to find them all in the dark.

"Gudgeon not turned the lights up?" he asked, turning on all the switches.

In the sudden dazzle, Mary was able to leave the piano and

come near the fire. She saw John, but thought, if she thought about it at all, that he had come in with the rest.

"Shall I read to you, darling?" David asked his mother.

"Yes, do. Mary, you must hear David read. He reads quite beautifully. Read us some Blake, darling."

"Do you mind if I go to bed now, gran?" said Martin, alarmed at the prospect.

"You aren't ill, Martin?"

"No, gran, of course not. But I think it's a good plan to go to bed early sometimes," he said virtuously:

"All right, Martin," said his young uncle. "I shall go to bed when you recite your French piece, that's all."

"Oh, shut up, David. It's better than your beastly Blake, anyhow."

'What, my young classic," said David, catching Martin by the wrist, "can't you abide the romantics? Have at you. I'll read some Milton. Where's your *Paradise Lost*, mother?"

"I had it a few days ago, because I was painting a picture of the Tree of Knowledge in the beginning," said Lady Emily, "and I couldn't get the serpent right.

I expect it's on my table."

"So it is. Now, Martin, sit down and listen to Uncle David."

"Which bit will you read?" asked Agnes.

"I am going to read the bit about Satan being turned into a serpent," said David. "And let it be a warning to you, Martin."

He at once began to read, remarkably well. But at the lines:

> *. . . they fondly thinking to allay*
> *Their appetite with gust, instead of fruit*
> *Chewed bitter ashes, which the offended taste*
> *With spattering noise rejected .. .*

Martin unfortunately was overtaken by violent giggles and fell into disgrace.

"You had better go to bed, Martin," said his grandfather.

"Sorry, grandfather, but it was so frightfully funny. I never knew Milton could be funny before. 'Spattering noise'—oh, gosh! Thanks most awfully, David. Good night, everyone."

He reeled from the room, overcome with laughter. "It is funny, too," said David. "But I was so busy listening to the beauty of my own voice that I couldn't stop to laugh. Don't you think I ought to pull off that job at Broadcasting House, mother?"

"I hope so, David. Wouldn't you like to go on reading? Only give me a glass of barley water first. Oh, hasn't it come yet? It must be earlier than I thought. Oh, here is Gudgeon with the drinks. He must have been waiting till you had finished reading, David."

"I think Milton cannot have been at all the sort of person one would want to know," said Agnes. "I don't think we should have had much in common."

"But he must have been attractive in some ways, Agnes," said Lady Emily, always ready to defend the absent. "He had two wives. Get me some barley water now, John dear."

"I don't think one would have liked them very much either," said Agnes, who seemed to nourish what in one so sweet-tempered was quite a venomous feeling against the poet.

"The first wouldn't have been so bad, but I couldn't have liked the second," said Mary. "Fancy the kind of woman that liked marrying a widower."

John gave his mother her barley water. David helped himself to whisky and soda and drifted over to the piano, where he played and sang snatches of music from revues and musical comedies with such masterful ease that Mary was more than ever glad the men had not been in the room when she was singing.

You must have had a black mammy for your fairy-god-mother, David," said John. "I don't see how else you got that nigger touch in your voice."

"Drinking rum and treacle does it," said David. He played a few chords and sang:

> *"Treacle make my voice so sweet,*
> *Fit to sing at de Judgment seat.*
> *Drinking treacle, drinking rum,*
> *Singing to de Lawd till Kingdom Come."*

"Is that a new spiritual, David?" asked his mother.

"Not yet, darling, but it will be soon."

"What does David mean?" asked Agnes.

> *"Treacle make my voice so clear,*
> *All de darkies come to hear.*
> *Drinking treacle, drinking rum,*
> *Dat's what for de darkies come."*

"Molasses, I believe, is the American term for treacle," said Mr. Leslie.

"Yes, father, but it didn't fit the poem, so they had to alter it to treacle. Anyway, you know what Americans are."

"Quite right, quite right," said Mr. Leslie, who certainly knew very little about it.

Lady Emily then began to collect herself for bed. As she insisted on carrying everything herself, her progress was like a paper-chase. Agnes, David and Mary dutifully followed her to gather what she let fall. At her door she said good night, taking David in with her to show him the moon through her window.

"Are you comfortable in your room, darling?" Agnes asked Mary. "It is a room I am very fond of. It is the one dear Gay always used when she came here alone."

"Who is Gay, Aunt Agnes?"

"Darling John's wife. We all adored her. You would have loved her and so would the children."

"I never knew John was married."

"Darling Gay died seven years ago. James was born just before she died and she thought he was the loveliest baby she had ever seen. Good night, darling, and sleep well."

Not till Mary was in bed did she remember with sickening shame her words about Milton's second wife. What must John have thought of her for sneering at widowers? Perhaps he was still getting Aunt Emily's barley water and had missed her silly priggish remark. Yet it was somehow true about widowers. Nothing you could do would give the word a romantic sound. Only quite elderly people ought to be widowers.

John had heard, but was more concerned with the possible remorse Mary might have than with his own feelings. It was obvious that the child, who after all had never met him before and did not know his family intimately, except Agnes, had never heard of Gay. Seeing her on such easy terms with David and Martin, he had taken it for granted that she knew about himself. Now what should he do? Pretend that he had never heard what she said, or find some way of telling her that no such mistake could hurt him in any way now? It might seem self-conscious to allude to it at all, yet he did not want to think of her possibly being disturbed at the recollection of her idle words. Perhaps Agnes or his mother could help.

What she had said was only thoughtless talk. What she had sung was his key to her. Even if the pure enchanting voice meant nothing, it was enough that it existed. "Bist du bei mir." Bitter waters flowed into his heart. The rose bloomed no more. `

CHAPTER VI

SOME ASPECTS OF DAVID

ON THE FOLLOWING DAY, amid indescribable tumult of plans and counter-plans, Martin and his uncles left. Lady Emily stayed in bed till they had gone, adding her share to the confusion by sending for each in turn, sending each to find the other and Mary to find them all, besides issuing contradictory orders through Conque to Gudgeon and Weston. By great personal exertion the party were at last dispatched, largely owing to Gudgeon, who had skilfully intercepted a message to Weston, which would have resulted in the car coming half an hour too late to take them to the wrong station. Just as they were leaving, Conque appeared, breathless, to say that her ladyship particularly wanted her seccotine and could Mr. Martin tell her where it was. Martin rummaged about in his pockets.

"Sorry, Conk," he said, "it's stuck to the lining and got all hard. I'll tell Weston to get some in Southbridge. Good-bye, Mary."

"Good-bye," shouted his uncles as they all drove off, leaving Mary on the steps. She went to find Agnes, who was said to be doing the flowers. This she did by walking about the garden with James and Emmy, and talking to Brown, the head-gardener, about his children. Meanwhile, the second gardener had cut the flowers for the house and they were subsequently arranged by Gudgeon.

"Good morning, darling," said Agnes, offering her niece a cheek which was so soft that Mary was always afraid of going right through it. "It is too sad that the boys have gone. You must help me with the flowers, because they take the whole morning, and I can't bear it if I don't do them myself."

"Did Nannie get her puffed wheat this morning?" asked Mary.

"Yes, she did. You were so tactful to Siddon, Mary. But the children wouldn't eat it, wicked ones," said Agnes proudly, "so they are to try shredded wheat."

Day followed day in delightful emptiness. Agnes and her mother did their embroidery and had endless conversations about plans for visiting neighbours or having a few people to lunch, plans which usually never got beyond their inception. Mary went for long walks alone, played tennis with the doctor and his wife, and spent much of her time with the children. She was a little shy of being too much with her aunts. Although Lady Emily and Agnes were as kind as they could be, they gave her such an unmarried feeling that she rather avoided sitting much with them during the day. In the evenings she played and sang for Lady Emily, whose habit of talking through all music did not prevent her enjoying it deeply. Mr. Macpherson usually came in two or three times a week when they were alone, talked business to Mr. Leslie after dinner, and then joined the ladies. He had taken a great liking to Mary, who enjoyed going about the country with him and sang Scotch songs for his special pleasure.

So June and part of July slipped away. It was lovely summer weather, and nearly every morning Mary woke to see the great meadow hidden in dewy mist through which the sun would have broken by breakfast-time. It would have been heavenly undisturbed peace except for David's week-end visits. It would have been even a little dull except for David's week-end visits. His job at Broadcasting House had not come off. He had had a trial there, and had rashly chosen to read the passage from Milton which had given such joy to Martin. When he came to the lines about the spattering noise, he remembered Martin's face, and sitting back in his chair, roared with laughter into the scandalized microphone. Joan Stevenson, the very competent young woman who was in charge of the department which dealt with Uplift Poetry Readings, had been shocked, or as she preferred to put it, Frankly, shocked, and took him back to her office in disgrace.

"You spoilt everything by laughing," she said with some annoyance. "Now they won't consider you at all."

"But why?" asked David, still weak with the thought of Martin. "Can't a man laugh without shocking you? Don't tell me you live here and never laugh."

"Of course we laugh," said Joan Stevenson, "but the microphone is, after all, well, frankly, almost a sacred charge. You haven't had the experience I have, David, and you don't quite realize what your action might have meant to hundreds and thousands of listeners, if this were a real broadcast."

"Of course when you talk like that it puts me off altogether," said David. "I don't mind talking aloud into that little box, which would have quite a nice face if you put some eyes and a couple of ears on it, but to think of reading aloud to all those people is, frankly, repellent, as you would say."

"David!"

"Oh, I don't mean you think the people repellent, I was only ragging," said David, a little nervous about the effect of his deliberate parody of Joan's earnest manner of speech. "I only meant, just think of millions of them, all over England. Of course most of them only turn it on to knit by, or read the paper by, or dance to—not that they would dance to Milton, I admit."

"No, David, you are being very unfair. Think what it means to all these homes to have beauty brought to them, and education of the highest kind, just for the asking."

"Listen, love," said David, quite untroubled by the pres-

ence of Miss Stevenson's secretary in the little office, "as for
education, that's all bunk. It just fills them up with ideas so
that they need never think at all. And as for beauty, I can see
the earnest ones listening to me reading Milton, their yearn-
ing eyes gleaming with lack of intelligence. And anyway they
could ask for it till they were black in the faces unless they
paid for a licence."

"I am very sorry you take it like that, David."

"Well, I'm sorry I laughed, but that bit is so frightfully
comic once you see it that way. Anyway, love, I don't think I
was born to live here. I don't like all your gentlemen friends
with their Fair Isle sweaters tucked into their flannel bags, all
calling each other Lionel."

A young man answering closely to David's description
came in.

"Not interrupting, am I, Joan?" he inquired, in so perfect
an accent that David smiled with pleasure. "I just dropped in
to hear the result of Mr. Leslie's trial. I must introduce
myself," he said, holding out his hand in a frank and boyish
way, "Lionel Harvest. I'm only a kind of humble underling of
Joan's. She is doing magnificent work, and we mere men have
to admire and feebly emulate."

David shook his hand warmly, assuring him with perfect
truth that he was delighted to meet him. He explained, taking the words out of Miss Stevenson's mouth, that he had
been turned down and was going to seek his luck at earning a
crust elsewhere.

"Oh, rotten luck, rotten luck," cried Mr. Harvest sympa-
thetically. 'Well, a rivederci," and off he rushed to tell his
friend Mr. Potter, whose hair waved quite naturally, that the
Stevenson had brought in another dud, and they might yet
succeed in a little conspiracy they were getting up against her.

"Little swine," said Miss Stevenson, becoming quite
human. "He and his gang are up against me because they want
this office for themselves. Why did you say you had been

turned down? I could easily have managed another chance for you. Do try again, David."

But David answered that his nerve was too much shaken.

"Besides," he said, "I should get an inferiority complex if I saw much more of Lionel. I can't think how he does it. I suppose it's partly the name. Lionel Harvest; it is quite perfect."

"He is a fine speaker, all the same," said Miss Stevenson, suddenly remembering to be loyal to a colleague.

"He reads Coventry Patmore quite perfectly, and is very popular with our listeners.

'Well, you'd better have lunch with me one day," said David, who had lost interest in broadcasting.

"I would love to, but you must let me pay for myself," said Miss Stevenson, who knew from her Oxford experiences the right way to treat men.

David was so enchanted by Miss Stevenson's attitude to life that he made a point of taking her out several times to the most expensive restaurants he could find. When Miss Stevenson saw that even a single portion of one dish was not infrequently as much as five and sixpence, or, in the case of game, as much as twelve shillings, she kept her head remarkably well, and David had little difficulty in persuading her that as a fellow-artist, for so he widely interpreted her work in the office and his own lamentable fiasco with Milton, she could eat his food with no loss of prestige.

But in spite of the attraction of his new friend, and partly because he again had no particular work in prospect, David was at Rushwater a great deal more than usual during June and July. His week-ends were more likely to be Friday to Tuesday than Saturday to Monday. His mother and sister were enchanted to see him, and it speaks much for Mr. Leslie's character that he did not more than once in every visit ask David why he didn't get some work to do. To see a young man of twenty-seven doing nothing, doing it happily and without apparent moral injury to himself or anyone else, was beyond Mr. Leslie's comprehension. But having said what he felt it his duty to say, he always succumbed to David's good humour and irresponsible charm. When David had explained to him that in taking a job he would be taking the bread from men who really needed it, his father could not but admit the justice of the plea. When his father suggested that he should give some of his time to the estate, he said very truly that it was Martin's job to learn to take care of what would one day be his own, and that Macpherson had Mr. Leslie and John working with him already and would not welcome a third and quite incompetent assistant. When Mr. Leslie said he could do with a good agent in Buenos Aires to keep an eye on some land he had bought there, thinking to start breeding from his own stock, David became very sweet and affectionate and shortly melted from the room.

For Mary these week-ends were an exciting joy. David kept her to her word about walks, and together they tramped all over the country within walking distance, David talking all the time, reading poetry to her when they stopped to eat their sandwiches and rest, amusing her with his account of his failure to get a broadcasting job.

One afternoon late they had been out on the hills all day and were coming back at a swinging pace down the long wooded slopes behind the village. A hillside where a copse had been cut down the year before was thick with wild strawberries. They stopped to eat them.

"You get no satisfaction out of them though," said David. "One or two at a time are nothing and one hasn't the self-restraint to gather quite a lot before one eats them, besides which I have nothing to put them in."

"Heroes always have a hat," said Mary. "They gather a few berries in it, or fill it with water at the rushing torrent."

"I'd like to see anyone filling my hat with water. It would all come out at the ventilation holes. I expect heroes went about in bowlers in those days. We used to have an old *Heir of Redclyffe* with pictures, and the hero always wore a bowler in the country. No, the only way to eat wild strawberries is to live somewhere like Switzerland where there is a poor but venal peasantry which picks enormous bowlfuls for your tea.'

"I'd love to eat them like that."

"I'll tell you what. I know a place in town that gets wild strawberries by air from the Tyrol or somewhere twice a week. Let's go up to lunch one day."

"Oh, David."

They pursued their way over the brow of the hill, down a sunken lane to the village, where they saw Mr. Banister with his bicycle in front of the vicarage.

"Evening, David, evening, Miss Preston," he called.

"Do you want any help, sir?" said David.

"Yes, do get me a bucket of water from the garden tap to test my tyre. Sit down, Miss Preston."

Mary sat down on a decayed garden chair while David got the bucket. The vicar slightly inflated his tyre and passed it through the water. Bubbles rose from two places. The vicar got out his mending outfit and began to patch.

"I have settled everything with my tenants," he said. "They are taking the vicarage for the whole of August and will be glad to arrange for Martin to do French with them. I have been seeing your father about it, and Martin is to go every morning for lessons and stop to lunch for conversation, except when there is cricket."

"Martin will be very grateful to you," said Mary.

"He hasn't the faintest wish to go abroad."

"By the way, David, the Boulles would like a paying-guest as well, some nice young man or woman who wants to study French seriously. So if you come across anyone, let me know. It would be an advantage to Martin to have someone to work with him."

"Judging by my own experiences at that beastly Swiss place I was at," said David, "if you once get two English pupils together it's all up with learning French. However, I'll remember."

After a little more desultory conversation Mr. Banister blew his tyre up again and put it into the water. One of the patches bulged. A column of bubbles rose from it and the patch floated up to the surface.

"I expect I didn't sandpaper it properly," said Mr. Banister, rather disappointed.

"Let me look," said David, rescuing the patch. "I should say you hadn't put any solution on it, sir."

"No more I did. I remember now that I picked this patch up with sticky fingers after I had put the first one on. I suppose the stickiness somehow made me think I had put the solution on. Well, well, to work again," said the vicar, looking wistfully at David.

But David didn't want to mend tyres, so he got up and said they were late and must fly. At dinner he told his mother, who always liked to hear village news, about the vicar's quest for a paying-guest for his tenants.

"Now, I am sure we can find exactly the right person," said Lady Emily, who had as usual come in late without her spectacles and was trying to eat mutton and red-currant jelly with a spoon and fork, apparently deluded by the jelly into thinking it was pudding.

"Agnes, who was that nice girl we heard about that was going somewhere abroad and it didn't come off?"

Agnes appeared to find the description perfectly clear, but could not be sure if it was a girl or a young man going in for diplomacy.

"Because," she said, "it was the day I got the cable from Robert, and I remember I left my letters in the garden shelter and they blew out on to the lawn, and then it rained. I was never sure if I got them all again, and I believe, mamma, that letter from whoever it was must have got lost, though I distinctly remember something about someone who was going abroad, but something had happened."

As this conversation did not seem to be leading anywhere in particular, David changed it by telling everyone that he was taking Mary to lunch in town one day.

"How nice," said his mother. "And then, Mary, you could go to Woolworth's and get the extra cups and the presents for the children. Let me see, the village concert is on Tuesday next week, so you'll have to go up this week."

"I'll drive you up on Tuesday, shall I?" said David, "when I go, and you can come back by train. Or else, come up by train on Friday and I'll drive you down."

"Now let me see," said Lady Emily, "if you go up with David you'll have all the Woolworth parcels to carry to the station afterwards, so you had better go on Friday and then David can drive you and the parcels down. Gudgeon, what are the trains to London in the morning?"

"Eleven-fifty from Rushwater is the best, my lady, arriving at two-ten."

"That wouldn't get me up in time for lunch," said Mary.

"There is the eight-fifteen, miss, arriving eleven forty-five."

"There you are," said David. "That gives you an hour and a half to play at Woolworth's, and then we'll have lunch and a cinema and drive down together."

"But, David," said his mother, who had been counting on her fingers with an anxious face, "that is not a human train. It takes three hours and a half, and Mary can't possibly catch a train at a quarter past eight."

"Can't you, Mary?" asked David, looking at her with disturbing appeal.

"Oh, I can easily get it, Aunt Emily," she said. "If I could have the Ford I'd run myself down to Rushwater and perhaps someone could fetch it."

Lady Emily, enchanted by the opportunity for further planning, then developed an elaborate arrangement by which the man who was going down to fetch a load of gravel from the station on Tuesday should drive the Ford as far as Mr. Macpherson's garage, while his gravel was being loaded, and Mr. Macpherson should drive up to lunch in the Ford and have Weston take him home; or, better still, Mr. Macpherson should drive the Ford up for lunch and Weston should walk down to the village at lunch-time and bring Mr. Macpherson's own car up; or even better, Weston should bicycle down and bring Mr. Macpherson's own car up, with the bicycle in the back seat. Having got so far, she was just wondering aloud whether it would not be better for the man who went to fetch the gravel to leave the car at Mr. Banister's, as he had said something about wanting to come up one morning, when Mr. Leslie cut across her.

"If Mary is going up to town for the day, Emily, and has to do your village shopping, Weston had better take her and bring her back. I don't want him on Thursday. If you don't, Mary can have him."

"That is much nicer," said Agnes. "David's car is lovely, but it is so dusty. I don't ever quite like an open car."

Mary thanked Mr. Leslie very much. She felt it would be too discourteous to refuse this offer, especially it as he rarely lent the car. It was very disappointing in a way, because she had frightfully looked forward to a few hours with David. To be sitting by David in a very fast sports car would have been bliss, but one had to remember one's manners and show proper gratitude. And in any case it would be very nice to motor both ways, and not have to carry parcels about with one.

"I remember now," said Agnes. "It was Dodo Bingham's letter, and she said her nephew had been going to Munich to a family, but his people wouldn't let him go because of the Nazis. Do you think he would be any use for Mr. Banister's tenants?"

David got up, and going round to Agnes dropped a kiss on the top of her head.

"No, love," he said. "You are so kind and perfectly adorable, but German is not French, look at it whichever way you will."

"No, I suppose it isn't," said Agnes. "But I knew it would come back to me. Do you know how sometimes you forget things and then you remember them again?"

David said he had occasionally had this peculiar experience, and so could fully appreciate her state of mind.

Mary lingered behind the others to thank Mr. Leslie again for his kindness. The less grateful she felt for it, the more grateful she ought to feel.

"That's all right, my dear," said Mr. Leslie. "David is bone selfish, always was. Expecting a girl to catch a slow train at eight-fifteen just to have lunch with him. But you girls will do it," he said, with unexpected insight, "and you make the young man worse than he is. John wouldn't do such a thing, and as for his eldest brother, a more unselfish boy—well, have a good time in town. You're a help to Emily. Like to hear you sing in the evenings. It sends me to sleep."

Mary was touched and pleased by Mr. Leslie's words about Lady Emily, though she hadn't felt there were adequate grounds for them. As for David being selfish, parents did not always see their children as they really were. And on Thursday she would have lunch in town with David.

CHAPTER VII
LUNCH FOR THREE

THE WORLD VERY OBLIGINGLY did not come to an end before Thursday, and Weston drove Mary to London, where she did Lady Emily's shopping and met David at a restaurant.

"Cocktails first," he said, putting his arm through hers and leading her to a bar. "What do you like?"

Mary didn't know, so David ordered two Snakes in the Grass, which he warned her had gone straight to many a stronger head than hers. David looked towards the door from time to time as they drank.

"Do you mind?" he said. "I've asked a friend of mine, Joan Stevenson. She is a highly-educated female, but otherwise harmless."

Mary instantaneously felt a raging jealousy of educated females, combined with hatred of David. Hateful of him to ask her to lunch as if it were to be a special treat for them both, and then ask an educated woman too. Hateful, selfish young man. In a moment she had thought of a dozen cruel and cutting things to say to him, but to her surprise her voice said:

"I hope she isn't too crushingly superior, David."

"Not a bit. As a matter of fact, she may be very useful to me, as I can keep in touch with broadcasting through her."

"But you told me they'd turned you down."

"One can always have another shot," said David, getting off his stool and going forward to meet Joan. He introduced the two girls. Mary's presence was almost as annoying to Joan as Joan's was to Mary, and each was conscious of angry and hopeless inferiority. In Mary, Joan saw one of those brainless society girls who have nothing to do but drink and dance and have a good time. A pretty creature if one liked that ordinary brown hair and blue eyes and that kind of rather generous figure. Probably she had an income of her own and never wore darned stockings. David had said a cousin of his, but that wasn't what she meant by a cousin.

In Joan Mary saw what anyone might call a good-looking girl if they liked that fair type with pale green-brown eyes and a hard sort of mouth. University women were always hard— unsympathetic and conceited as well. She might be useful to David, but that was no reason for her to have such a very well-tailored silk suit. But probably she earned a huge salary and had everything made to measure.

Mutual hatred passed between the girls in waves. Hatred for David also permeated the air, but to none of these currents did David appear to be attuned.

"Cocktail, Joan?" he asked.

"No, thanks. I can't work if I drink cocktails," said Joan looking at Mary's glass.

"One more before we go in to lunch, David," said Mary affectedly.

"On your own head be it," said David, ordering one.

"In my stomach, I hope," said Mary with an insane giggle caused by jealousy. The cocktail was brought and

Mary, feeling that one was really quite enough, pretended to sip it, said in a bored voice that the second one never seemed so good as the first, and asked David if they were never to have lunch. David seized an arm of each to guide them to the lunch-room. He should have fallen a charred corpse, or stood convulsed, rooted to the ground, so strong were the angry waves that must have passed through him, instead of which he put his ladies at a table in a corner and seated himself between them.

Lunch was made even more uncomfortable for Mary and Joan than it need have been, as each made it a point of honour to pretend she could not touch anything that the other liked, so that neither got more than half of David's delightful meal. The caviare which Mary ate with relish was only pecked at by Miss Stevenson, who said she had eaten it fresh in Russia, where she had once been on a long vacation, and could never bear to eat it in any other way. It was almost impossible to find fault with the omelette of which both ladies greedily partook, but over the wine fresh difficulties arose. David inquired if they both liked white wine.

"No, thanks, David, water only for me," said Mary in a pure and aloof way.

"I'd love a Barsac or a Vouvray, David," said Joan. "Let me look."

By this means she was able to spend two or three minutes over the wine list, her shoulder touching David's, while they discussed names. The wine waiter, having condescended to let them amuse themselves, then brought hypnotic influence to bear, so that they ordered what he had always meant them to have.

"Are you frightfully busy, Miss Stevenson?" asked Mary graciously, while cutlets were being served. "I expect you are broadcasting every night."

"I am not an announcer," said Joan, helping herself to saute potatoes. "I arrange the poetry readings."

"Oh, office work," said Mary. "No, no potatoes," she added, glancing at Joan's plate.

"Do you find them fattening?" said Joan. "I am terribly lucky. I can eat whatever I like without having to worry."

"I expect some day I'll get to that stage," said Mary. "Oh, David, James was too sweet this morning. He had Emmy and

Clarissa in a little wooden cart we found in the old bicycle shed and was pushing them about. James is David's little nephew," she explained to Joan, "and Emmy and Clarissa are his nieces. Such darlings, and we have the greatest fun together."

"You must come down and see them some day, Joan," said David.

Joan said she would love to, which made Mary fume at her bold-faced readiness to accept, but her week-ends were always booked up months ahead, which made Mary equally furious at her want of enthusiasm, but she thought she could spare a week-end late in August when she would have her holiday, which smote a cold chill to Mary's heart. Didn't David remember that Martin's birthday was late in August and they were to have a dance? He did, and told Joan she had chosen a perfect time, as they were to have a dance for his young nephew.

"Cheers," said Miss Stevenson, at which schoolgirl exclamation Mary raised her eyebrows, which, though Joan didn't see it, gave her great inward satisfaction, and nerved her for further conflict.

David had left the choice of pudding to his guests. Joan asked, in what Mary considered a very affected accent, for crêpe Suzette. This gave Mary a good opening to say that, thank you, David dear, she had simply gorged and couldn't eat any more, but might she just have coffee and perhaps a *fine* with it. *Fine* was rather a shot in the dark, but to her great relief it appeared to be correct, and her self-esteem perked up its head still further.

"Madame's crêpe will take a few minutes," said the waiter.

"Cigarette?" said David, offering his case to Joan, who took one, and then to Mary.

"No, thanks, David. You ought to know by now that I don't smoke. Don't you think it spoils one's palate for good drink?" she asked Joan politely. At the same moment her satisfaction burst and collapsed. David ought to have remembered that she didn't smoke, considering how much they had been together lately. It was heartless of him to forget like that, and now she had given herself away to that horrid smart woman, who would think that David had never noticed whether she smoked or not. She would like to explain to her that David had really offered her a cigarette not from forgetfulness, but because he didn't want to emphasize his intimacy with Mary and his mere friendliness with Joan. Also she had been a fool to say anything so crude about smoke spoiling one's palate. It was true it was a nasty and a satisfactory slap in the eye for that Miss Stevenson after all the fuss she had made about the wine, but it should have been more delicately done.

David talked about his novel till the crêpe came, when Mary, though wishing she was eating one too, at least had the satisfaction of seeing the enemy more or less gagged by food, while she was able to talk to David about his book with the understanding of one who has been present at the inception of an Idea. David was also having coffee and a *fine*, which was another snub to Miss Stevenson and a bond between Mary and David.

They sat on talking for a little. David mentioned a ballet which Mary hadn't seen. Joan had seen it in Paris. David mentioned a symphony which Joan hadn't heard. Mary had heard Toscanini conduct it, though she omitted to say it was on a gramophone. Joan mentioned a banned book. David knew a man who had bought fifty copies in France and smuggled them over in an aeroplane, but Mary was here inspired to say that she had read it in typescript and found it simply dull. Why people were, persuaded to read crashingly dull books just because they were banned, she really could not think. For this appalling lie fire from heaven should have descended on her, but as nothing happened, she was defiantly glad that she had told it and shown that she was really in things just as much as that Miss Stevenson.

"Well, I almost envy you your chance of reading all those horrid books," said Miss Stevenson, getting up. "I have to go back to work now. Are you coming my way, David?"

"I suppose we are going to our cinema, David," said Mary, planting a last barb in the enemy's breast. "We could drop Miss Stevenson." That at least should rankle.

"Will you mind frightfully if we don't?" said David. "I want to see a man about my novel, and I know I'll find him at the Café Royal till half-past three."

The blood of many generations of soldiers ran in Mary's veins. Inclining graciously towards Joan, she said:

"Could I take you anywhere? I have the car."

Nor was Joan wanting in the stoicism of the Red Indian who makes no sound while his sinews are torn from him. She accepted with becoming gratitude. David saw them both into the car.

"Good-bye, Joan. I'll look you up soon," he said. "I've an idea about your holiday. Good-bye, Mary. I'll be down to-morrow."

Both ladies gave him frozen smiles and murmured something unintelligible. Luckily the journey only lasted a few minutes. Miss Stevenson thanked Mary for the lift, and both ladies mentioned how glad they were

to have met each other.

"Beg pardon, miss," said Weston, as he put the dust rug over Mary's knees, "Mr. Leslie asked me to call at Mr. John's office after lunch for a letter. Will that be all right?"

"Certainly, Weston."

They drove into the city and stopped at a building in a dark, narrow street. John happened to be going in as they drew up.

"I've come for a letter for Mr. Leslie, sir," said Weston.

"Mary, what a charming surprise. Will you come up and see my office while I finish father's business? I shan't be long, Weston."

Mary saw no reason not to, so she went upstairs with John, whose office, being exactly like any other office, we need not describe. It is enough to say that it had a large window of frosted glass looking on to a well, on that hot day it was almost airless, the furniture was bleak and efficient, the tear-off calendar was several days in arrears.

"Sit down," said John. "How's everyone?"

"Very well. Clarissa has got another back tooth and Nannie has had to give Ivy a piece of her mind." 'What did Agnes say?"

" 'Oh, Nannie, how annoying of Ivy."

Mary imitated Agnes's plaintive voice so exactly that John began to laugh.

"I'll just finish my letter," he said, "and then I'll show you the rest of the place if you like. It isn't much of a show, but I am thinking of moving if things go on well."

He rang for his secretary and began dictating a letter to her. Mary looked about her, but finding no entertainment her thoughts naturally returned to the battlefield of lunch. It had been the most horrible lunch she had ever had. In spite of scoring several distinct hits, she only felt lowered in her own esteem. She had been spiteful, affected, a liar and a prig. She hated that Joan person more than anything on earth except David, who was perfectly horrible. Asking her up to town, expecting her to come by the ridiculously early train, inviting a strange woman who put on airs to meet her and— Then the most horrible thought of all, which she had not yet thought of adding to her grievances, came thundering over her mind. There had been no wild strawberries. It was to have been her own special party for wild strawberries, brought by air twice a week from the Tyrol or somewhere, and David hadn't so much as thought of them. But he had let that girl choose her own pudding, the greedy pig. It was true that he had offered her a pudding too, and she might have said Wild Strawberries if she hadn't been so stupidly snobbish, pretending she couldn't eat any more. But that didn't in the least affect the awful, heart-rending fact that he had entirely forgotten his promise.

"Get that typed at once, Miss Badger," said John, "and put those papers in with it and bring it in here when it is ready. No," he added, as she left the room, "I'll ring for it in about ten minutes."

For as he turned from his table to his guest, he saw her sitting upright in the office armchair with tears pouring down her face.

As the secretary shut the door, Mary looked up with a start.

"Oh," she said in a desolate voice, trying to dab her tears away. But nothing would check them now, nor indeed did she much want to check them, it was such a blessed relief to dissolve all one's past wickedness in tears, to wash away the splinter of glass in one's heart that had made one behave so disgracefully. And John didn't matter.

John stood with, his hands in his pockets in considerable perplexity. Why Mary Preston should come into his office in excellent spirits and be discovered ten minutes later in tears was a mystery to him. The only probable explanation was that she had suddenly felt unhappy, and he only hoped it wasn't his fault. He hastily reviewed his conduct for the past quarter of an hour. He had seen Mary in his father's car, and on an impulse had asked her to come upstairs. They had walked up together to the first floor. Here he had taken her straight into his own office and given her the chair which was officially the most comfortable one. She had then given him a short account of the nursery at Rushwater, and a very good imitation of his sister Agnes. No cause for tears in all this. Had he perhaps been rude in sending for his secretary almost at once and dictating a letter? No, she had come up quite realizing that he wanted to finish a letter which she was to take down to Mr. Leslie. So, being no further on than he had been a minute earlier, he took the plunge and diffidently asked her what the matter was. Mary, her face slightly mottled with emotion, replied in a low, choked voice:

"David's lunch."

This did not make matters much clearer. If she were poisoned she would be writhing and fainting, not shedding a steady rain of tears. In any case it would be extremely unlike David to poison anyone. The kind of restaurant he went to might surfeit people, but would be above poisoning them.

'What happened at lunch?" he asked. "I mean, I don't want to ask questions, but I must do something to help you. You can't go on like this."

"Oh can't I," said Mary in a thick voice. "Well, I jolly well can. Unless," she added, with a sudden and touching humility, "you have anyone coming to see you here. If you have, I'll rush down into the car. I could quite well finish crying there."

"No one will come in here," said John, "till I ring. And I want you to stay here till you feel happier. Don't bother to tell me if it makes you unhappy. Only if it's anything to do with David, perhaps I could help."

Thus encouraged, Mary gave a great gulp and rubbed her eyes with the small damp ball which had been her handkerchief. John pulled a chair up to her and sat down, as if he were a doctor preparing to hear a patient's symptoms.

"You see," said Mary, whose utterance became clearer with every word and whose complexion was reassuming a more uniform tinge, "David promised to take me out to lunch and give me wild strawberries. He knew a place where they get them sent over from the Tyrol or somewhere twice a week. So your father very kindly lent me the car and I did your mother's shopping and then I went to lunch with David—and he had forgotten about the strawberries."

Upon which she made a sound resembling that usually written as boohoo.

"How rotten of him," said John. "But you must have some another day. Tell him to take you out again, and rub it in well how low and caddish his behaviour has been."

"There will be no other day," announced Mary, to whose voice her late excesses had imparted a fine resonant timbre.

John looked startled. The whole situation was becoming alarmingly melodramatic. Surely the girl was not quarrelling with David because the young ass, who was as selfish in his pleasant way as anyone John knew, had forgotten to give her wild strawberries. One didn't quarrel with a cousin by marriage on such meagre grounds. Then into John's mind came a little spiky thought. One didn't burst into tears over such a trifle unless one were very fond of a person. Could it possibly be a kind of lovers' quarrel that David and Mary had had? He had not been down to Rushwater himself since the week-end of Mary's arrival, but he had an idea from his mother's letters that David had been there a good deal. Had David been philandering as usual? John felt a rush of annoyance with his younger brother, an annoyance which he at once recognized as unreasonable, but could not control. Hadn't David enough charming friends without having to try his hand on this girl with the clear, small voice? What David needed was a rough shaking and a little responsibility.

"Have you and David had a row?" he hazarded.

"Oh, no," said Mary, in an airy way which deceived no one, certainly not herself, for she added penitently, "At least David has been most thoughtless and unkind, but I have been a liar and very rude, so we are about equal."

"Tell me about your being rude," said John, hoping that to talk about herself would be the quickest cure.

Mary looked steadily at him, and apparently given confidence by what she saw continued:

'Well, you'll think me very silly, but when I got to the place where we were to have lunch, David said he had asked someone called Miss Stevenson, and I was disappointed because it was to have been just us. And she was a horrid woman who had been at college and does something about broadcasting, and I hated her. And then however much I tried to be nice it came out like rudeness, and I hated myself more and more and I hated David. And it was all so silly and I am so dreadfully ashamed and I shan't know what to say to David."

John couldn't tell her that David, if he knew his younger brother, would be unconscious of anything beyond the fact that he had taken two presentable young women out to lunch, that he would not for a moment realize how much his promise of wild strawberries had meant to Mary. Nothing so definite as warning Mary that no one had ever yet penetrated David's armour of egoism occurred to him, but he felt that no one was taking care of the girl properly. She ought not to be in a position where David could treat her as he treated the many charming girls whom he admired.

"Will Weston mind being kept waiting?" Mary asked anxiously, while she repaired some of the ravages of grief.

"Not a bit. If you start by four o'clock you will have plenty of time. Did my father come up to town too?" he asked. "No, how stupid of me, he would have called for the letter himself.'

"Oh, nó, David wanted me to come up by that early train from Rushwater, and I had a lot of shopping to do for Aunt Emily, so Mr. Leslie said I might have the car, for which I was very grateful, because it was a treat and made me much less tired."

"How like father," said John. But his unsaid thought was, How like David. He had evidently taken it for granted that Mary would get up at some unearthly hour and take that slow, early train, which John himself knew well and loathed, and then carry an armful of parcels about London, just for the pleasure of having lunch with him. David's whole scale of values was wrong. He was so used to thinking in terms of expensive girls who had their own cars and thought nothing of motoring a hundred miles to have a meal with him that he could not realize how different Mary was—or didn't want to. He wished that David were there now so that he could give him what Nannie called a piece of his mind, but at the same time he knew that it would be quite useless and that David would inevitably disarm him by his ingenuous surprise and charming contrition. Too much charm altogether, he thought.

"I believe a cup of tea is what most restores females," said John, ringing. "Is that the letter, Miss Badger? Thanks. And can you get some tea for Miss Preston and me?"

"Isn't it rather early for tea?" said Mary.

"It is half-past three. Miss Badger has tea in her room every day from three o'clock onwards. The tea is good, I see to that. And we rather affect an Abernethy biscuit in our office. Does that meet your views?"

Miss Badger shortly produced tea on a tray. Mary, partaking of it, was much refreshed in body and mind.

"I was an awful idiot," she said. "I expect it was really drinking that Snake in the Grass cocktail that David gave me. Did he tell you that he got turned down at Broadcasting House? They gave him an audition or whatever they call it, for reading English poetry aloud, and he chose that bit of Milton he read us when you were there, and he laughed so much that he couldn't go on, so it wasn't—"

Here she quite suddenly stopped. Her face went bright pink, her mouth remained slightly open, and her general appearance was that of one struck with madness. John was seriously alarmed. A fit of crying was a reasonable affair, but why the mention of David's Milton reading should induce paralysis and insanity, he couldn't conceive. The child couldn't be dazzled by David to such an extent that to speak of him made her self-conscious. Then Mary, gazing dumbly at John, saw a tide of colour mount to his face also. He tried to speak, but only produced a kind of click. Silent agony pervaded the room till Mary, with burning cheeks and her voice almost as inaudible as it had been half an hour ago, managed to say:

"I said something frightfully stupid that night David was reading. I don't know if you heard it and if you didn't don't ask me about it, but if you did, please forgive me, because I hadn't the very faintest idea."

"As a matter of fact I did hear, but please don't think that I minded. You were perfectly right about Milton. No one in their senses could have thought of marrying such an exasperating widower, and as I am, thank heaven, not in the least like Milton, I don't see that there can be any comparison. Besides, the world is full of widowers, and if no one was to mention Milton, or, for that matter, Henry the Eighth, what would we all talk about?"

Mary's face relaxed and she gave a sigh of relief. John's kindness, as also his courage in mentioning that somehow almost funny word widower, were tremendous.

'Thanks most awfully," she said. "And I am so very sorry about Mrs. Leslie, if you don't mind my saying so. Aunt Agnes told me how darling she was. I do so wish she hadn't—"

She stopped again, feeling foolish. What business was it of hers to intrude on John's past? And how utterly stupid what she was going to say. But John apparently hadn't minded.

"So do I," he said. "In fact, I wish it all the time. But she did. You must let Agnes talk to you about her. Agnes in a way came closer to her than even my mother did. If it hadn't been for Agnes's kindness I could hardly have borne it when Gay died."

"Aunt Agnes is kind to everyone. It was the greatest luck in the world that Uncle Robert married her. I think one is very grateful for kindness," she added musingly. But whether she was thinking of Agnes's kindness or of John's, who can say? John wondered if she was thinking of David; the thought of kindness might lead one to think of unkindness. Then he blamed himself for the thought..

He took Mary downstairs and put her into the car. Then he went back to the office, from which the good Miss Badger had efficiently removed the tea things, and went on with his work. Between six and half-past he rang David up at his flat and found him in.

"Hullo, David," he said. "Are you going down to Rushwater for the week-end? You are? Then I want you to see Macpherson for me," and he gave David a message about some cottage repairs.

"Right. I wish you had been at lunch with me to-day. I took Mary and Joan Stevenson out and we could have done with another man. I rang you up, but you were out."

"Mary told me. She came round to fetch a letter for father. I gathered that the lunch was a great success, except that you forgot some strawberries that you had promised her."

"By Jove, so I did. But, anyway, they would have been two days old. They only get them on Tuesday and Friday."

"Take some down to-morrow, then."

"Yes, rather. When do we see you down there, John?"

"Not this month. I'll be down in August for Martin's celebrations."

"Well, dine with me before then. I'll tell you all about my novel. I was talking to a man today who seems rather keen—"

When David had finished anticipating all he wished to say when his brother dined with him, John stood in thought for a moment. He had done his best to help David to repair his forgetfulness; whether David would think of it again was another question.

Mary drove back to Rushwater with very mixed feelings, the chief of which was shame, not only at her extremely unladylike behaviour at lunch, but at her subsequent babyish behaviour in John's office. Her comfort under the first affliction was that she didn't think David had noticed, though this again led to a feeling of considerable mortification that he hadn't. Her comfort under the second affliction was that she had at last managed to clear up the affair of her silly ignorant remark about widowers. John had been so kind about it that there would not be even a faint discomfort in meeting him again. It was partly the word widower that made one self-conscious. Why a widow should raise an attractive or pathetic image in one's mind, or at the worst something rather bold and dashing, while widower seemed to have a vague connection with the word mother-in-law cannot be explained. Brightness falls from even Clive Newcome when we have to envisage him as a young widower in mourning. As for David Copperfield, his creator most wisely sent him abroad almost at once, and while he was still in England surrounded him with events so overwhelming that we never have time to think of his widowerhood.

She only got back in time to run upstairs and dress, and did not see her relations till they met for dinner. Mr. Leslie showed genuine pleasure at having her back. Agnes and Lady Emily folded her in the softest of embraces. Mr. Macpherson was with them for dinner.

"Well, Miss Mary," he said, "did you have a good time in London?"

Mary said she had had a lovely time. David had given her a delicious lunch and there was a very nice girl called Miss Stevenson who was frightfully clever and worked at broadcasting. Having paid this lip-service to the hateful Miss Stevenson, she felt that she had gone far towards appeasing her conscience in the matter of her bad behaviour at lunch.

"Don't know what they want all these girls for," said Mr. Leslie. "Taking jobs from the men. Glad you don't want to have a job, Mary."

"I am afraid I did have a job for a bit," said Mary, "in a library."

"Oh, books, that's all right. No harm in a girl reading a bit. It's all this education I object to. Same everywhere. All these young people going to the university and coming away half-baked. Can't even talk English. Heard a fellow on the wireless once, talking about a cattle show in the West. What do you think he said? Macpherson, this will amuse you. He said it was held at Westhampton Pollingford."

Mr. Leslie laughed loudly and fiercely. Mr. Macpherson

gave a short bark and applied himself to inward meditation on the enormity of this announcement.

"Where was it really held?" asked Mary.

"He must have meant Wumpton Pifford," said Agnes. "How very peculiar. That was where Rushwater Rinaldo got a prize. I suppose he didn't know any better, poor thing. There was apricot jam for tea to-day and darling Clarissa called it dickybob."

"Dickybob, eh?" said Mr. Leslie, coming into the conversation again after his laugh. "What did the child mean? Can't she say dickybird yet?"

"No, father," said Agnes, not displeased at this opportunity of praising her gifted younger daughter again, "it was apricot jam and darling Clarissa called it dickybob."

Mr. Leslie made no comment, but appeared to think poorly of his youngest grandchild's mental powers. Gudgeon came round to Mr. Macpherson.

"Beg pardon, sir, it's Mr. David on the phone from London, and he would wish to speak with you if you are here, sir."

"Excuse me, Lady Emily," said Mr. Macpherson, getting up.

"Might have known we dine at eight, interrupting Macpherson's dinner like that," said Mr. Leslie.

"But, Henry," said Lady Emily, who was getting into frightful difficulties with a chicken wing, "time always seems so different in London. Walter, take this plate and cut through the joint for me on the sideboard. Don't you know," she continued to the company at large, "how one is sometimes lucky with chickens and sometimes isn't. Their joints sometimes go into all the wrong places. Turkeys are worse, and ducks worst of all. Do you remember, Henry—thank you, Walter, that is perfect now—a duck there was at papa's a great many years ago?"

"Can't say I do, my dear."

"You must, Henry. It was quite soon after we were married, and we went to stay with papa and there was a duck."

She paused so long that everyone thought the story had come to an end.

"Dare say there was," said Mr. Leslie. "Sort of thing one would have."

"No. Wait," said Lady Emily impressively. "It was not a duck, it was a turbot, a very large turbot, and mamma .had it placed on the table and papa said to one of the footmen, 'Take it away and serve it from the sideboard."

The end of this remarkable anecdote was received with respectful silence.

"Turbots don't have joints, Emily," said Mr. Leslie. "But I must say your father was quite right in having it served off the table, quite right."

"They don't have joints, Henry, but they have bones, and I dare say it was the difficulty of getting into the chicken's joints that made me think of a turbot's bones."

"Extraordinary the way one thing does make one think of another sometimes," said Mr. Leslie. "Well, Macpherson, what had David to say?"

"A message from Mr. John about those cottages."

"John? Thought Gudgeon said David."

"You were correct, Mr. Leslie. David rang up to say that he couldn't get away this week-end as he expected, so he gave me the message Mr. John had asked him to bring. I'll tell you about it after dinner. He sent his love to you, Lady Emily, and I was to tell you he regretted very much his inability to be with you this week-end."

"It is very sad," said Agnes. "I wanted David to see Emmy on the pony. She looks so sweet."

"Well, it will be sad not to have David to read to us," said Lady Emily, shaking white sugar over her savoury. "It was very naughty of Martin to laugh so much when David read Milton aloud to us so beautifully. Never mind, we shall be very busy getting ready for the concert in the racket court and the supper. Mary, were you able to get all the things we wanted at Woolworth's?

"Yes, Aunt Emily."

"Mamma," said Agnes, who had been gently trying to attract her mother's attention, "that was sugar you put on the cheese souffle."

"I thought it was pepper. Conque will not give me my right spectacles. Walter, bring me a clean plate and I'll just scrape off the parts that got sugar on them and put them on the plate, if you will hold it near me. That's better. Now you can take it away. Papa always used to put port wine into his cheese."

"Very sensible thing to do," said Mr. Leslie. "Sensible man, Lord Pomfret."

"But not sugar, mamma," said Agnes firmly. "Grand-papa never put sugar into his cheese."

"Of course he didn't put sugar into his cheese," said Mr. Leslie, with some heat. "Man would be a fool to do that. You don't know what you are talking about, Agnes."

His daughter, who had shown unusual liveliness in dealing with her mother's behaviour over the savoury, had relapsed into her customary happy indifference and only smiled lovingly and abstractedly at him.

CHAPTER VIII
DAVID MAKES AMENDS

THE WEEK-END passed in a frenzy of preparation. For many years there had been a concert in the racket court, given by tenants on the estate, followed by a supper and presents for all the children. The whole affair was oranized by Mr. Macpherson and some of the farmers wives, and as the procedure, and indeed the programme, was almost unvarying from year to year, Lady Emily had no reason to trouble about it. But her genius for hindering and meddling was too strong to resist. Every year she would descend uninvited upon .the committee as they sat in Mr. Macpherson's office.

"Here I am, come to disturb you all," she would say, smiling deliciously, while she unwound her scarves and took the chair from which Mr. Macpherson, the chairman, had risen.

After inquiring about the health of all the husbands and children, with variations on the subject of her own family, she would ask what they had been arranging, admire the plans, suggest impossible alterations, or something entirely different, and after holding up all business for the best part of an hour, drift out again. The committee had finally, with great cunning, arranged a well-advertised meeting which they secretly called "Her Ladyship's Committee," at which they agreed to everything she said without any intention of taking it seriously. Other meetings were held less publicly and so the work was done.

This year she had wanted Mary to sing. Mary was terrified at the thought and confided in Mr. Macpherson.

"That's her ladyship all over," he observed disloyally. "Why, the whole point of the affair is that the entertainment should be provided by the tenants themselves and some of the local people like the postmaster and the stationmaster. I would well like to hear you sing a good Scots song, Miss Mary, but the drawing-room is your place, not the racket court. I'll make her ladyship see reason."

In making this statement he showed a rashness alien to his disposition. But whether he made Lady Emily see reason (which no one else had ever succeeded in doing), or whether he spoke with authority, as he occasionally did, no more was said of Mary's taking part. In any case, she knew that she could not have sung, for her worst fears were realized. David had evidently been disgusted by her disgraceful behaviour, though he had been too polite to say so at the time. He had told her he was coming down to Rushwater, but sooner than spend a week-end in company with such an unrestrained, ill-bred girl, he had given up the pleasure of seeing his parents. It would probably have been far happier for everyone if she had never been born, or had died some time ago.

She then drifted into an agreeable reverie in which Miss Stevenson came to stay at Rushwater and the house caught fire. Miss Stevenson's bedroom was cut off by the flames. Hastily damping a blanket in her water-jug, Mary flung it round her head and ascended the smoke-filled stairs. What though the blanket made it impossible to see and tripped her up at every step, what were such trifles? "Miss Stevenson," she cried at Miss Stevenson's door. There was no answer. Dashing in, it was but the work of a moment to wake the sleeping girl, damp a blanket in the water-jug, fling it round her bead and drag her to safety. But from the staircase came an ominous crackling sound, and a lurid light filled the room. Rushing to the window, she beheld David on the terrace. It was but the work of a moment to strip the sheets from the bed, tear them into strips, knot them together and tie them to the bed-post. "You are the heavier," said Mary to Miss Stevenson (it was her one moment of revenge), "go first." Swiftly Miss Stevenson, wrapped in the blanket, slid down the rope into David's arms. No sooner had she reached the ground than Mary, throwing away her blanket, prepared to follow her. But careless of her own safety—for had she not seen Miss Stevenson in David's arms?—she recked not that the licking flames had reached the bed-post. The frail ladder to which she clung gave way. She fell. Her back was broken, but she felt no pain. David's arms were round 'her. "I am the mashed fireman," she said with bitter gaiety. All marvelled at her courage. "Is Miss Stevenson safe?" she murmured, fighting the pain—no, there must not be any pain—the blackness which threatened to overwhelm her. "I don't know, and I don't care," said David. "Something wrapped in a wet blanket came down. But, oh, Mary, Mary, it was always you that I wanted."

To this fascinating picture her mind returned at intervals during the week-end, with much satisfaction and considerable elaboration of details.

Agnes, with the exercise of much diplomacy, persuaded her mother that they would never have enough presents for all the children, so Lady Emily occupied the days before the concert in painting a number of little cardboard boxes which Agnes had had the foresight to ask Mary to get in town, and filling them with sweets. It rained all Sunday and Monday, which helped to keep her within doors. On Tuesday they woke again to pouring rain, so her activities had to be confined to sending contradictory messages which no one delivered.

Dinner was to be at seven, the concert from eight to ten, supper from ten to eleven. At five minutes to eight a procession with umbrellas, mackintoshes and overshoes set out for the racket court, which could not be approached except on foot. Lady Emily, in regal purple and amethysts, black lace on her hair, hobbled with the aid of her stick and her husband across the hundred yards of dripping garden in excellent spirits. Conque followed her with cushions and shawls. Once arrived at the racket court, Lady Emily sat down in the little entrance, while Conque took her galoshes off and relieved her of some of her wraps.

"Come along, Emily," said Mr. Leslie impatiently, "they are waiting to begin."

His wife wound herself up in her shawls and they went through the racket court to their places in the front row,. followed by Agnes and Mary, with the cushions and extra wraps.

"That's right," said Lady Emily, sitting down slowly. "Now that cushion behind me, Agnes, and that shawl over my knees, and Conque—where is Conque?—oh, I remember, I told her she could go up to the gallery when she had taken my galoshes off. Mary, find Conque and ask her if she has brought my little footstool. Oh, Mr. Banister, good evening. Wait a minute, Mary, I'll ask Mr. Banister. Mr. Banister, you haven't a hassock about you, have you?"

"No, Lady Emily, I'm afraid I haven't."

"What a pity. You have such a lot at church, in fact I'm always falling over them, and I somehow thought you might have one. Then, Mary, please find Conque."

But before Mary could go, Mr. Macpherson came up with a small footstool.

"I doubted whether your ladyship would have brought your footrest," he said, patiently, "so I just brought one up with me from the office. Miss Mary, come away with me a moment; I want to speak with you."

Mary followed him, stupidly wondering if David had suddenly died and sent a message to Mr. Macpherson to tell his family. But while she was heroically going through the evening without letting them know what had happened, so that they might not spoil the pleasure of their dependants, she was recalled to reality by what Mr. Macpherson was eagerly saying. The schoolmistress who played the accompaniments had suddenly been laid low with a temperature. Would Mary save the situation by taking her place? Knowing that nothing very difficult would be expected of her, she said yes at once, to Mr. Macpherson 's visible relief. He conducted her behind the green baize curtain to a little space at one side of the platform where the performers were assembled. They were all very kind and helpful, the postmaster in particular.

"You won't find it's like a London concert, Miss Preston,' he assured her.

Mary said she was sure she wouldn't.

The curtains were then drawn aside, discovering Mr. Macpherson, who announced that Miss Preston had kindly volunteered to replace Miss Stone, who had gone down with a touch of the old enemy, flu. Loud applause followed, which redoubled when Mary mounted the platform. While she waited at the little upright piano for the audience to settle itself, she saw Lady Emily insisting on spreading half her shawl over Mr. Banister's unwilling knees, and Agnes picking up her mother's bag and stick. In the front row of the gallery she could see most of the servants, including Ivy, to whom Nannie had given lofty permission to come, indicating that churchgoers, having little chance of salvation in the next world, might as well enjoy themselves, if enjoyment it could be called, in this. Gudgeon she could not see anywhere, but looking at the programme, which was pinned to the piano, she saw in the second half:

SONG (*by special request*)—MR. GUDGEON

The performance now began. Mary had no difficulty in reading the music provided, but had to exercise considerable ingenuity in following the soloists. All the performers, she discovered, regarded anything played by piano alone, whether as introduction, intermezzo between verses and phrases, or closing melody, as unnecessary padding, put in by the composer to lessen their chances. Taking this attitude, most of them plunged straight into their items, sometimes not even waiting for the key, in their anxiety to distinguish themselves. The audience enjoyed everything. The heat became stifling. A racket court is never at the best of times a well-ventilated place, and crowded as it was with people in wet shoes and coats, it felt like a conservatory in which the favourite plants were damp wool and rubber.

In the interval Mary joined her party, who were loud in admiration.

"You're just splendid, Miss Mary," said Mr. Macpherson. "We've yet another piece of ill news, though. The young man that was to have done the comic solo, the last number on the programme, has had a tooth out, and he is in that state of agony that I had to advise him to go home. It is a pity, for the comic is a good note to end with. You couldn't sing us something, could you, Miss Mary?"

"Oh, I'm very sorry, but I couldn't possibly," said Mary. "I don't mind playing, because no one listens to me, but I couldn't stand on the platform. Oh, please not."

'Well, we'll have to see what we can do. Maybe I'll sing myself. Time now, Miss Mary."

The concert proceeded through its interminable length. The singers never had a second copy of their music, and if they did not know it by heart, looked over Mary's shoulder and sang down her neck. The postmaster gave a comic reading in stage Scotch which produced roars of enthusiasm. Gudgeon arrived with his song. He was as unruffled on the platform as he was at the dinner-table.

"I am well acquainted with both music and words of my item, miss," he said to Mary in a conspiratorial aside, "so shall leave the music with you. Be kind enough to follow me and all will go well. I shall return to the piano to turn for you myself."

He then took up his position on the platform. While he was acknowledging the applause which greeted him, Mary was able to cast her eye over his song. It was a Victorian relic called "The Body in the Bag." Its theme was the adventures of a gentleman who sought to dispose of a tom-cat which had died, in his establishment. While playing the opening bars, which consisted of two or three chords with the written instruction "ad lib. till ready," Mary glanced ahead and was smitten with horror. The Song would obviously be a popular success, but what would Aunt Emily and Aunt Agnes think? However, it wasn't her fault, so she steeled herself to go through with it. The accompaniment being written for the class of accompanist who acquires his technique through a popular manual called "Vamping in Six Lessons," she was able to give her almost undivided attention to Gudgeon's rendering. It was that of a master. Every word was clear, every point was not only made but underlined, and his gracious waits for laughter made it impossible for his audience to miss a word. During the chorus which followed each verse, Gudgeon had to imitate a trombone, which he did with great skill, joined in ever-increasing numbers by his hearers. True to his word he came and turned over for Mary in every verse, in spite of her whispered hint that she knew it by heart now. Two verses before the end he paused dramatically.

"Kindly continue the *ad lib.* till I recommence, miss," he said to Mary. Then, advancing to the edge of the platform, he addressed Lady Emily in a respectful but penetrating voice.

"I thought you might like to know, my lady, that there are only two verses more to come, and these contain what we may call the crux of the item."

"Thank you so much, Gudgeon," said her ladyship. "Oh, and Gudgeon, did you think of seeing that Mr. Leslie's other shoes were sent to be mended? Not the other ones, you know, but the *other* ones."

"Yes, my lady. Walter took them over to Southbridge on his bike this afternoon."

"Oh, thanks, Gudgeon."

"Thank you, 'my lady. Now, miss, if you will be so kind," he added, turning to Mary.

The crux of the song, to use Gudgeon's unimpeachable phraseology, was that after the cat's body in a sack had been left on doorsteps, dropped into rivers, thrust up chimneys, and always returned, the owner went back with it in despair, only to discover when he opened the sack at home that he had been mistaken about his cat and there were seven little bodies in the bag.

> *"There was I with the bodies in the bag,*
> *The bodies in the bag, ta-RA-ra,"*

sang Gudgeon triumphantly. Such of the audience as were not singing in the chorus explained to each other that it was "bodies" this time, not "body," so that by the time the applause died down there was hardly a single member of the audience who did not clearly understand what it was he or she had been laughing at.

The items that followed were commonplace in cornparison. While the postmaster's daughter was delivering herself of a monologue, Mr. Macpherson came up to Mary in the little space beside the platform.

"It's going on well," he observed, "but I wish I had put Gudgeon at the end. It would have been a fine windup. I doubt if his dignity would have stood for it though," he said, chuckling. "Well, Miss Mary, there's but the one more song. Just keep your seat at the piano and as I said, I'll maybe give them The Wooing O't' myself."

The monologue and the following song were disposed of. Mary, sat idly at the piano, wondering what sort of a voice Mr. Macpherson had, when the agent walked up to the front of the platform.

"Ladies and gentlemen," he said, "our last item is unfortunately cancelled, as the gentleman is at present in bed with the face-ache. I had thought of singing to you myself, but I doubt if you'd have stood it. I now have much pleasure in announcing that a young gentleman from London will oblige with a song."

The applause was deafening as the newcomer mounted the stage, and putting a piece of music on the stand, said to Mary:

"Can you play this?"

"David!"

"Why not?"

"Oh, David!"

"Oh, Mary," he mocked. "Look, love, can you read this thing?"

"No, no, I couldn't possibly," she said, quickly getting up. Probably she couldn't. The newest jazz hit isn't in everyone's technique. And even if you had the jazz gift, which you know you haven't, how could you play with your fingers trembling and your eyes feeling as if they must be crossed with the violence and suddenness of your emotions?

"No, I didn't suppose you could," said David. "I only got it by post from America this morning. I can hardly play it myself. However, we'll give it a try. Get another chair and you can turn over for me."

Mary obediently fetched a stool from the back of the platform, where the seats provided for the Cheerio Trio (a revolting combination of clarinet, violin and female cello, with whose performance Mary had hardly been able to keep slowness, if one may coin such a phrase to express the opposite of keeping pace) had been piled. David pulled the piano further towards the front of the stage, slewed his chair round, and plunged into fireworks of finger-work, singing all the time in a heartrending voice. For Mary there was the pleasure of leaning across him two or three times to turn over.

Nothing could have pleased the audience more than Mr. David's unexpected appearance and his crooning voice. Shrieks, stamps, whistles and yells called for an encore.

"No more. Not a drop," shouted David, blowing kisses to everybody.

Mr. Macpherson, who had an eye on the time, had the curtains closed, and the audience simmered down.

"That was a grand song, David," he said. "You were a good lad to come. But why didn't you let us know?"

Without waiting for an answer, he went back to the hall to superintend the placing of the trestle tables and the unpacking of sandwiches, cakes and beer, while Mrs. Siddon looked after the large tea urns.

The Leslie family and Mary walked back to the house. The rain had stopped. David gave his mother his arm, while Agnes, Mary and Mr. Leslie walked behind. Mr. Leslie was loud in his praise of Mary's kindness and skill.

"Played like a Paderooski," he said. "Success of the evening. Good girl."

"Thanks awfully, Mr. Leslie, but really Gudgeon was the success."

"Oh, Gudgeon. 'Body in the Bag.' Ought to have warned you; he sings that song every year. Hope you didn't find it a bit shocking, eh?"

There was hot soup and an informal supper in the diningroom. Mary, happening to come in last, saw that the only empty place was between David and his father. In front of the plate was something large, wrapped in tissue paper, tied with a huge bow of ribbon.

"What is it?" she asked as she sat down. "Not a present for me?"

"Open it," said David.

She untied the ribbon and loosened the paper. Inside was a lair basket of tiny strawberries.

"Oh, David! Wild strawberries."

"Are you pleased?"

"Oh, David! How too heavenly."

"They are to make up for forgetting the other day."

"Oh, David, did you really think of that?"

"Of course I did," said David, honestly believing what he

said for the moment. "I was no end of a brute to forget my promise the other day."

It certainly was worth seeing Mary look so pleased and so pretty as she shared her strawberries. David had been lunching that day with Joan Stevenson at the same restaurant, and had been reminded by the proprietor that wild strawberries could still be got. This again reminded him of John's suggestion, so on the spur of the moment he ordered a basket to be sent to his flat and decided to run down to Rushwater with it. When he arrived the whole party were at the concert, so he told the under footman, who was temporarily in charge, to put the basket on the supper-table, went over to the racket court and, as we have seen, made his appearance just at the right moment.

"Excuse my not being dressed, mother," he said. "I motored down and I am famished. I didn't have any dinner. Did I miss a lot of good stuff at the concert?"

David is hungry because he went without dinner to bring me srtrawberries, thought Mary. A thought that wrung one's heart, yet how pleasantly.

"Gudgeon was in great form," said Mr. Leslie. 'Body in the Bag' as usual. Good song, that."

"It seems too sad about all those kittens," said Agnes plaintively. "He really ought to have noticed that it wasn't a tom. I mean, days beforehand you can see the poor creature is going to have kittens. Darling Clarissa is going to have a kitten this winter for her very own. It will be too sweet."

"Darling Agnes, there is no one like you in the world," said David, admiringly.

"Well, I expect you will all be glad to get to bed," said Lady Emily, who had managed to trail a purple chiffon scarf through her soup and was washing it in a wine glass. "Gudgeon's song is too delicious and so was yours, David. You must sing it to us to-morrow night."

"Sorry, mother, I shan't be here. I'm rushing off at cock-crow to-morrow. I only came down for fun."

"Oh, very well, darling. Agnes, give me my stick. This wet weather doesn't help my stupid knee. Blow out the candles, David. Most of the servants are over at the racket court, and I told the others they could go to bed."

Escorted by her husband and daughter, she limped from the room. Mary and David blew out the candles and went towards the door.

"Did you really like the strawberries?"

"Oh, David, I adored them. But I wish you hadn't gone without dinner."

"That's all right," said David, who having eaten what amounted to a hearty meal at a cocktail party from six to half-past, quite honestly meant what he said.

"I was so unhappy when I thought you had forgotten," said Mary, unable to resist the temptation to prolong this pleasant moment.

"My poor child, what a rotter you must think me."

"Oh, I don't. I think you are—

"What?"

"I don't know. Rather David-ish, I suppose."

If David slid his arm round one in the half-light of the doorway, if one burrowed one's face for a moment into his collar, that didn't count as kissing. Of course, it didn't, thought Mary, indignantly, while undressing. Kissing is rather horrid, she thought, with memories of film stars, their lips glued dispassionately together. But just to be near a person for a moment and feel his cheek against your hair is quite, quite different. In fact I wouldn't mind who knew, she told herself, loftily and untruthfully.

In due time Lady Emily redeemed the promise she thought she might have given, and asked the dull Lady Norton, Mr. Holt's friend, to lunch. Lady Norton was indeed almost duller than is humanly possible, but she really loved flowers. She and Lady Emily spent some of the afternoon in the garden, exchanging names of flowers and promises of bulbs and seedlings. Mr. Banister, who came in to tea, was admitted as a fellow-gardener on the strength of some seeds which he had once brought back from the Holy Land. He was afraid that Lady Norton would inquire further about the seeds which, either because he had lost them, or because he had planted them at the wrong season, he never could remember which, had not come up. But Lady Norton was so anxious to tell him how she and her husband had once intended to visit Jerusalem at Easter, but had been unable to do so because of a General Election, that the subject of the seeds was dropped, much to Mr. Banister's relief.

"May I stay and have a little talk with you, Lady Emily?" he asked, when Lady Norton had taken her depressing leave.

"Yes, do, Mr. Banister. Mary, did I promise to go over to Norton Manor one day?"

"Yes, Aunt Emily. You really did ask her to let you come because you wanted to see her poppies."

"Did I? Well, I suppose I did. Agnes, what is one to do when people are as dull as that? But she really understands gardens and is going to give me some seedlings."

"That will be lovely, mother. Only you know Brown will be offended. He minds things very much."

"The concert was a great success," said Mr. Banister. "I am sure we are all more than grateful to Miss Preston. And David coming down like that was great luck. He gave us just the right spirit. And he gave me some good news which he may have mentioned to you.

"No, I don't think so," said Agnes. 'What was it?"

"He really is a kind-hearted boy," said the vicar. "I happened to mention to him—you will remember, Miss Preston, you were there at the time, when I was mending my bicycle in the front garden—I mentioned to him that my tenants would be glad of a suitable paying-guest who wanted to study French. As Martin will not be sleeping at the vicarage they will have a bedroom to spare."

"How will they do that?" inquired Lady Emily, with great interest. "You have only five bedrooms at the vicarage and there are five of them, I understand. Will you have enough beds? I could always lend you one, and there is Clarissa's crib that she grew out of last year, and it is in perfectly good condition except that the moth got into the blankets. But, after all, a larger one folded would do just as well. Agnes, remind me to speak to Siddon about it."

"I am afraid they won't have much use for a crib, Lady Emily. The youngest child is sixteen."

"No, I see. But still I don't see how they are going to manage about the bedrooms. Monsieur and Madame Boulle can have your room, of course, with another bed moved into it, and then there is the dressing-room for him, and then the three other bedrooms for the three young people."

"I really don't quite know, Lady Emily."

"Well, I can ask Madame Boulle when I go to call on her. I shall certainly call on her as soon as she is settled."

"Mamma," said Agnes, "don't you want to know what Mr. Banister's good news is?"

"Of course I do, Agnes, only we had to settle the question of the beds first. What is the news, Mr. Banister?"

"David tells me that he has found a guest for them, a friend of his who wants to spend a fortnight studying French."

"How delightful," said Lady Emily. "I must ask the Boulles to bring him up here for tennis."

"It is a young lady, Lady Emily, a Miss Stevenson. David tells me that she works at broadcasting in London."

"Then perhaps she will know some nice bed-time stories for the children," said Agnes.

"I don't know whether she does the Children's Hour," said the vicar. "I rather gathered from David that she was on the executive side. She sounds a brilliant young woman. She got a first in economics and was secretary to Professor Gilbert for a year before she took up this work."

"When is she coming?" asked Mary, afraid that her silence might be observed.

"Let me see, he did say. Yes. The second fortnight in August."

"Then she will be here for Martin's dance," said Lady Emily. "I must ask them all to it. It won't be a big dance, Vicar. Just neighbours, about sixty or seventy people, I think, and the band from Southbridge. John and David will be here, of course."

"Good-bye, Mr. Banister," said Mary. "I am going to see Clarissa put to bed. I hope you'll have a splendid holiday."

She ran upstairs to the nursery, determined not to think about David for a single minute. Hateful David. Horrible Miss Stevenson. Sneaking into Rushwater by back doors. Probably she spoke perfect French already. Such a very brilliant person would. She knew David's week-end invitation was rather vague, and she had found this clever way of worming herself in.

Clarissa was just going to be bathed, and Nannie graciously allowed Mary to assume her flannel apron and soap Clarissa's divine slippery body.

And of course David wanted her, or he wouldn't have told her about the Boulles wanting a paying-guest. He didn't think his Miss Stevenson was good enough to ask to his mother's house, so he installed her at the vicarage. The word install gave Mary considerable pleasure, conveying as it did a flavour of illicit relations and *petits soupers*.

She helped Clarissa to walk out of her bath and sat her on her lap to be dried.

Hateful David. How dared he think that she wouldn't mind if he .put his arm round her? Of course she didn't like it, but no one made a fuss about that sort of thing nowadays.

Perhaps he thought she had put her head on his shoulder
because she liked him. Good heavens, didn't he know that it
was a gesture which meant nothing, absolutely nothing? Here
she laughed so loudly to show her scorn of the idea that
Clarissa began to laugh too.

"Angel!" said Mary, buttoning up Clarissa's dressing-gown
and pushing her feet into her bedroom slippers, "you don't go
behind people's backs and be a hateful selfish pig, do you?"

She kissed Clarissa with great satisfaction in the nape of
her neck and lifted her into her tall chair. Nannie coming
back found Miss Mary telling Clarissa "This Little Pig went
to Market" while she ate her biscuits.

"There, baby, isn't it kind of Auntie Mary to bathe you?"
she said.

Clarissa took the mug of milk in both hands and tilted it
to her mouth. After a long and satisfying draught she set it
down on the edge of the table and it fell onto the floor.

"Oh, baby, you are a naughty girl. That's the second time
she has done that, miss. She is just showing off. Ivy, come and
wipe this milk off the floor and empty the bath, and then you
can go and fetch James and Emmy from Mrs. Siddon's room.
They've been having tea there, miss."

Mary wiped Clarissa's milky mouth with her feeder and
lifted her onto her lap again. At such moments, when one's
world crashed about one, and one realized that everything was
a hollow sham and particularly David, a fat, speechless
Clarissa on one's knees was a great comfort.

"You've heard our disaster with the canary, miss?" said
Nannie.

"No, Nannie, what happened?"

"Well, miss, you remember we were getting a little wife for
him. It turned out there was a mistake and she was another
little gentleman. So our Dicky quite took against him and
pecked him so badly that we had to put him in another cage.
And this morning there was our poor little new gentleman

lying dead on the floor."

"Oh, Nannie, how sad."

"It was, miss. Ivy cried so she could hardly wash up the breakfast things, and she's been quite upset all day," said Nannie, in whose eyes Ivy had evidently reinstated herself by this proper display of emotion. "But I was brought up to believe that all things work together for the best if you look at them rightly, and James had a lovely funeral with the poor little gentleman, didn't he, Ivy?"

"He looked so sweet in the coffin, miss," said Ivy, beginning to cry again. "Master James had the box his new shoes come in, and he lined it with moss ever so nice, and you'd have said the poor little bird was only sleeping, he looked that peaceful. It was beautiful, miss."

"That'll do, Ivy," said Nannie, becoming brisk again. "Now, baby, say good night to Auntie Mary."

Clarissa was suddenly taken shy, so Mary kissed her all over the back of her soft neck and went away. Yes, she thought, as she dressed for dinner, that was what life was like. Canaries were pecked to death and David liked a girl like Miss Stevenson. If she had known what he was going to do, no, what he had already done, she would have thrown his strawberries on the ground and stamped on them, if it hadn't been for the mess.

CHAPTER IX

LADY EMILY PAYS A CALL

AT THE END OF JULY Martin came home for the holidays. He had been growing in every direction during the summer term and was looking extremely handsome. As the Boulles were to arrive at the vicarage on the first of August, there was no time to be lost, and Martin threw himself with energy into the business of rounding up the village eleven and arranging for the cricket match which was to take place on his seventeenth birthday between the tenant farmers and the estate employees, stiffened by David, Martin and John. There was to be .tea in the racket court in the interval. A dinner party at Rushwater House, followed by a dance, would conclude the festivities. If the preparations made the Leslies think with a pang of their eldest son's coming of age, they resolutely put the thought away from them.

Agnes, who was ordering a new evening dress for herself, wanted to get one for Mary, but Mr. Leslie, hearing of it, insisted that it should be his present.

"Get what you like," he said. "Don't think if it will last or not. Just get something that will make you look your best. Must do us credit, you know. Go up to town with Agnes, and she'll see you get the right thing. Good taste, Agnes."

Indeed Agnes's clothes, joint product of her own taste, an inspired dressmaker, and a wealthy husband who liked to see his wife well turned out, were always perfect. The commission was much to her liking, and she wrote to John to suggest that they should lunch with him in town. John was delighted and a date was fixed. Mary, while feeling that life as far as she was concerned was over, found the prospect of a new dress not unattractive. Besides, one might see David in London.

The question which now agitated Lady Emily was, should she call on Madame Boulle before Martin went for his first French lesson or after. None of her considerable social experience in the past appeared to be the slightest help to her in this matter. On the very day when the Boulle family were to come into the vicarage she was still undecided.

"If I call before Martin goes," she argued at lunch, "they might think I was coming to see if they looked good enough for Martin, but if I don't go till after he has had a lesson there, it may seem rude. When papa was being a Governor in India, people used to come and write their names in the book, but that, of course, was so many years ago, and none of us were French. Mr. Banister says they are very nice simple people, but that doesn't make it any easier. Henry, what would you do?"

"About what, Emily?"

"Calling on the Boulles."

"Calling on who? Oh, Banister's tenants. Yes, my dear, call on them, of course."

"Ask them to tea, mamma, and we could have the children down," said Agnes.

"Children?" said Mr. Leslie, lifting his eyes from the peach he was peeling. "Thought their young people were all grown up. Played tennis and so on. But call on them by all means."

Lady Emily and her daughter exchanged glances expressive of the difficulties of a world where papa would join in the conversation without being fully aware what it was about. Mary suggested that Lady Emily should call on the following day, stay just long enough for civility, and ask them all to tea and tennis the day after. After a great many impracticable suggestions this plan was adopted, and Lady Emily professed herself much relieved.

Accordingly, accompanied by Agnes and Martin, who was very unwillingly pressed into the expedition, Lady Emily descended upon the vicarage next afternoon.

Madame Boulle, a stout, middle-aged woman with masses of grey hair, was in the drawing-room and greeted her guests in excellent English.

"But how kind of you to visit us," she exclaimed. 'We are already installed and everything is of the highest comfort. And this is your grandson who is to study with us? Bien. What is your name, sir?"

Thus addressed, Martin turned bright red and mumbled "Leslie."

"Naturally, it is Leslie," said Madame Boulle. "But we shall not call you Leslie, you will be as a son to me. I assure you," she added, turning to Agnes, "that, a mother myself, I shall give to your son the care I should give to my own."

"He isn't my son, Madame Boulle, he is only my—"

"Assuredly. I wondered that you should have a son already so old. Naturally he is your young cousin."

"No, I'm sorry," said Agnes, with a distinct feeling of guilt at spoiling the relationship which Madame Boulle had arranged, "he is only my nephew."

"Ah, I renounce," cried Madame Boulle. "It is too complicated. Tu m'expliqueras tout vela plus tard, mon petit, n'est-ce pas," she said to Martin, who at once hated everyone with a deadly hatred which he was at no pains to conceal.

"I feel already that he is my son," Madame Boulle explained. "I must now present to you the rest of our family. Henri, Pierre, Ursule, Jean Claude," she cried through the open doorway.

No one answered. Madame Boulle said that they were all doubtless in the garden and begged her guests to step that way.

"Ah, you are cripple?" she inquired, seeing Lady Emily's stick.

"Not exactly," said Lady Emily, "but I have so much arthritis. I went to Aix once, but it didn't seem to do me any good."

"*Aix*," said Madame Boulle. 'We all know about Aix. A rabble of doctors who only want to profit by the English. Let me tell you. Do you know Droitwich? No? Then later I shall tell you about it. I have a particular knowledge of all England. But here is my husband and young ones."

The rest of the Boulle family who were seated under a tree in the garden got up as the visitors approached. Professor Boulle was a tall, good-looking man with a melancholy face and courteous manners. If he rarely spoke it was because of his conviction that anything he said would be interrupted or ignored. Pierre, a young man of about twenty-five, was like his father, though not quite so silent, and Ursule was stout and like her mother, but not so talkative. In Jean Claude, Martin recognized with horror the image which David had set up on the night when the plan was first mooted. He was about Martin's height, but extremely bony. He was wearing khaki shorts and a pullover, socks and sandshoes. His face was incredibly spotty, and on his upper lip, cheeks and chin lay a thick yellow down.

"You two young people will be comrades," declared Madame Boulle, an assertion which was met by her son with a weary acquiescence, by Martin with a scowl of rage. "Jean Claude is, as you see, Boyscout. He is also impassioned for nature."

"I adore nature too, maman," said Ursule with a giggle.

"You will all three make some excursions on foot," said Madame Boulle, "you, Ursule, and Jean Claude and Leslie."

"But you mustn't call him Leslie," said Lady Emily. His name is Martin."

"Ah, Martin. Nom Bien français, par exemple. But I shall call you Martine, as you are an English lad."

Ursule giggled violently and whispered something to her mother.

"Tais-toi, Ursule," said Madame Boulle angrily. "Have I not told you repeatedly that it is very ill-bred to whisper in company?"

"But, maman, if you call him Martine, everyone will think he is a girl," giggled Ursule.

"Ursule, one does not argue with one's mother.

When you are married and have a house of your own you can say what you like. Till then, obedience."

"All the same it is true what Ursule observes," her father remarked.

"Ah, but Henri, this is too much. To encourage Ursule in impertinence on the first day of our arrival. Will Martine then be Sir Leslie when he inherits?" she asked, turning to Lady Emily.

"Inherits what?" asked Lady Emily, bewildered by this change of subject.

"Inherits of his grandfather, the present Sir Leslie."

"My husband is only Mr. Leslie," Lady Emily began, but was cut short by a torrent of words from Madame Boulle, who was firmly convinced after studying a Debrett which she had found in the vicarage, that Martin, in virtue of being an earl's great-grandson on his mother's side, would naturally come into a baronetcy at his father's death. Lady Emily and Agnes tried to explain, but were overwhelmed by Madame Boulle's display of knowledge. It appeared that she had in her youth been a governess in English families of the highest distinction, and since her marriage had continually received scions of the nobility as paying-guests.

"You have not abolished your hereditary peerage as we unfortunately have," she said, "therefore Martine will be, if not Sir Leslie, at least an honourable."

Martin, goaded almost beyond bearing, said in a loud voice that tides were an awful nuisance. At this Jean Claude became transformed. He clenched his large hands, his spotty face turned scarlet, the pale fluff on his face seemed to stiffen. Coming close up to Martin he drew him aside, and putting his face right into Martin's said in a low, threatening voice:

"You are a republican then?"

"Good Lord, no. We don't have a republic here, you know. King George. Roi George," he kindly explained.

Jean Claude's anger evaporated as quickly as it had risen.

"That is well," he remarked ominously and said no more.

Lady Emily now collected her party and said goodbye, issuing an invitation to tea and tennis to all the Boulles for the next day.

Madame Boulle accepted with voluble ecstasy. It was, she explained, many years since she herself had taken part in a party of tennis, but Pierre, Ursule and Jean Claude all played magnificently. As for her husband, he was an artist, and could never be depended on.

"But I thought Mr. Banister said he was a professor," said Lady Emily.

"Ah, perfectly. He is a professor, but in soul he is an artist, a poet. Although my own family is of ancient date, bearing the particule, I yet feel it a distinction to have married an artist soul. Pierre inherits from my husband. He is also artist, but not in the arts, no. On another scene. Oh, one will hear of him in the world."

Without further explanation she conducted them to the front gate, followed by Jean Claude.

"Eh, bien, say farewell to your comrade, Jean Claude," said his mother.

But Martin, overcome by fear that Jean Claude might kiss him, for such he had heard was the custom of foreigners, bolted into the car, where he sat speechless, glowering at his relations. They, to his great surprise, took the Boulle family as a matter of course, and talked of other things, so that Martin had to nurse his anger and reflect that whatever he had let himself in for, it was entirely his own fault. As soon as they got back he went in search of Mary, who was leading Emmy about on the pony. To her he poured out the horrors of the afternoon's expedition.

"David was right," he declared gloomily. "That young Claude or whatever his name is, is the most glastly spotted sight you ever saw, and what's more he is mad. He wanted to know if I was a republican and old Madame wanted to know if I would be Sir Leslie when grandfather died. The old professor didn't look so bad, nor did the eldest son, thank heaven. I'm to have my lessons with him, I believe. But the girl is a fat giggling pest. About twenty, I suppose, and thinks she's a hundred. I say, Mary, they're all coming up for tennis tomorrow. What on earth shall I do? I've got to go for my first lesson to-morrow and then have them up here in the afternoon. Oh, gosh, what ghastly holidays these are going to be. And when I think it's all my own fault too."

Overcome by despair he flung himself onto the ground and began pulling the heads off daisies.

"Never mind, Martin," said Mary, "here is Ivy coming to fetch Emmy. Will you take the pony round to the stables and I'll get my tennis shoes and we'll have a practice for to-morrow."

Emmy was taken to bed and Martin, bestriding the pony with both feet well on the ground, conducted it thus to the stables; to the intense joy of the groom. Then he gave Mary fifteen in each game and beat her, so life seemed less hopeless.

It was, however, with a sinking heart that he set out for the vicarage next morning. His chief fear was that someone would kiss him, if not Jean Claude then Madame Boulle in her maternal mood, or even the professor. But to his great relief he was received by Pierre, who took him to the vicar's study, examined him in what he knew and set him to work. Pierre was quiet and undemonstrative. Martin was soon at ease in his company and felt the French lessons would not be so bad after all. The only thing that disturbed him was that Pierre would look at him now and then with a curious appraising glance, take breath as if he were going to say something, then resume his lesson again and go on as if nothing had happened. Finally Martin put it down to the queerness of foreigners and took no further notice.

At lunch, however, his old feeling of suspicion returned. Madame Boulle welcomed him as ce cher petit Martine with enthusiasm. Ursule giggled and Jean Claude looked just as unprepossessing as he had done on the previous day. After they had begun the professor came in and went quietly to his place.

"What is the soup to-day?" he inquired.

"Lentil soup," replied Madame Boucle. "These lentils, Martine, are a particular kind which I get from France. They cannot be got in England, nor in Germany, nor in Russia—"

"But I assure you I have often met them in Germany, Madeleine," said her husband.

"On the contrary, I assure you, Henri, that these lentils can only be got in France. They are very expensive, Martine. Living is expensive everywhere. One has to spend an enormous amount on food in France. Food is more expensive in France than anywhere else."

"Food is also very expensive in Spain," the professor ventured.

"Possibly."

Martin, who could understand their conversation quite well, prayed inwardly that they would go on talking for ever, so that he need never open his mouth. It was one thing to talk with Pierre in the study, where he had somehow expressed himself in what felt to him easy and idiomatic French. But to say anything before the giggling Ursule or that ghastly Jean Claude was unthinkable.

Madame Boulle, a conscientious woman, was just going to address a remark to Martin which would force him to take some part in the conversation, when Jean Claude stretched over the table for a bottle of gherkins and took some out with his own fork. His mother was unable to let pass so excellent an opportunity for edification.

"Jean Claude, only very ill-bred people take gherkins with their own fork. And you should offer them to others before taking them yourself."

"But, maman, they were in front of me, so why shouldn't; I help myself? It takes much longer to pass them round and then help myself. afterwards. Besides, I do not know that any-one wants them."

"Jean Claude, how often have I told you not to argue with your mother? You are only a child. Some day, as I am always telling Ursule, you will have a home of your own and then you can behave as badly as you like.

But while you are under my roof I demand obedience."

"The roof belongs to Monsieur Banister," said Jean Claude in a low defiant voice which luckily his mother did not hear. He then relapsed into a fit of sulks.

"Martine," said Madame Boulle, turning to her guest, "do you want some mustard?"

The blow had fallen. Crimsoning to the ears Martin muttered, "Merci."

"As you are English," said Madame, "I know that you mean Yes, please. All English make this mistake once, it is entirely natural, and I only point it out to you that you may not repeat it. This is French mustard. French mustard is known all over the world. It is everywhere considered the best. This particular kind of mustard is very expensive. I get it from a special shop in Paris."

"What we had last week was better, Madeleine," said the professor.

"Listen, Henri. I have been a housekeeper for many years and I assure you—"

"But, Madeleine—"

"It is no good example to Martine to discuss the food at table. I have often begged you not to, Henri. Well, Martine, you are not very talkative, are you?"

Another horrible crisis.

"Non, madame," he said, with a forced unnatural smile.

Pierre now spoke for the first time.

"Ursule, have you heard from René lately?"

"Yes," said Ursule, for once without her giggle. "He wrote to say—"

"Pierre," interrupted his mother, "how often have I told you that it is very ill-bred to discuss at table a per son of whom the other guests know nothing. If you wish to talk about this Rene you can do so afterwards."

At this moment Martin, sorry for his gentle instructor, who was being thus unmercifully baited, forgot his shyness and haltingly asked Pierre if he liked tennis. Although, to Martin's embarrassment, the whole family stopped talking and eating to listen to what he said, Pierre answered him so kindly that he became valorous, and wallowed and plunged in the French language till the end of lunch. When coffee had been drunk, to the accompaniment of a disquisition from Madame Boulle on the superiority of French coffee to all other coffee, and the extreme expense of good coffee in France, Martin made his excuses and left for home. Pierre came with him to the door. He again looked as if he wanted to say something, so Martin waited. Again he seemed to think better of it, but said in English, which he spoke as fluently as the rest of his family:

"It was nice of you, Martin, to come to my rescue. You are just the sort we want."

He went into the house and Martin went home, puzzled and interested. But as he changed into his tennis things, his fear of the family as a whole began to grow again. Suppose Madame lectured his grandfather as she did the professor. Suppose, which was very likely, Ursule giggled all the time.

Suppose Jean Claude came in his shorts and socks. Thank heaven David wasn't here to jeer at Martin in his self-inflicted torment. In a frenzy of. annoyance Martin took a book and went across the garden to the churchyard, determined to see his guests without being seen. The vicarage, a modern house which Mr. Banister had obtained permission to build because the old vicarage was too large and expensive to keep up, was about half a mile away at the other end of the village. To reach Rushwater House the Boulles must necessarily pass the church. Just inside the low churchyard wall was a large bush, from whose shelter Martin had often defied the search of nurses, or shot peas at his village friends. He perched himself on the wall with one eye on his book and the other on the village street, which was white and empty in the after-lunch sunshine. Not only his eyes but his thoughts were divided. Part of his attention was given to Shelley, who happened to be in fashion among the higher intellectuals at school, part of it wandered to the Boulles, and especially to Pierre. Martin's blood boiled at the thought of Pierre's treatment at lunch. To Martin, who so long as he did not grossly transgress the bounds—as in the unfortunate affair of Milton—was allowed complete freedom in his doings and his conversation, it was incredible that a grown-up man of twenty-five, who was almost a professor, should submit so tamely to his mother. It was also incredible to Martin, child of his age and country, that any mother should have the nerve to talk like that to her sons. Pierre was a very decent chap. If only all French people were like him one could get on very well indeed. Martin wondered again what it was that Pierre had meant by saying, "You are the sort we want." Perhaps he only meant the sort of pupil, though it was a funny thing to say.

The sound of Madame Boulle's voice in the distance recalled him to the present. He slipped Shelley into his pocket and dropped off the wall, worming himself into the bush till he was invisible from the road. To his intense relief Jean

Claude was now dressed like any other boy in grey flannel trousers, flannel shirt and tweed coat, with a white scarf round his neck. Probably the others had only been his boy scout clothes. Martin breathed again. At least he would not be eternally disgraced before the servants. Ursule, in a short silk tennis frock, looked quite presentable, though not elegant, and the rest of the family would pass muster anywhere, though Professor Boulle's alpaca jacket perhaps left something to be desired.

"Mais voyons, Ursule," he heard Madame Boulle say as they passed, "how often have I told you that no wellbrought-up girl should eat chocolates in her bedroom. The nourishment that I give you is healthy and sufficient. If you are hungry, you have only to say so. Chocolates are an unnecessary expense. By that I do not include chocolate as drink, which is healthy and fortifying. All English chocolate is excessively bad. The French chocolate is the best in the world and I must procure some from Paris, although the price augments daily. Have you read, Henri, in to-day's paper that the price of chocolate already remounts to—"

Here her voice died away into the distance as the party turned into the grounds of Rushwater House. Martin bounded away by the churchyard gate and was at the house to meet them when they arrived.

At tea Professor Boulle fell an immediate victim to Lady Emily, who treated him with the respect due to a professor with the soul of a poet and an artist, a respect to which he was little accustomed at home.

"How is it," she asked, "that you all speak English so well, Professor?"

"My mother was English, and my wife, after taking her degree, taught in English families for some years before our marriage. We have always kept it up. But I can assure you, Lady Emily, that your grandson will not hear a single word of English while he is among us."

"No, I'm sure he won't. And you all speak such beautiful French," said Lady Emily, who appeared to be much impressed by this phenomenon.

"One's maternal language," said the professor with a smile.

"But you said your mother was English."

"Madame, you confound me by your quickness."

"Some more tea, Madame Boulle," said Agnes, who was pouring out.

"Thank you, I will. You will observe, mon petit," she said to Martin, who started nervously at being thus addressed, "that I here conform to the English custom by which `thank you' may be a term of assent, not of dissent as in French, as in effect I pointed out to your grandson, Lady Emily, at lunch-time. Your tea is indeed delicious. Tea is a speciality in the English nation. English tea is the best in the world, though excessively dear. I procure mine from a shop in London. It is a special brand which they reserve for me. Tea has never been in the genius of the French nation. Jean Claude, before helping yourself to cake you should offer it to others."

"Eh Bien, en veux-tu, maman?" said Jean Claude, pushing the plate sulkily at his mother.

"Ah, par exemple," ejaculated Madame Boulle. "It is not for me, it is for the young people, for Miss Preston, for your comrade Martine. Martine has already made excellent progress with his French, Lady Emily. He is an intelligence, ce petit Martine. He will make a niche for himself in the world."

But Lady Emily had resumed her conversation with Professor Boulle. They discovered that he possessed an autographed copy of a poem by Ronsard which her father, the late Lord Pomfret, had translated very badly, printed at his own expense, and presented in large quantitities to all the leading French universities. She was delighted to find this link and made herself so enchanting to the professor that he informed his wife later that Lady Emily was petrie d'esprit et de grace.

Agnes had Pierre next to her, and felt sorry for him.

His mother obviously had a crushing effect upon him, and he seemed the member of the family least able to resist. Where Ursule was impertinent and Jean Claude sulked, Pierre was invariably polite, but he felt keenly the impression his mother might make on other people. Agnes, incapable of clarifying her thoughts, could not have explained this to herself, but her instinctive kindness drew her to talk to Pierre about what she felt would really interest him.

"I am sure you like children," she said. "I would like you to see mine. James is seven and Emmy is five, and darling Clarissa is two and a half. They are such darlings. James is going to school next year and I shall miss him terribly. Emmy has a pony and she is going to be very good-looking."

"Then she is like you, Mrs. Graham?"

"Yes, partly like me and partly like her father," said Agnes, on whom Pierre's gallantry made no impression at all. "Would you like to see them after tea?"

"I should love to. But what about the tennis?"

Agnes looked round.

"Your brother and sister, and Mary and Martin will be four. I shall take you to see the children and then you can join in afterwards."

"I am going to the tennis with the young people," said Madame Boulle as they all got up. "I shall be umpire. Fairplay," she added waggishly.

Martin and Jean Claude exchanged looks. Although they had no particular liking for each other, a bond of sympathy was being forged between them in their distaste for Madame Boulle's masterful ways. However, she could do no harm on the tennis court, and no one need take any notice of what she said, so they all went off, leaving Lady Emily and the professor deep in a discussion of books.

Agnes took Pierre into the kitchen-garden where the children were again engaged in trying to catch goldfish in the pond. Pierre was an immediate success with the three children. He took off his coat, appearing in a short-sleeved tennis shirt, and plunged his arms into the water, pretending to grasp the unconscious fishes as they glided below, out of reach. Agnes watched them benignly from the further edge, with Clarissa on her lap, thinking of nothing at all.

It was inevitable that one of the children should fall into the pond sooner or later. Emmy reached over too far, shrieked, and fell in. For one instant Pierre thought of his white flannel trousers, then saw Agnes's lovely face, pale with terror, as she clasped Clarissa to her bosom with a vague idea of sheltering her from danger. He walked into the pond, which was only two feet deep, picked out the still shrieking Emmy and put her on land. Roused by her cries, Nannie and Ivy came running.

"Emmy you *are* a naughty girl," said Nannie, shaking her charge. "Ivy, run and get the pram rug and put it round her and I'll carry her in. That's what comes of leaning over too far, Emmy, and now the poor French gentleman is all wet. You *are* a bad girl."

Ivy hurried up with the rug and Nannie took the still shrieking Emmy away to hot bath and bed.

"Oh, Monsieur Boulle," said Agnes, still clasping Clarissa to her breast and looking like Niobe protecting the last of her children, "you are wet."

Pierre, as he wrung some of the water from his trouser legs, wished that he were lying drowned at Mrs. Graham's feet if she would give his corpse such another glance, say to it such exquisite words. The poor young man stood damp and adoring before her, not knowing what to do next.

"Ivy, take Mr. Boulle straight to the house the back way and tell Walter to find him some dry things, Mr. David's or Mr. Martin's, and then come back and take the children while I go to Emmy. Darling Clarissa, we will stay with James till Ivy comes back, won't we?"

Pierre suffered himself to be led indoors, delivered to

Walter and conducted to Martin's room, where he changed into a pair of Martin's white trousers, which were a good enough fit. Walter, waiting to show him the way to the tennis court, wondered what kept the French gent so long. If he had looked into the room he would have been none the wiser. Pierre, leaning against the foot of the bed, one leg in Martin's trousers, was thinking of Mrs. Graham. Her kindness, her beauty, the vision of her all pale and dishevelled—this was, of course, poetic licence, as Agnes was incapable of such discomposure—with cet amour d'enfant pressed to her bosom, had entirely upset the romantic young man. The soul of an artist to which his mother had alluded expanded within him. What a picture she would make.

Recovering the balance which his artistic distraction had nearly caused him to lose, he finished getting into Martin's trousers, meditating a poem to the goddess. But he had got no further than

O toi qui . . .

when Walter knocked at the door to ask if he could do anything for him.

When he got to the tennis court he found that the others had just finished a set. Mary and Jean Claude had been beaten by Martin and Ursule. Lady Emily, Madame Boulle and the professor were watching them.

"Where is Agnes?" asked Lady Emily.

"I think Mrs. Graham is in the nursery, Lady Emily. Little Emmy fell into the fish-pond and got wet."

"Ah, mon Dieu!" cried his mother. "That is frightful. You must take the utmost care, Lady Emily; that she does not catch a pneumonia. To fall into water is excessively dangerous. I have never permitted my children to go near the water for that very reason, until they could swim."

"There is hardly room to swim in the fish-pond," said

Lady Emily, "it is so small and shallow. Is Emmy all right, Monsieur Boulle?"

"I think so. I lifted her out and her mother and the nurse took her to the nursery at once."

"You didn't get wet, I hope," said Mary.

"Only my legs."

"What an ass you were to get in," said Martin. "I'd have hoicked Emmy out by her petticoats, the silly little idiot."

"But you will infallibly catch a bronchitis if you are wet, Pierre," shrieked Madame Boulle.

"No, maman. I have a dry pair of trousers on, Martin's, I think."

'Well, come on, let's .have another set," said Martin. "Here, Jeane Claude, you're the worst. You can sit out for a bit and Pierre can play with Mary. Come on, Ursule, we'll lick them again."

Madame Boulle, in spite of her experiences among the highest English families, was amazed at the coolness shown by Lady Emily. A grandchild in danger of drowning, a young man in danger of a pneumonia and a bronchitis, and she was entirely calm, not even impressed by Pierre's bravery. Bravery in the face of danger, Madame Boulle explained, was the characteristic of her family. Her great-grandfather, the comte de Florel, had been renowned for his bravery in the face of the most frightful dangers. Bravery was a special characteristic of the French nation. The English had a sang froid, a phlegme britannique, admittedly, but such courage as Pierre had shown was peculiar to the French in general and the house of de Florel in particular. Madame Boulle wept with emotion. To console her Lady Emily mentioned the dance which was to be held on Martin's birthday and hoped they would all come.

"Mr. Banister told me," she said, "that you would have an English girl staying with you, a friend of my son, David, so I hope you will bring her too."

Madame Boulle cheered up at once and accepted for her

family. Miss Stevenson, she said, was coming to them about the middle of August and would undoubtedly be delighted to come to the dance. She then embarked on an account of a toilette de bal which she had had as a young girl, which lasted till the set was over. Mary and Pierre had beaten Martin and Ursule.

"Jean Claude isn't much good," said Martin with the unfeeling frankness of his age. `We'll play again tomorrow, we four."

Pierre became pale inwardly. He knew he ought to be working, but if he came up to tennis he might see Mrs. Graham. While he was trying to make up his mind between romantic affection and duty, a hubbub broke out, caused by his mother. This lady asserted that no English laundry could wash Pierre's white flannel trousers. French laundries were the best in the world, but as there was no French laundry near at hand, she would take the trousers home and wash them herself.

"I have a real talent for washing," she explained. "I shall tell you my method, Lady Emily, as it is practical and excellent. To begin with—"

"I'll send the trousers over when they are washed," said Lady Emily, getting up without taking the slightest notice of Madame Boulle. "My French maid shall wash them. It was too kind of you to get poor Emmy out of the pond, Monsieur Boulle, and I am sure Agnes is most grateful. Children always fall into that pond. All my children fell in. It has been too delicious to have you all, and I am so glad you are coming to the dance."

Her farewell was in the nature of a royal dismissal. The Boulles made their adieux and went back to the vicarage. Pierre was even more silent than usual, which following on the events of the afternoon gave his mother cause for alarm. He retired early to his room, having been struck with an idea for a sonnet beginning

Belle éplorie ... .

but before he could get any further his mother knocked at his door.

"Pierre, tu ne tousses pas?" she asked anxiously. "Non, maman."

"Tu n'as pas de fièvre?"

"Non, maman, je t'assure."

"Tu n'as pas froid?"

"Non, maman, je suis couché," cried Pierre, jumping on his bed till the springs creaked so that his mamma should be satisfied of his whereabouts. There was a moment's pause during which he hoped she had gone away. But her voice reached him again through the door.

"Si tu es couch, Pierre, dis-moi, est-ce que tu transpires?"

"Oui, maman," shouted the unfortunate young man at the top of his voice. A sound of approval was heard and Madame Boulle's footsteps departed. For a couple of hours .Pierre wooed the muse, but in vain. Towards midnight he sought his couch and went to sleep at once.

CHAPTER X

THE RISE OF THE LILIES

DURING THE NEXT FEW DAYS, Mary noticed that Martin's attitude towards the Boulle family was changing. He made no more fuss about going to his lessons, and either brought the younger Boulles back to tennis or stayed down at the vicarage with them for the afternoon. At the same time his attitude towards his own family also underwent a change. A kind of eighteenth-century courtesy to his elders, a deference to ladies, characterized his deportment. Mary wondered if Madame Boulle had been giving him lessons in manners, but felt so sure that any suggestion of politeness from the lady would only drive Martin to deliberate savagery that she dismissed the idea.

Meanwhile, there was no news of David except that he had been away somewhere. He wrote an affectionate note to his mother now and then, with messages for all the household, but gave no details of his movements. He was certainly coming down for the dance and very likely earlier, but couldn't say for certain. Mary pined in secret, but the presence of the Boulles, the preparations for Martin's birthday, and the thought of the new frock, left her but little secret time in which to pine. For quite a week she said "David" when she had put out her reading-lamp in bed, but having once forgotten to do so, she felt a little self-conscious about beginning again.

The day for the visit to Agnes's dressmaker and the lunch

with John was fixed. After breakfast, Martin drew Mary mysteriously aside.

"Can you do some shopping for me in town?" he asked.

"Yes, of course. What do you want?"

Martin gave her an unexpected commission to buy white and yellow satin for him, but would not explain why he wanted it.

"It's absolutely secret at present, Mary, but I'll let you know before the dance. It is frightfully important that no one should know, so don't tell Aunt Agnes."

Mary promised, amused and mystified, but coming to the conclusion that there was to be some sort of dressing up she thought no more about it. The visit to the dressmaker was eminently satisfactory. A number of exquisite nymphs slank about the room in rapturous creations. As Mary had never had an expensive evening dress before she found it difficult to choose among so many, but Agnes took command and made her have a soft flowery confection. Agnes herself was going to have a white lace dress. Mary immediately wanted to change her mind and have one like it; but Agnes was firm.

"Don't wear lace or velvet while you are young, Mary," she said earnestly. "Girls always want to, and it is so foolish. When Emmy comes out I shall have great fun dressing her, and darling Clarissa too. Clarissa will look well in greens and Emmy, I think, will be able to wear pink. It is a difficult shade, but she has just the right colouring. I shall make her wear a pink with a shade of orange in it."

To Mary's deep and excited gratitude Agnes then bought her shoes and stockings such as she had never dreamed of having.

"And now we will go to John," said Agnes.

"Oh, Aunt Agnes, I have a little private shopping to do. Can I do that on the way?"

So they stopped at a large shop where Mary did Martin's shopping while Agnes sat in the car.

"Where are we having lunch, Aunt Agnes?" asked Mary, getting in again with her parcels. It might perhaps be the place where she lunched with David before, and David might be there.

"At John's flat. It is easier than a restaurant and I can leave you there while I have my hair done, unless you want to go to a cinema."

John was waiting for them in his disgracefully comfortable fifth-floor flat with a view. Mary had not seen him since the memorable day at his office and was relieved to find how easy it was. She would have been surprised if she had known that John was sharing her feelings. He was glad to see that she looked well and pretty and was evidently not fretting for David. Probably, he thought, I was mistaken about it, and vaguely felt the happier for the thought.

Agnes and John had a good deal to talk about at lunch, so Mary listened and enjoyed her food.

"How much longer have you got the flat, John?" his sister asked.

"Only till the end of the year. Then I don't know what I'll do. My tenants are giving up the Chelsea house then, and I am inclined to sell it."

"John, you mustn't sell that house. Couldn't you live there again?"

"I don't know. I haven't lived there since Gay died, and I would rattle about like a pea in a pod."

Mary noticed with interest that he didn't have at all what she called A Voice when speaking of his dead wife.

"You wouldn't get a man to share it with you,. would you?" Agnes went on. "I can't bear to think of that lovely house going out of the family. I wish I could take it myself, only there wouldn't be room for the children. We really need so many rooms now. A day nursery and a night nursery, and a room for James, and a room for Ivy. And when Emmy is a little bigger she will want a room for herself. And when I have some more babies it will mean another nursery as well."

John laughed and asked if Agnes didn't find her household difficult.

"Oh, no," said she in surprise, "it is quite easy. And when I have some more babies I shall get a second nurse as well as Ivy. It is really no trouble."

Mary, who had been rehearsing the words for some time, now asked John how David was. To her own surprise, it was quite easy to mention him. John said he had been quite well when he last saw him.

"I really wanted to talk to you about David, Agnes," he said. "It is no particular business of mine, but I am a bit worried. We'll have coffee in here while I tell you."

"If you are bored, Mary, you'll find heaps of books in the library," said Agnes, when coffee had been served.

Mary, taking this as a hint, got up. John opened the door for her, saying:

"It's nothing private, Mary, so come back if you don't like my books. Or there is the piano."

"Thank you, but I'll be quite happy with the books," she said, and passed into the library. She wandered about the room for a few moments, looking at pictures and admiring the view. A pile of music on the piano attracted her attention and she began to turn it over. She picked up one sheet, looked at it, shrugged her shoulders, and laid it down. Then she took a book and sat down on the sofa near the window.

Meanwhile Agnes and John were discussing the subject of David.

"After all," said John, "David has a perfect right to live as he likes. He is quite independent and there is nothing wrong with him at all, except his endless frittering away of himself. I'm not sure that the bees are any better than the drones. I hold no brief for myself as a bee. It suits me to be one. If I lived as David does I'd go mad. Conversely, I dare say David might go mad if he worked regularly, but I don't think so. He has discovered that in spite of his money and his charm—and I realize exactly how charming he is, Agnes—he can't get a novel written, let alone published; he can't get a broadcasting job because he won't take it seriously, his experiments with films and plays have all come to nothing. If it didn't make father so unhappy I wouldn't mind so much, but last time I was down at Rushwater he talked to me about it, and I promised to see if I could do anything. Can you suggest anything?"

"I'm afraid not, John. You see, he won't listen to any of us. Gay was the only person he ever listened to. He had a kind of respect for her that he hasn't got for us. Of course, I could write and ask Robert."

"Do you think," asked John, ignoring his sister's last remark, "that he could have that feeling for any other woman? If he really cared for a woman and respected her as well, he might pull up a bit."

"I don't know, John. You see, I don't know the kind of women he meets. The ones he has brought to Rushwater from time to time have been very charming, but not really what I would call the right sort. Robert would not have liked them at all."

"I know, I know. Of course he will marry whom he pleases, whenever he does marry, and of course mother and father will be angelic about it, whoever she is. He has been about lately with a Miss Stevenson. Do you know anything about her?"

"Only that she is a friend of his. We heard about her from Mr. Banister. Mr. Banister has let the vicarage to some French people called Boulle, and David told him he knew a girl who would like to come as a paying-guest to study French. I believe she is something to do with broadcasting."

"I have seen her with him. She looks the usual rather hard-boiled sort. Quite attractive. You don't think, Agnes," said John, looking hard at the tablecloth, "that David is at all attracted by Mary?"

"Mary? Oh, no. Why?"

"I don't know," he said, getting up and walking about. "I had an :idea that they might care for each other."

"Oh, no, John. Mary certainly doesn't think about David, and as for David, he hasn't been down to Rushwater since the concert. Oh, John dear, I do wish I could get you two boys married."

"Agnes, you are insatiable. Just because you are rather fond of Robert you won't be happy till you have married us all off, including Martin. Marry David, if you like—and if you can— but I have had my day, Agnes. I had Gay and I was lucky."

"John, come here and sit down again. David certainly doesn't care for Mary. Do you at all?"

John looked at her.

"I wonder what is in your head, Agnes. I don't know the answer to your question."

"Is Gay the answer?"

"No, I don't think so. If I could care for anyone as I cared for Gay, I would risk it, with the little I have to offer. When I heard Mary sing at Rushwater I loved her for her voice. Then I thought that she and David cared for each other, never mind why. So I didn't think much about her again. That's your answer."

"If David and she don't care for each other, would that change your answer?"

"Oh, my God, don't ask me," said John, getting up again impatiently.

"I'm sorry, darling," said Agnes in her gentle voice. "But next to Robert and the children you know you come, always. We will talk about it again when you come to Rushwater. Now I am going to leave Mary here for an hour while I have my hair done. She will be quite all right here if you are busy, and I'll come and fetch her. Good-bye for the present."

After seeing Agnes out John went into the library.

The afternoon was hot and sunny. The light filtered through John's gay-striped outside blinds. The roar of

London, at its lowest in August, was not disturbing, and the room was very quiet. Looking round, John saw Mary asleep with a book on the sofa. Her slumber was so light that the mere sense of his presence broke it, though he had made no sound. Momentarily bewildered she sat up, struggling with the unfamiliar surroundings. To John her abandonment in summer drowsiness, her short-lived perplexity on waking, her self-conscious return to reality seemed infinitely touching. He apologized for disturbing her. Mary said in a confused way that she was ashamed of herself.

"Has Aunt Agnes gone?" she asked.

"Yes. She told me to amuse you till she comes back. She said she would be about an hour."

"But is that all right? I mean, wouldn't you rather be doing your work?"

Again this childish humility before someone who, so she evidently thought, did real work. John remembered how, in the middle of her storm of grief in his office, she had offered to go and finish crying in the car if he had a business appointment.

"This is Agnes's day," he reassured her, "and yours. I kept it for you and now she has deserted me, so if you will help me pass the time that will be very kind."

"What a lot of music you have got," said Mary. "I was looking at it after lunch."

"Did you see one of your songs there?"

"Yes, lots that I know. Which one specially?"

"The Bach one."

"Oh, 'Bist du bei mir.' Isn't it a darling?"

"I bought it after I had heard you sing it at Rushwater."

"But I never sang it when you were there."

"Yes, you did, truly. The evening David made up his spiritual about treacle and rum."

"But that was after dinner before the men came in. I was just singing for myself, so that Aunt Emily and Aunt Agnes could talk comfortably," said Mary, beginning to feel alarmed.

"I came in before the others. The room was dark except for mother's reading-lamp and the fire. You were singing in a little pool of candlelight at the far end. It was the loveliest voice I had ever heard. It gave me the peace you were singing about. I went and sat with mother and Agnes till you had finished. They understood."

"I would have stopped if I had known."

Mary's distress and confusion were so painful that John felt almost sorry he had spoken.

"I would apologize for eavesdropping," he said, "but I really can't be sorry for hearing something so precious. You couldn't possibly sing that song again, could you, Mary?"

"Oh, no."

"The music is here and no one will come in."

"Oh, I couldn't. Besides it is the wrong key."

"Perhaps I could transpose it," said John, sitting down at the piano.

"Can you do that?" asked Mary, interested.

"I can do one semitone up and one tone up," said John gravely. "As for going down, that has me beat. What key do you want?"

Mary mentioned a key.

"Up, thank goodness," said John. He played a few bars. "Would that do?"

"Oh, please, I couldn't possibly," said Mary, backing behind an arm-chair in her agitation.

"Well, if you can't," said John, playing through the accompaniment as he spoke, "no one else will. Never mind, I heard you once. Perhaps I shall hear you again at Rushwater, after dinner, by candlelight. Three o'clock in the afternoon isn't the most tactful moment to ask anyone to sing. I oughtn't to ask for peace so soon after lunch. Death, of course, I don't want. `. . . . zum Sterben and zu meiner Ruh,' " he sang, and shut the piano.

"It isn't rudeness," said Mary. "Honestly, it isn't. It is only awful self-consciousness. I wouldn't mind singing to Aunt Emily or Mr. Leslie, but to you I couldn't."

"Why not?"

"You would listen."

John laughed.

"By your way of arguing you could only sing to people who didn't listen to you."

Mary nodded her head. "Yes. Or to people who I don't know are there," she added in a half-voice, a remark which John pondered over afterwards. They talked about Rushwater, and Mary described the concert and made John laugh again.

"And at supper," she said, "David gave me a huge basket of wild strawberries to make up for forgetting them. Wasn't it nice of him?"

"Delightful."

Then Agnes came back to pick up Mary. John gave them tea and they drove back to Rushwater. Even Agnes was a little tired by the heat and her exertions at the hairdresser's, so they drove mostly in silence. Mary thought how silly she must seem to John, first crying in his office, then going to sleep in his flat and being too shy to sing. But somehow it didn't matter what one did with John. He always made one feel safe and comfortable.

When she got back, Mary gave the parcel of shopping to Martin, who thanked her warmly.

"If you like," he said, rather diffidently, "I will tell you what it is for, only it is frightfully important, frightfully secret. You will have to swear not to tell anyone.'

"It isn't anything Aunt Emily would mind, is it?"

"Oh, no. I am sure she would agree if she knew about it, but we aren't sure about grandfather."

"Does Madame Boulle know about it?"

"She is terribly keen and so is the professor, but they don't know about this special bit. We are doing this on our own and if it comes off it will have an enormous effect."

"What is it, Martin?"

"I mustn't tell you, Mary, or I would, honestly. But I'll ask Pierre and the others, and if they say it's all right I'll let you in."

Mary couldn't make head or tail of his mystery, but gave her faithful promise not to betray whatever it was to anybody. Martin disappeared after dinner, probably to the vicarage, for when Mary went to bed she found a tightly folded rather dirty note on her dressing-table. At the head of it was what looked like the boy scouts' badge and below was written in what was obviously Martin's writing disguised:

They agree. Three o'clock to-morrow at the Temple. Silence. Secrecy.

The Temple was a monument which had been erected by Mr. Leslie's grandfather as a neat finish to the little hill on which it stood. In nature it partook of the pyramid, the pagoda and the mausoleum. It was built of a yellowish stone which flaked and crumbled with agreeable ease, as several generations of destructive children had found. Its lower story was lighted by four enormous sash windows which no human power had ever succeeded in opening. From the ground floor a wooden ladder staircase led through a trap-door to an upper chamber whose windows, of semicircular shape, were on the level of the floor, having been designed more with a view to exterior proportion than to any possible convenience for people using it. The walls of this uncomfortable abode sloped inwards and the building was crowned by what can only be described as a serrated peak. To all children it meant romance, not unmixed with terror. Every young Leslie had at one time been shut up in the top room by an elder brother or sister, and there shrieked itself into hysteria at the thought of dying forgotten among the spiders and daddylonglegs which infested it. Nearly every older Leslie had tried to climb the pinnacle and had to give it up. All grown-up Leslies took no interest in it at all, considering it, as indeed it was, stuffy, dirty and inconvenient. Therefore it was a safe place for mysteries.

It was a blazing hot afternoon when Mary walked up the hill by, winding paths under the beeches. At the top of the hill was a slight depression like an empty dew-pond, where the Temple stood. This again was a guarantee against spies and interfering grown-ups, as no one could cross the grassy hollow without being seen from one of the semicircular windows.

Mary found the Temple door shut, and knocked. There was no answer. She knocked again impatiently, for the sun was beating down on her back, and the paint of the door was hot to the touch. There was a scuffling noise inside, and Martin's voice said in a hoarse whisper:

"Would you mind knocking twice very loud, three times softly, and then once loud again."

Mary obligingly complied with this request, upon which the door was opened by Jean Claude.

"Hullo, Jean Claude," said Mary. 'What's it all about?"

"Password," said Jean Claude, looking straight in front of him.

"Orleans," whispered Martin.

"Orleans," said Mary obediently.

"It is well," said Jean Claude. "Follow me."

He lead the way up the ladder through the open trapdoor into the upper room. None of the semicircular windows were made to open and the heat was stifling. Bluebottles buzzed in an angry perfunctory way in old spiders' webs. The white-washed walls were covered with the graffiti of the junior branches of the Leslie family. On one wall David had painted, when he was about fourteen, a romantic scene of a princess leaning out of a tower with a knight riding past. On another wall John, at some earlier epoch, had written in blue and red chalk the words:

Ding, long, bell,
Fräulein goes to hell,

which Agnes had vainly endeavoured to erase. Sums, unkind

remarks about brothers and sisters, ostentatious and incorrect Latin verses jostled each other. James had already begun to contribute with a very poor chalk drawing of Clarissa in her perambulator.

Martin, who had followed Mary up the ladder, now shut the trap-door with a bang, raising clouds of dust from the floor, causing whitewash to fall in flakes from the ceiling, and making the room even more unbearable than it had been. Pierre and Ursule were sitting on a wooden box and other boxes were lying about.

"I suppose we must go through the formalities," said Jean Claude to Martin, who nodded.

It may here be mentioned that except when Madame Boulle's eye was on them, English was the invariable medium of communication between Martin and the young Boulles. To Pierre, Ursule and Jean Claude it was almost a matter of indifference which language they spoke. To Martin it was a matter of great importance to his own mental comfort that he should speak French as little as possible. Alone with Pierre it was different, he made one feel clever and idiomatic. But to talk a halting stuttering French to Ursule and Jean Claude was not in Martin's plan. It might even raise Jean Claude from the position of inferiority in which his tennis had placed him, a state of things not to be encouraged. So Martin made no effort at all to practise the language which his mother was paying for him to learn, considering, if his conscience ever made itself felt, that by swotting away with Pierre for three hours every morning, and sitting through family lunch every day, he had amply fulfilled his mother's wishes. At any other time Pierre, who though mild was conscientious, would have done his best to encourage a more general use of French among the young people, but his adoration for Mrs. Graham and his unfinished sonnet lay heavy on his mind and prevented him from paying his usual attention to duty. While waiting for Mary, he had been trying his hand at literary composition on the wall.

Et pourtant son regard me trouble étrangement he had written with a stump of pencil, and was then assailed by doubts as to whether someone else had not already written it. However, even a last line of a sonnet was worth clinging to; one might get the thirteen previous lines later on if the Muse were propitious.

"Alors, fais ton devoir, Ursule," said Jean Claude.

Ursule, giggling wildly, approached Mary and ran her hands down her dress.

"Just to see if you are a spy with concealed arms," she explained, giggling more than ever.

"What on earth are you all doing up here and what is it all about?" said Mary.

"Sit down, Miss Preston," said Pierre. "We regret any inconvenience which we may have caused you, but it was necessary. If you are to help us, you must be of ourselves and share our secrets. We cannot be too cautious."

"Well, what is it? A treasure hunt?"

"Oh, Pierre," said Martin, "may I tell her?"

"But she must have guessed already," objected Pierre. "Did you not notice our password, Miss Preston?"

"Yes."

"Did it convey nothing to you?"

"No. I know Orleans is somewhere in France. I've never been there."

"Then, Martin, you may explain," said Pierre. "We are royalists," said Martin in an awed voice.

Pierre, Ursule and Jean Claude immediately stood up. "A bas la republique," said Ursule, giggling.

"A bas la republique," said the others and sat down again.

"Mary," said Martin eagerly, "you don't know how important this is. We can help enormously in England. All the Boulles are royalists and they are working to restore the monarchy. You would like to see a monarchy in France, wouldn't you?"

"Certainly. I always thought it must be silly to have a President who has to wear evening dress in the daytime."

A pained expression on Pierre's face warned her that though a royalist one was still French, and could not hear the matter of the President's official clothes treated lightly.

'Tell me some more," she said hastily.

"Well, Pierre and Jean Claude are camelots du roi," Martin went on, "and I can be one, too. You only have to sign a form. Pierre was once nearly arrested by a policeman for selling *L'Action Française*, that's the royalist newspaper, you know. There is bound to be a great royalist reaction soon, and we are to help at the English end. Do you know why Jean Claude has his name?"

"No."

"The duc de Guise is Jean," said Martin impressively. "And what about the Claude?" asked Mary.

"Oh, of course, if you're going to laugh," said Martin sulkily.

"I'm so sorry, Martin. I didn't mean to. Tell me what you are going to do here."

The four royalists then all began to talk at once in two languages. Mary finally made out that the night of Martin's dance had been chosen for a royalist demonstration. The satin which she had bought in town was being made into a flag by Ursule. They had meant, they explained, to use the royalist flag, tricolore with ecusson fleurdelisé, but as this would take too long to make it had been decided to have golden fleurs-de-lis on a white standard. At a given moment Jean Claude carrying the flag, followed by Martin and Ursule, was to advance into the ballroom. Pierre was to cry "Vive le roi" from the balcony, thus lighting a candle which would run like wildfire from one end of England to the other, leap the Channel, snatch up the duc de Guise from his estates in Belgium, raise the barricades in Paris, sweep France at the elections, and restore the rightful heir to the throne of the Capets.

"But where do I come in?" asked Mary.

"We want you to ask the band to stop for a few moments suddenly, in the middle of a dance. It will make much more effect like that," said Pierre.

"What do your father and mother say?"

"We haven't told them," said Jean Claude. "They do not understand the necessity for action. They will applaud afterwards, but we cannot expect them to risk their lives for a gesture as we shall."

"Besides," said Pierre, "maman might think this plan of ours rather too exalted. She is very practical. It was she who thought of the dustbin."

Seeing that Mary looked puzzled, Martin volunteered an explanation. "Madame Boulle is frightfully practical," he said enthusiastically. "She has painted La Republique on her dustbin. Isn't it splendid? So that every time she chucks anything dirty into it she is insulting the old republic."

"You will help us, Miss Preston, won't you?" said Pierre, his soft brown eyes alight with enthusiasm.

"Well, if you are sure it won't upset Aunt Emily. After all, it is her house. No, I don't think I can join unless you let me tell her."

Another bilingual discussion took place and it was decided that *vu* the improbability of Lady Emily ever noticing anything that was said to her, it would be quite safe for Mary to tell her that the Boulles and Martin wanted to have a sort of pageant half-way through the dance which would only take a few moments. Martin and Jean Claude felt that this attitude was cowardly, but Pierre, older and more experienced, assured them that deception in a good cause was on the whole a virtue. This important affair having been settled, the conspirators separated, the three Boulles going back to the vicarage and Martin returning with Mary. On the way down he poured out a flood of information about the royalist movement, which Mary secretly found rather tedious. However, it was better than having to listen to cricket averages.

"There's one awful nuisance," said Martin gloomily. "That friend of David's, whatever her name is, is coming down three days before the dance. We can't let her in because we don't know if she is sound or not, and it will be an awful nuisance having her about. I say, Mary, couldn't you make friends with her and take her for walks or something?"

A wave of anger swept over Mary as the hateful Miss Stevenson was recalled to her mind.

"I'm afraid I can't, Martin," she said. "I shall be frightfully busy helping Aunt Emily. You'll have to get Madame Boulle on to her."

CHAPTER XI

INDIGNATION OF A TOADY

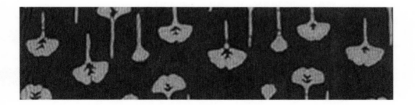

THREE DAYS before the dance Lady Emily came in to lunch with a distracted expression.

"A really frightful thing has happened," she announced. "Get me my bag from the drawing-room, Martin, and I will tell you all about it."

Martin, who was having a day off from his French lessons to devote himself to details of the cricket match, got up and went in search of it.

"It is a most extraordinary letter from Mr. Holt," she went on. "It came this morning and I didn't open it for some reason or other and when I got downstairs I took it out of my bag and read it and now I can't find it anywhere. Oh, thank you, Martin, perhaps I did put it in my bag. Yes, here it is. He is so very peculiar. I am sure he asked me to invite Lady Norton here, didn't he, Agnes?"

"Yes, mamma. At least, I remember your saying after Mr. Holt had gone that you must ask Lady Norton to Rushwater. I remember it so well, because it was the day James got his tunic so wet trying to catch goldfish in the pond, poor darling. He had to have his tunic changed at once, but Nannie was very prompt and luckily he didn't catch cold. Ever since I had him inoculated last winter he hasn't caught half so many colds."

"Then why does he write in such a peculiar way?" said her

ladyship. "Where is that letter? I had it in my hand a minute ago."

After considerable tumult the letter was discovered by Mary in Lady Emily's table napkin, which was on the floor.

"Thank you, Mary. I suppose I had it in my hand and then while I was talking I put it on my lap and then it fell on to the floor with my table napkin. They do slip so. I sometimes think of telling the laundry not to put starch in them, but they never have the same appearance without it. And now I am afraid I can't see it without my spectacles. It is really astonishing how Conque can't remember anything. So I must tell you about it. He is so much annoyed with me that I feel quite unhappy at the idea of having hurt him. Oh, here are my spectacles in my bag, after all. Conque must have put them in just before I came downstairs. David, darling, this is very nice. Where do you come from?"

For David was standing in the doorway looking pleasantly at his family. He walked round the table, dropping a kiss on Agnes's head and touching his father and Martin on the shoulder. He greeted Mary and put himself in between her and his mother.

"From London, mother. I'm simply famished. Has Gudgeon any food for me? Oh, Gudgeon, I've some suitcases with me. I want them taken to my room. I've come to stay till after the dance, mother, if that's all right. How's the bull, father?"

"He's going to the Argentine at the end of the month."

"Splendid. How's the French, Martin? Can you recite 'Le Chéne et le Roseau' yet?"

"Oh, shut up, David."

"David," said his mother, "you must help me. I have had such a peculiar letter from Mr. Holt and I want all your advices. Henry, I want you to tell me what I ought to do."

"Can't tell you, Emily, till I hear what it's all about."

"Listen to what he says:

Dear Lady Emily,

*'I must confess that I have been much hurt at hearing from
an old friend, Lady Norton, that you had invited her to
Rushwater without asking me also. As it was through me that
you met Lady Norton in the first place—'*

Now that," said her ladyship, folding up the letter, putting
it into her bag, and gazing into the past, "is perfectly true. He
would introduce us at a flower show, at Chelsea, I think, or
perhaps at Vincent Square, but I know it was the year the blue
Meconopsis came out, and I found her insufferably dull. I
would never have done anything about her if he hadn't asked
me to, and I must say I found her even duller than I had
thought, though she knows a great deal about poppies and is
going to send me some seed. Isn't it peculiar?"

"But you haven't finished reading us the letter yet, Aunt
Emily," said Mary, voicing the feeling of the party.

Lady Emily hunted in her bag, found the letter, reopened
it and continued.

" *'As it was through me that you met Lady Norton in the
first place, I should have thought you would naturally include
me in any invitation to her.*

*I regretted that I saw so little of you and the garden on my
last visit, and hope Mrs. Graham's children, who absorb so
much of her time, are well.'*

Then he is mine sincerely."

"What a horrid little man, Aunt Emily."

"Well, Emily," said Mr. Leslie, "I really don't know what
advice you want. I always disliked the fellow, and now he has
written you a very offensive letter."

"But I mean, what am I to do? I feel so sorry for him, feeling hurt like that. Of course, we didn't see much of the garden and this time I must see that he does."

"This time? What are you talking about, Emily?" said her
husband.

Lady Emily's face coloured slightly.

"I know what you have done," said David, suddenly pointing an accusing finger at his mother. "You have asked the little toadstool here again."

"I didn't mean to, David," said his mother deprecatingly. "But it is terrible to think of anyone feeling as hurt as that over such a trifle, especially anyone so universally disliked as Mr. Holt, so I felt I must invite him."

"And what is more," said David, fixing her with his glance, "by the pricking of my thumbs I can tell you what else you have done. You have asked him to stay the night for Martin's dance."

"My God, Emily, you haven't?" said Mr. Leslie in alarm.

"Henry, you mustn't mind. It is really a kindness to have him."

"Well, I do mind, Emily," said Mr. Leslie, getting up. "Kindness is one thing and your family is another. You treat this house as if it were the Ark, Emily, inviting everyone in."

"At least she doesn't ask them in couples, sir," said David. "A female Holt would be appalling."

"That's enough," said his father. "If Mr. Holt comes into this house, I go out of it."

He took a cigar from the sideboard and went out, almost slamming the door.

"How very annoying," said Agnes peacefully. "It will mean quite a lot of work to soothe papa down again. Mother, darling, I think I shall take the children to Southbridge to-morrow. They all want new shoes and I must get James's hair cut. His hair always seems to grow so much faster in the country. I can't think why unless it is that I don't have it cut so often. Come and have your rest now."

Agnes and her mother went off. Martin followed them, saying darkly to Mary:

"Must go. Frightfully important. You know what."

"What the dickens has Martin got in his head now?" asked

David. "It's always some queer idea in the holidays. Last summer he was a Socialist and at Christmas he was a United Irishman, or something of the sort. At least he would read Yeats aloud and feel melancholy about Deirdre."

"It's something he and the Boulles are interested in. I don't quite understand it," said Mary truthfully.

"Well, boys will be bores. Tell me all about yourself, Mary. I've had a marvellous time over my novel. A man

I know is really keen to film it, and I have a chance of getting a dramatic version broadcast. That's why I've been away all the time. I was so busy."

"Is your novel really written, then?" asked Mary.

"Oh, no, that's the whole point. I shall do the film version and the dramatic version, and then with that success behind me it will be as easy as anything to write the novel. People often do, you know. 'The Story of the Play.' How is Martin's party getting on?"

"It is going to be lovely. Your father has given me a divine dress and Aunt Agnes gave me shoes and stockings. I am looking forward to it frightfully."

"Catch!" said David, throwing a parcel at her. In her surprise she missed it. "Oh, butterfingers. You are as bad as mamma." He picked the parcel off the floor and put it into her hands.

"For me?" said Mary, opening it without waiting for .an answer. In the tissue paper was an evening bag of the finest embroidery with gay flowers and birds rioting on it.

"Oh, David, how perfectly lovely. And it exactly goes with my frock. How perfectly divine. But really you oughtn't to give—"

"Now, don't say your mother told you never to take presents from gentlemen unless they offered honourable matrimony, because that is quite out of date. Do you really like my parcel?"

"Oh, I do, I do. Last time you gave me a parcel it was

strawberries, and the time before that my own hand done up in a silk handkerchief. Do you remember?"

"Your own hand? Oh, yes, of course, I remember. At Rushmere Abbey. I can't give you anything as perfect as your own hand, but this will pass muster, I hope." "I simply love it."

"Let me see if your hand is still perfect," said David. He took Mary's hand and looked at it attentively.

"Perfect," he said. "Will you honour me by letting me claim it at Martin's dance?"

"Why, of course. Are you booking dances already? I don't expect I'll know many people except you and John and Martin and the Boulles.

"Not bad people those Boulles," said David, putting a rapid and businesslike kiss into Mary's palm, shutting her fingers on it, and apparently losing interest. "Madame Boulle is a bit garrulous and the girl is a giggling gawk. I like the Professor though and the elder son. The younger son isn't as spotty as I hoped." He took a peach and began to peel it.

"I didn't know you knew the Boulles," said Mary. Her heart was beating so furiously at David's kiss that she could hardly bear what her common sense told her was only a pretty gesture. She was not sure whether she wanted to press the palm so lately saluted to her own lips, or to smack David's face with it.

"I saw them to-day when I dropped Joan Stevenson there," he said, his mouth full of peach juice.

If Mary had been overcome by David's pretty gesture, his appalling treachery now turned the daylight to fiery darkness and the summer noises to thunder. He could bring that horrid Miss Stevenson down in his sports car, and then, fresh from her embraces, or, to be fair, fresh from sitting next to her while he drove, could bring Mary a present, throw it at her as if he were scattering largesse to beggars. If it hadn't been that her present evening bag was distinctly shabby, she would have thrown this Greek gift on the floor. She hated David more

than she had ever hated him before. She would take care to
fill her programme for the dance, even if it meant sitting out
with Mr. Holt.

"What about a walk this afternoon?" said David.

"With Miss Stevenson?" asked Mary. She hoped that her
tone expressed a cold lack of interest, but when you are nearly
choking with emotion at the sound of David's alluring voice,
your frigidity is remarkably apt to sound like hoarseness.

"Joan? I should think not. She can't walk fast, and I must
stretch my legs. Come on."

"Right, David, that will be lovely," said Mary.

The Boulle family and Miss Stevenson came up to tennis
after tea. Ursule was already in a state of giggling devotion to
Miss Stevenson and insisted on taking her arm as they
walked. Miss Stevenson, whom her three years at Oxford had
familiarized with every sort of crush, was not displeased by
Ursule's artless homage, but found her weight rather exhaust-
ing. As David and Mary were still out walking Madame
Boulle took upon her the duty of presenting Miss Stevenson
to the rest of the family.

"Lady Emily," she said, "may I present to you Miss
Stevenson, of whom you have doubtless heard from Mr.
David. Miss Stevenson is an officer of the broadcasting, and
is thus in touch with all the most interesting movements of
the day. It is really ridiculous that Miss Stevenson should
come to us to acquire French, for she already speaks with
astonishing correctness and hardly any trace of that English
accent which, although disagreeable when exaggerated, is yet
rather attractive to a French ear. I will tell you, Martine, that
in France we call English la langue des oiseaux on account of
the effect, a twittering and sibilant sound as we may say,
which it produces on our ears. German, on the contrary, we
call la langue des chevaux, because it has a certain heaviness,
a clumsiness, not unlike the neighing of a horse. A horse's
neigh is in French hennir, qui se prononce aussi ha-nir, mais

je to conseille d'éviter ce dernier, Martine, which in fact I only
signal to you that you may be aware of the fact, for it is a question sometimes asked in exams. The word hennir was doubtless in the mind of your Swift when he wrote about his talking horses, his Houyhnhnms."

"Onomatopie, " said Professor Boulle, but no one took any
notice of him.

"How clever of you to say that word," said Lady Emily to
Madame Boulle. "It is one of the words I have always read to
myself and never dared to say aloud."

Everyone present then explained how they pronounced the
word Houyhnhnms, except Ursule, who giggled.

"At Broadcasting House," said Miss Stevenson, "the correct pronunciation has been standardized as Winnim. It will
probably be in our next authoritative list."

"Nevertheless," continued Madame Boulle, "there are certain faults, small perhaps in themselves, but which would
infallibly strike a French ear, which I have already indicated to
Miss Stevenson, and of which she will cure herself rapidly, for
she has an excellent ear. Martine has not so good an ear, but
he is a good lad," she added colloquially, to Martin's horror. "I
am glad to see that he is much with my young people apart
from lessons. Thus will he acquire an easy and natural way of
speaking French, which is recognized as the most pure and
beautiful language of the civilized world. The French of
Touraine is particularly noted for its purity. My ancestors, the
Fiords, have lived in Touraine since the eleventh century and
have always been renowned for the purity of their speech."

"Come on," said Martin, unable to bear it any longer, let's
have a set. Me and Ursule, and Pierre and Miss Stevenson."

While they were playing David and Mary came back. Jean
Claude immediately pounced on Mary and drew her aside.

"Our banner is nearly finished," he said excitedly. "Ursule
has sat up two nights to finish it. We have slightly changed
our plans. Instead of bringing it on a stick, which is more dif-

ficult to hide, I shall have the flag folded inside my coat.
When you stop the band, Martin, Ursule and I shall advance
up the ballroom. Pierre will call from the gallery 'Vive le roi,'
and we shall answer 'Vive le dauphin,' and I shall unfurl the
flag. It will make an effect, don't you think?"

"It will be splendid," said Mary. "But I thought the
dauphin died in the French Revolution."

"Louis the seventeenth undoubtedly died in the infamous
prison to which his father's murderers had sent him," said Jean
Claude passionately, "but so long as a King of France has a son,
that son is the dauphin. You have heard of the comte de Paris."

"Wasn't he a son of Louis Philippe or something?" "Your
history is very old-fashioned," said Jean Claude pityingly.
"The comte de Paris is the son of the due de Guise, Jean the
third, the lawful king of France. His name is Henri, like my
father's. How does that strike you? Here in the family Boulle
we have a Henri and a Jean. Striking, is it not? The Boulle
family has always been celebrated for its loyalty. So has the
family of Fiord, my mother's family. The Florels have been
celebrated for their loyalty since the days of Clovis."

Mary, reflecting with sorrow that Jean Claude would probably get more and more like his mother as he got older, apologized for her ignorance and expressed profound approval of
the royalist plans. She asked what they would do after the
demonstration.

"Nothing," said Jean Claude simply. "That will be enough.
The English will recognize our courage and our convictions
and rally to us. The English have a great admiration for
courage. Except for the French they are doubtless the bravest
and most courageous nation in the world."

"Come on, Mary, and have a game," said Martin, suddenly appearing. 'That Miss Stevenson can't play for nuts. You
and I will take on David and Ursule. We'll have a nursery set
for Jean Claude and Miss Stevenson afterwards. Is everything
all right?" he added, looking significantly at his fellow-con-

spirators. Jean Claude, who did not appear to bear any grudge for Martin's opinion of his tennis, nodded portentously.

"I'll let you know any further plans by a note on your table," said Martin to Mary, as they went on to the court. "It is not safe to talk."

"Why did you have a boy scout's badge on your letters about the meeting in the Temple?" she asked.

Martin looked at her with lofty contempt.

"Don't you know a fleur-de-lis when you see one, my good girl?" he inquired.

"Sorry, Martin."

After two more sets, in neither of which Jean Claude or Miss Stevenson were asked to play, the party broke up. Miss Stevenson had made a great success with Mr. Leslie, who liked to hear how things were done, by telling him all about her work at Broadcasting House. Pierre had sat with Agnes, feeling like Geoffroy Rudel with the Princesse Lointaine, though he would have been hard put to it to explain exactly why. Agnes, finding in him a sympathetic audience, had told him all about Clarissa saying dickybob for apricot, and how James's hair seemed to grow much longer when it wasn't cut, and how Emmy had been none the worse after Monsieur Boulle had so kindly rescued her from the pond.

"I do hope you didn't get cold," she said, for the sixth or seventh time. "I always think it is so annoying to be wet. I remember when James was little we went to the Isle of Wight and I got quite wet. We were out walking and it came on to rain, and I hadn't Nannie with me, so I put my umbrella over James and my husband turned his coat collar up. It was so disagreeable."

Pierre went home quite intoxicated by the thought of the lovely young matron protecting her lovely child, even getting so far as composing parts of a line of poetry which was to begin, "Dieu pluvial!" and to end, by a pretty fantasy, "ce doux agneau." But as for the middle, the muse was unfavourable.

CHAPTER XII

MANY HAPPY RETURNS

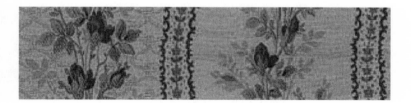

ON THE MORNING of Martin's seventeenth birthday the sun rose in an unclouded sky. Haze lay over the garden and meadow, foretelling a perfect August day. Martin's room faced east and sunlight poured through the uncurtained windows on to his bed, where he lay deep in slumber, the bed-clothes kicked off during the hot night, his pyjama jacket cast aside. As the sun crept over his bare skin he began to move and stretch luxuriously, still half-asleep. A wasp flying round the room pinged angrily about his head. Rousing himself Martin made a slap at it and missed it. It sailed angrily away, hit itself violently against the window, discovered the open casement and flew out. Lulled by the silence Martin was just dropping off to sleep again when he remembered what day it was.

"Good Lord," he said, sitting up in bed and pushing his hair back, "I'm seventeen.

He contemplated this fact for some moments, sitting hunched up with his arms round his knees. To be seventeen was practically as good as being grown-up. One could now drive the Ford, or indeed David's sports car if he would let one, with impunity. Seventeen was an age at which anything might happen. Romance, adventure lay before one. Everything was going to be perfect.

John had come down yesterday, and it had been a ripping evening with David singing his amusing songs and playing

the piano for them to dance after the grandparents had gone
to bed. There was to be cricket all today. He could hear the
distant noise of hammering as the men finished putting up
the extra seats in the field. It was amusing how, if one both-
ered to get up, one could look across the garden at the men
working and see the hammers fall long before the noise they
made reached one; something to do with science. Then after
the cricket a dinner party and one's health drunk. Then the
dance—

Martin straightened his arms and legs and shot out of bed.
He had almost forgotten. Not only was it his birthday, but it
was The Day. The flag with fleurs-de-lis was finished, though
pressure had had to be put on Ursule, who had suddenly
transferred her interest to that Miss Stevenson and been
found giggling at her feet when she ought to have been working. All plans were made and his seventeenth birthday would
also be a dedication of himself to the cause of fallen royalty.
From a pocketbook on his dressing-table he drew a newspaper cutting about the duc de Guise and the comte de Paris.
What though the peculiarities of newspaper photographs
made the duc look like a bald man disguised in a beard and
the comte like a lowbrow criminal. Martin knew better. Even
the English Press recognized the power in these two men.

"French Government," he read aloud to himself, *"take duc
seriously as they did his father. Duc de Chartres was retired from
the French army forty years ago because he was its most brilliant
general. Duc de Guise is tall, good-looking, sixty. Owing to
father's brilliance was forbidden to serve in French army."*

"Tyrants!" he muttered. Then placing the newspaper cutting on the mantelpiece he stood erect.

"Mon roi," he said, with devoted respect, to the duc de
Guise, and saluted.

"Mon dauphin," he added, with chivalrous respect, to the
comte de Paris, and saluted.

He then observed a moment's silence to the memory of

young Daudet, basely done to death by traitors. How it made one's blood glow to feel that Pierre, Ursule and Jean Claude were doing the same thing, possibly at the same moment. While such loyal hearts beat, the cause of the golden lilies was not lost.

Had Martin been able to fly over the vicarage and look in at the windows, his faith would have received a shattering blow. Pierre was indeed worshipping a photograph, but it was not of king and dauphin. It was a cutting from the Tatler representing Mrs. Robert Graham chatting to a friend at the Buckingham Palace garden party. Agnes's beauty was of that rare kind that can survive even a Press camera. The delicate proportion of her features, her lovely, all-embracing smile, her exquisite figure, to all these the Tatler's photographer did full justice.

"Moi, j'aime la lointaine
Princesse,"

murmured Pierre, locking the photograph away in a drawer so that it should not see him shave.

Ursule, in dressing-gown and bedroom slippers, was sitting on the foot of Miss Stevenson's bed, listening to words of wisdom.

"Marriage is such a large subject," said Miss Stevenson as she drank her morning tea. We must talk it over together. I believe immensely in getting views on every subject from every angle. Yours will interest me very much, Ursule. I believe that in France the companionate marriage is not yet fully recognized, but it will doubtless come. We naturally have to be careful at Broadcasting House, as the great mass of our listeners are still full of prejudice. We find it particularly necessary to keep the personnel of the Children's Hour on a high moral standard. In my department the standard is officially very high, but the mere fact of divorce does not attach the same stigma as it does in the Children's Hour."

Ursule giggled admiringly.

As for Jean Claude, he was still asleep.

Nor were Mary's thoughts of a nature proper to the day. The previous days had been a tumult in her breast. She had had glorious walks with David, who had helped her over several stiles in an unnecessary way, though if he cared for her enough to help her over when she could obviously quite well get over alone, it would have been more tactful, she thought, to have done it in a more lingering way. Merely to hold out your hand with your back almost turned and say, "Jump, my good girl," could hardly be read as an expression of deep devotion, however hard one tried. Against this must be set the fact that he had given her that lovely bag. But one could not forget that he had brought Miss Stevenson to Rushwater. On the other hand, he had taken no notice of Miss Stevenson since their arrival, had not played tennis with her, nor looked her up at the vicarage, nor talked about her.

Then John had come down yesterday, as kind and reliable as ever. He had played tennis with her and David and Martin, and played very well. He had been very kind at dinner and hadn't said anything about her singing, for which she was profoundly grateful. David had been the singer, and after the grandparents' departure for bed had entertained them all with the latest songs, including some new and very indelicate verses to his spiritual of Drinking treacle, drinking rum. Then he had played jazz music quite divinely for the others to dance.

"How well you dance," John said to her. "You are the most feather-footed person I ever met."

"But how very well you dance too. Even better than David."

"You see I had the advantage of being in the navy. I had to leave it because I was too tall and banged my head on everything, but before I left they taught me how to dance. You will dance with me again to-morrow night, won't you?"

David had asked her if she had her present quite safe.

"Rather," she said, "it is put away, wrapped up till to-morrow. I'm going to use it for the dance."

"Oh, the bag," said David, "that's nothing. I meant the present I gave you in your perfect hand. Is it quite safe?"

Flaming with embarrassment Mary had escaped to Agnes with an incoherent mumble. How dared he think that she cared for a kiss in her hand? How adorable of him to remember what she had thought so lightly given. And, thank heaven, he would never know that she had kept her hand under her cheek when she went to bed that night until the position became too uncomfortable.

Agnes's only thoughts on Martin's birthday morning were a mild regret that Emmy and darling Clarissa were not old enough yet to come to the dance, and a determination to do some more match-making for John. She had been pleased to see John and Mary dancing together last night, and had even faintly exerted herself to keep Martin as her own partner, that John might have more opportunities.

To Mr. Leslie and Lady Emily, Martin's seventeenth birthday must inevitably bring the thought of Martin's father. Mr. Leslie looked in on his wife on his way down to breakfast.

"Morning, my dear," he said. "Lovely day for Martin's cricket. D'you know what it reminded me of?"

"Yes, Henry. It reminded me too. It was a hot day like this, and I remember the noise of the men hammering at the seats over in the cricket field."

"It brings it back," said Mr. Leslie, looking out of the window. "Wish it could bring other things back. Martin gets more like him every day, Emily. When I heard Martin's voice on the stairs this morning, I could have believed—Oh, well, must get down to breakfast," said Mr. Leslie, blowing his nose. "Don't get up too soon, my dear, you've got a long day."

At the door he met John, coming to say good morning to his mother.

"Morning, John," said his father, going out.

"Good morning, sir," said John. "Good morning Mother

darling. Many happy returns of Martin's birthday. Anything wrong with father?"

"Thoughts, John. Martin gets more like his father every day. There are things you remember all the time, and then you find you are only remembering them now and again, but they don't hurt the less."

"I know, I know."

"One has to get one's happiness from seeing the joy of the young," said Lady Emily, half to herself.

You get your joy by making joy for other people, darling," said John.

"I wish I could make it for you."

"Perhaps as one gets older one takes one's joy altruistically," said John, in his turn thinking aloud. "I must say though I sometimes wish I could get it selfishly, just for myself, as Gay used to give it to me, when I was young."

Lady Emily found nothing to say. John's last words fell dead on her heart. It terrified her that he could speak of his youth as a perished thing. She was conscious of the mother's age-long cry, "What do you know of grief who have not lost your child?" The vision to which she had so often, so steadfastly barred the way rose before her: her first-born, wandering somewhere beyond life, wanting her, thinking she had forsaken him, not knowing that it was he who had left her to grow old without him. She thrust it away, remembering that John was in need of help and was alive.

"Darling John," she said, "what miserable conversation we are having for Martin's birthday. Don't talk about when you were young like that. It makes me feel too old."

"You think I am young because I am your offspring, mamma. Other people don't. Good morning, Mary, do you think I am young?"

Mary, also looking in on her way downstairs to breakfast, was taken aback by this question.

"Are you much older than David?" she asked cautiously.

"Seven or eight years. It depends on which of us had a birthday last."

"Then you can't be very old. Aunt Emily," she said, as John left the room, "I forgot to tell you Martin and the Boulles want to do some kind of little show to-night. It will only take a few minutes, and they wanted me to ask you if you minded. I think they are to dress up and recite, or something."

"Of course they can. Will they want somewhere to dress up? I'm afraid they'll have to use one of the bedrooms, as the downstairs rooms are all being used. Conque could help them. She is splendid at making clothes. Ring, Mary, and I'll tell her. Or if she is at breakfast, as she always is when I want her, I will tell her when she comes up, if you will write it on a piece of paper for me. There is some paper over on the table, and I know I had a pencil here not long ago, but everything gets mixed up in the bed-clothes."

"I don't think they need any help, Aunt Emily, thank you very much. It's all arranged. I'll tell them you say it's all right."

When Martin got down a little late for breakfast he found everyone eating. He was greeted by a chorus of many happy returns of the day and a pile of presents by his plate. His grandfather and John had given him cheques which would go far towards solving the problem of the motor bicycle. David had brought down a box of shirts, socks and ties, the latest and chastest of their kind. Agnes gave him real pearl studs and engraved cuff links. Mary had knitted a scarf and a white sweater edged with his school colours. There were letters and telegrams from various relations and friends.

"Oh, thanks most awfully, everybody," said Martin, happily embarrassed. "Thanks awfully, grandfather, for the cheque. Thanks awfully, John, it's awfully good of you. Thanks awfully, David, they are ripping. Thanks awfully, Aunt Agnes, they are absolutely it. Thanks awfully, Mary, they are simply it."

He sat down to his breakfast in a happy dream of scouring England with an open exhaust. Nannie and Ivy then appeared with James, Emmy and Clarissa.

"Say Many Happy Returns to Mr. Martin, James," Nannie said. "And me and Ivy both wish you many happy returns, Mr. Martin."

"Oh, thanks awfully, Nannie, that's awfully good of you."

"Come along, James, and give your present to your cousin," urged Nannie again.

James pushed into Martin's hand a spirited but highly inaccurate water-colour drawing of two railway engines meeting in a head-on collision.

"Oh, thanks awfully, James. That's a ripping picture. Thanks most awfully."

"I did mean to buy you some transfers," said James, "but they cost sixpence, and I am saving up to buy some new paints, so I did a picture. Oh, many happy returns of the day."

"Thanks awfully, old chap. It's simply splendid."

Emmy and Clarissa were then brought forward. Emmy, on being told to say Many Happy Returns, burst into tears and ran to Ivy.

"Oh, wicked one, wicked one," said Agnes. "Ivy, give Emmy's present to Mr. Martin."

"Oh, thanks awfully, Emmy," said Martin, opening an envelope in which was a representation of a swan, embroidered in red and blue cotton on a piece of cardboard, "it's simply splendid."

"You bad better take Emmy away, Ivy," said Agnes. She is in one of her crying moods. It is so annoying. Come and give Martin your present, Clarissa."

Clarissa's contribution was a small bunch of dead daisies, tightly held in her hot hand.

"Oh, thanks awfully, Clarissa. It's the nicest present I've had," said Martin.

"She picked them herself for Mr. Martin," said Nannie

proudly, "yesterday afternoon, and nothing would make her let me put them in water. She slept with them all night, Mr. Martin, and first thing this morning she was sitting up in bed holding them tight, and she would have them all through breakfast, so Ivy had to feed her with a spoon."

Martin picked up his small cousin and kissed her. Everyone felt inclined to cry. Nannie removed Emmy and Clarissa.

"Wait till you come of age, my boy," said David.

"This is nothing. You'll have to kiss Siddon and Conk and the whole lot of them and make a speech."

The door opened and to everyone's surprise and, it must be said, slight annoyance, Lady Emily came in, leaning on her stick, a black lace scarf thrown round her head and shoulders.

"Well, here I am, come to disturb you all and talk about plans," she announced with a mischievous face. "Many, many happy returns of the day, dear Martin."

Martin sprang up and hugged his grandmother.

"I've brought you a present," she said, sitting down next to Martin and giving him a little box. "It belonged to papa, and your father would have had it, Martin, so I have been keeping it for you."

Martin took out of the box a large gold watch, as thin as a biscuit, with a gold chain.

"Oh, gran," he said, awestruck, "is it really for me?" "Really for you, Martin. Let's see what time it is." She took the watch from him and pressed a spring. A clear bell-like sound struck nine times, followed by three quarters.

"A quarter to ten," said Lady Emily, handing the watch back to Martin.

"Oh, gran, I say, it's simply splendid. I say, you oughtn't to give me such a ripping present," said Martin. "It's top-hole."

He made it strike again with an air of proud mastership.

Clarissa will love to hear it," said Agnes.

"No, Agnes," said David firmly. "The watch isn't mine, but

as Martin's uncle I insist on exercising my authority. That divine watch is not to go near your children. Do you hear, Martin? If they get within a hundred yards of that watch, James will take it to pieces, Emmy will break it and Clarissa will drop it into her bath. Won't they, Agnes? And then you will say, 'Oh, wicked ones, I must get you another watch to play with.'"

Whether David intended it or not, his imitation of Agnes made everyone laugh and destroyed the slightly emotional atmosphere which the gift of Lord Pomfret's watch had created.

"I remember your father very well with that watch, Emily," said Mr. Leslie. "He used to wear it in the evening. Men didn't wear wrist-watches then. Silly habit. Your father would never have worn a wrist-watch. Sensible man, Lord Pomfret. Never wore those stupid white waistcoats without any back, either."

"Because they weren't invented then," said David in a stage aside, thus causing Martin to utter a wild guffaw. Mr. Leslie looked suspiciously at him, but remembering that it was his birthday, he held his peace.

Lady Emily then proceeded to drive everyone mad who had the patience to listen to her, by rediscussing plans that had long been made, reopening questions that had been settled days ago, and finally suggesting that the whole vicarage party should be asked up to dinner. Mr. Leslie, David and Martin went out of the room while she was talking, saying something about cricket. Agnes, seeing no end to the trouble in which her mother was proposing to embroil them, suggested visiting Mrs. Siddon and talking about the tea-arrangements, knowing well that Siddon, through long practice, was capable of countering any of her ladyship's projects which interfered with her own excellent plans.

"Will you come out for a bit, Mary?" said John. "The cricket doesn't begin till twelve o'clock."

They strolled down the garden to where a low brick wall separated garden from field and woodland. On the other side of the wall ran the little stream known as Rushmere Brook, which had supplied water to Rushmere Abbey and the fishponds. At one end of the wall was a red brick gazebo, or summer-house, approached by a short flight of steps. John suggested that they should go into it, as the sun was already very hot. A wide, low, unglazed window with a broad sill overlooked Rush-mere Brook, and here they perched themselves. The hammering in the cricket field was finished and all was still.

"What is Martin up to just now?" asked John. "He was very mysterious last night."

"It is rather a secret, John. Something he and the Boulles are doing."

"Are you in it, too?"

"Not really, but I promised to help them and not give them away, so do you mind if I don't tell you? It is nothing they oughtn't to do, only a romantic kind of idea. They are going to have a kind of little pageant to-night, and I asked Aunt Emily and she said it would be all right."

"I wish you had known my elder brother, Martin's father. Martin is so absurdly like him. I've never known a man I liked better than my brother. We had frightful rows of course, when we were growing up, but they never meant anything. Gay was devoted to him too. Our people were old friends, you know. She was only a child when he was killed, but she adored him. In a way I fell in love with her later on because we both cared for him so tremendously."

"What was Gay really like, John? I have seen photographs of her, but when I ask Aunt Agnes about her, she can't explain."

"Dear Agnes," said John, laughing. "I can imagine her difficulty in trying to explain anything definite about anybody. It's difficult to describe Gay. Don't think poorly of me if I say that I am beginning to forget."

He looked out over the stream and was silent for a moment. It was unbelievable that Gay, his childhood's friend, his young love, his adored wife, should be slipping away from him, but so it was. If he tried to think of her look, her voice, he could no longer make a vision of her. Someone whom he had loved past words was becoming a gentle shade, melting away from him month by month, day by day. Time devours everything, but each mortal believes that his own memory can enshrine immortality. He holds the dear image in his heart, but while he yet holds it the laurels fade, the image is dimmed. Of one thing he was certain, that if he could see Gay again, tell her that he was losing her hour by hour, missing her less bitterly if one were to face the truth, thinking necessarily of so many things in which she had no part, she would understand as she had always understood.

"I can only explain Gay to you," he said, breaking the silence, "by saying that she understood everything and was absolutely fearless."

Mary made no answer.

"And," said John, bitterness coming into his voice, "if I could tell her that I am forgetting her, she wouldn't think it unkind. She would laugh at me and tell me not to make a merit of grieving. I suppose all of us like to make capital out of our griefs." His voice became harder as he scourged himself. "After all, the disconsolate widower is hardly a romantic figure after seven years, is he?"

"John, how dare you!" said Mary passionately.

"How dare I what? Laugh at myself? Haven't I the right?"

"No, you haven't. As long as you remember Gay at all, you have no right to laugh at Gay's husband so unkindly. And even if you had forgotten Gay altogether, it isn't fair to talk so untruthfully and horribly about yourself, when you are so kind."

"Am I kind?"

"Of course you are. You were kind to me when I made such

a fool of myself in your office, and when I tried to tell you how sorry I was for having been such a beastly prig about Milton, and not asking me to sing again when you knew I was frightened, and helping Martin not to go abroad when he didn't want to. How dare you run yourself down like that?"

"I suppose I was showing off. One does, even at my age," said John, more touched than he cared to admit.

"Be quiet," cried Mary, in exasperation, shaking his arm with both her hands. "If only everyone were as kind as you are, it would be much happier for everybody. And I'm not going to make a fool of myself again in front of you, but if I do, it will be all your fault."

Her brimming eyes showed the truth of what she said.

"Do you mind drying your eyes at once?" said John in his normal voice. "If you are going to cry, I can't bear it, and I shall say a good deal that I probably oughtn't to say."

"If it's swearing," said Mary hopefully, "I am pretty good at it myself. Daddy swore frightfully about things like meals or boots—not about real things"

"No, not swearing, you dear goose. Quite, quite other things; but if you don't know what they are, I shan't tell you. You keep Martin's secret and I'll keep mine. Come back now. I shall be wanted for the cricket.'

For the benefit of such readers as are not interested in cricket, we shall not describe the game. We will merely say that the home side lost, which however, as Martin contentedly said, is the next best to winning, that Martin played a useful and steady game and made the highest score for his side, that David did some fine fancy batting and made a spectacular catch, and that John was bowled almost at once. Lady Emily came down to the pavilion before lunch and enjoyed herself enormously, interrupting conversations and ruthlessly tearing people from chairs where they were perfectly comfortable to put them in chairs they didn't like, next to people they didn't want to know. David said afterwards that he had seen his mother limp up to the umpire between overs and offer him a mackintosh square to stand on, but this statement was rightfully disbelieved. John and Agnes, who perhaps alone realized how deeply their parents felt the anniversay, and how all their joy in Martin was mingled with grief for Martin's father, admired with loving anxiety their courage and self-forgetfulness.

Lunch was cold, and people came in and out as they felt inclined. Mary felt so happy about nothing in particular that she extended the hand of friendship to Miss Stevenson, whom she met wandering about alone, and took her up to Rushwater House for chicken and cider cup.

"I'd love to come," said Miss Stevenson with obvious gratitude. "The Boulles are not very keen on cricket, so they aren't coming till this afternoon."

"How are you getting on with them?"

"Quite well. I am working with the professor every morning, and he is an excellent tutor. As for conversation, if I had known how well the whole family talked English, I'm not sure if I would have come here. However, Madame Boulle is splendid at jumping on one's mistakes. I have asked her to be merciless. It is so good for one to be pulled up every time one makes a howler. I feel I am really fighting something. Ursule is an interesting girl, too."

"Isn't she rather greedy?" asked Mary. "Martin says she is always talking about food."

"That is very interesting, too. She evidently has a repression of some sort which takes that peculiar form. But it is more her attitude as a half-way type that interests me. She is modern in some ways, extremely domestic in others. I want to get her to stay with me in my flat before she goes back to France. What do you think of David?"

This sudden question nearly made Mary jump.

"He's very nice," she said, noncommittally. "A bit vague about things."

"I find him extremely interesting. The predatory male

type, softened by civilization. Frankly, very attractive to women. Are you in love with him?"

With great presence of mind Mary answered, "Are you?"

Miss Stevenson appeared to find this question perfectly normal.

"Not yet," she replied, "but I expect to be. I shall suffer, of course. One always does with men of his type. Beautiful tyrant, fiend angelical. He is not really my type. I would like you to meet my friend, Lionel Harvest. He is tremendously attractive, too. He tried to get me out of Broadcasting House, but since he has failed, he has become definitely more appealing to me. I am the maternal type."

To her own interest, Mary found that she was no longer madly jealous of Miss Stevenson. She envied her hideously, her detached attitude, her implication of knowing all about men and life, but she no longer wanted to hit or kill her.

"Just now I am rather worried," said Miss Stevenson.

"I am getting up some poetry readings about gardens and I want someone to do a preliminary talk. I can get hold of plenty of amateur enthusiasts, or people who can write beautiful prose, but what I want is someone who knows the literature of the garden as well as being a practical gardener."

"Would you mind someone who was a bore?"

"It would interest me. I collect bores. They are nearly always the result of early repressions and as I am the maternal type I understand them. Have you one?"

"Not yet. But there is a Mr. Holt coming for the night who is an awful old bore, but he knows everything about Herbals and Perennials and all that sort of thing."

"Let us meet," said Miss Stevenson. "Does he dance?"

"Oh, I shouldn't think so. He is quite old and fat."

"Splendid. I don't dance myself. It is probably a kind of exhibitionist pose in me, to conceal the fact that I don't dance well. He will be useful to me, I am sure. Thank you so much for giving me lunch, Miss Preston."

Tea for most of the company was in the racket court, but Gudgeon withdrew such guests as he thought suitable from the throng and brought them into the house, where Agnes was dispensing tea. Pierre Boulle had attached himself to her and was passionately handing to the guests the cups she filled. Sometimes their hands met across a saucer and Pierre becamee pale with emotion.

"Lady Dorothy Bingham, Miss Bingham, Miss Hermione Bingham," Gudgeon announced.

"Dear Dodo, this is too lovely," said Agnes. "Dear Rose, dear Hermione, how delicious to have you. Have you had tea? Monsieur Boulle, do look after my cousins."

Lady Dorothy was a cousin of Lady Emily's, and the very same Dodo Bingham whose letter about the young man who wasn't allowed to go to Munich had been lost in the garden. She and her nice pretty twin daughters had come to spend the night, and as they were only asked to make up the numbers at the dinner-table, we shall not pay much attention to them. The girls both had a very happy time and were a great success, and as they all went home in their car early next day, we need not trouble much more about them.

Mr. Holt was the next arrival. He came in a very evil mood, having had to travel by the branch line to Rushwater and be driven up in the Ford. The calculated effect of his arrival was entirely spoilt by finding a large room full of people talking at the tops of their voices, through which even Gudgeon's clarion tones could not penetrate. He stood swelling with rage for a few moments, alone and neglected, till Mary caught sight of him.

"How do you do, Mr. Holt?" she said. "I am Mary Preston. I was here the last time you came."

"Doubtless, doubtless," said Mr. Holt, offering her a flabby hand. "I fear I am almost an intruder here among so many."

"Of course not," said Mary. "Lady Emily isn't receiving guests herself, because she is rather tired with the heat. You will find her on her long chair by the window. Come and have some tea."

She piloted Mr. Holt to the tea-table and did her best to placate him by describing Miss Stevenson, whose importance at Broadcasting House she greatly exaggerated, and her anxiety to meet him. Her wiles were successful, and in a short time Mr. Holt became his own simple, selfish self again.

"Now," he said, "I must not further delay in presenting my respects to my hostess. Will you conduct me thither, Miss Preston? Ah, there she is, in her chair. Dear Lady Emily, how grateful I am to you for bidding me to your delightful house once more. And on such an occasion as our young friend Martin's birthday, too. But before you take me to your garden, of which I unfortunately saw so little last time I was here, may I lay a humble petition at your feet? I am again going on to my dear friend, Lady Norton, but I fear she cannot have me till the day after to-morrow. May I therefore trespass upon your kindness for two nights instead of the one for which you so kindly asked me? I should also beg your chauffeur of his kindness to convey me thither."

Lady Emily, who had closed her eyes during the latter part of this speech, now made a delicious despairing grimace at Mary.

"Of course you must stay, Mr. Holt," she said. "As for Weston driving you, I'm sure he will if he is free, but I'll have to ask my husband. Come and tell me all about Lady Capes. I haven't heard from her since you were last here. Or you want to see the garden, don't you? Dodo, darling," she called to Lady Dorothy Bingham, "I know you hate cricket. Will you take Mr. Holt round the garden? He is a tremendous authority."

"Of course," said Lady Dorothy in a deep voice. "I need some exercise after motoring all the way," and seizing on Mr. Holt she carried him away. As she knew a great deal about gardening, had an excellent opinion of her own genius, and was a powerful walker, Mr. Holt derived but little pleasure from the expedition. The pleasant saunter with an admiring hostess which he had promised himself was changed to a brisk walk with a woman who contradicted and bullied him, and except for being a duke's daughter was in every way abhorrent to him. His evil mood, which Mary's flattery had dispelled, came upon him again in full force, nor was it softened by being put in what he considered an inferior bedroom and having to wait for his bath while David soaked interminably.

So it was with no particular pleasure that he found himself placed at dinner between Lady Dorothy whom he feared and Mary whom he considered beneath his notice. David was on Mary's other side, and never had he been more charming and amusing.

"You look quite divine in that frock," he said to her .after the fish, "not so lovely as Agnes, but quite divine."

Agnes was indeed radiant in loveliness. Her white neck and arms, her exquisite complexion, her dark hair and eyes, were like something out of a Victorian novel. Her white lace dress, her diamond necklace and earrings, all helped to make a vision of dazzling beauty.

"You will give me a lot of dances, won't you?" David continued. "I want to have a good lump of them, about half-way down your programme. Where is your bag? Do you really like it?"

Mary showed him the bag he had given her, lying on her lap.

"I got one like it for Joan," said David. "It is a jolly thing, isn't it?"

Again Mary nearly burst with rage and mortification. The bag which was her special present from David turned out to be only the duplicate of Miss Stevenson's. Probably David had bought six, had bought a hundred, had given them to every girl he had ever met. Miss Stevenson had been perfect-

ly right in calling him fiend angelical. Before she could think
of anything really cutting to say, David had begun to talk to
his cousin, Hermione Bingham, on his other side. Mary
turned to Mr. Holt, but he was firmly engaged by Lady
Dorothy, so there was nothing for it but to eat her dinner and
try to look happy. There was evidently little chance of talking
to Mr. Holt, which, much as she disliked him, would be better than being odd man out. Mr. Leslie, on Lady Dorothy's
other side, was indulging in a heavy flirtation with Rose
Bingham, whose impertinent vivacity had great charm for
elderly gentlemen. Beyond Rose, John was talking to Agnes.

"Don't you think Mary looks lovely in the frock I chose for
her?" said Agnes, whose methods were simple and direct.

"Yes, delightful."

"I want you to be very nice to her to-night," his sister continued. "I want her to have a very happy evening."

"There will be lots of younger men," said John, half seriously.

"But not so nice as you, John dear. It was at a ball that I
got engaged to Robert. He took me in to supper and a waiter
spilt some coffee all down his shirt-front and I said, 'Oh,
Colonel Graham, that coffee will stain your shirt So he asked
if he could have the next dance but two, and he went straight
back to his rooms and put on a clean shirt and came back and
proposed to me."

"Darling Agnes, that is very helpful. And what did Robert
say exactly when he proposed? That might help me too."

Agnes looked gratified.

"I don't exactly remember," she said, "but it was something
about mother, and I said that sounded very nice, so we got
engaged."

Not really very helpful, after all, thought John. Besides, he
wasn't at all sure if he had the courage to think of getting
engaged, even if Mary would look at him. In the summer-
house, in the still morning heat, Gay, that gentle ghost, had

slipped from his grasp, leaving him alone and free. His thoughts which had lingered for so many years among shadows of love had now all winged their way back to his heart, free for fresh adventure. He had known, ever since he heard Mary sing in the candlelit drawing-room, that she might give a haven to these thoughts, but some feeling of loyalty to Gay, some fear of using Mary's compassion, had held him back. Gay had withdrawn herself now, content to be forgotten. Could Mary care for him except through pity? Kind she had called him, but gratitude for kindness can be very far from love. Shaken and bewildered he could only let the evening bring forth its own fruits. If they were bitter, he could taste them without shrinking. He looked across the table at Mary, still deserted by both her neighbours, and was deeply disturbed by the smile she sent him. Such open and confident affection as he read in her look made him half-afraid to trouble her serenity.

Before he could reply to Agnes, Mr. Macpherson had claimed her to take part in a discussion with Lady Emily and Martin. Lady Emily had told Gudgeon that the servants must come in and drink Martin's health after dinner, and Martin, who till now had borne up under his birthday honours, felt that this was too much.

"Oh, I say, gran," he remonstrated, "if I saw Gudgeon and Conk drinking my health, I'd feel an awful fool."

"But they will be so disappointed, Martin," said his grandmother. "Conque told me to-day how much they were all looking forward to it. When papa and mamma had their golden wedding, papa had all the servants in and everybody cried."

"Oh, I say, gran, we don't want Conk crying," said Martin.

"It is so sad that Nannie and Ivy can't both be here," said Agnes, "but someone must stay with the children. Ivy went to the concert, so Nannie is coming in this evening. She will be able to tell the children about it at their breakfast to-morrow."

"I'm afraid you'll have to, Martin," said Mr. Macpherson. "It's expected, and there's no more to be said."

Martin became as nearly sulky as anyone is on his seventeenth birthday. But besides a general wish to please his grandmother, another thought struck him.

"All right, gran," he said, not ungraciously. "Let them all come. And I'll give them a health to drink."

Lady Emily was delighted and laid her hand approvingly on Martin's arm. Gudgeon, who had been filling a number of glasses with such port as he considered suitable for the staff, then ushered in the housekeeper's room and the servants' hall in a body. Mr. Macpherson made a short speech of congratulation and Martin's health was drunk by everyone.

Martin, flushed and stammering and looking more attractive than ever, got up to speak.

"Thanks most awfully, everyone," he said. "Grandfather and gran have been jolly good to me and so have Uncle John and Aunt Agnes and David. And I wish it was my father making this speech, but as it isn't, it can't be helped. It's most awfully decent of you all, it's awfully decent of you, Gudgeon, and Siddy and Conk and everybody, and I'm most awfully grateful. And now I want you all to drink another health. Gudgeon, give them all some more of the fruity port. I'm going to ask you all to drink to our king and all the royal family."

Everyone stood up. Martin, looking straight at Mary, emptied his glass and threw it on the floor defiantly. Mary understood. Others might be drinking to King George, to whom Martin wished every possible good, but only Mary knew that as he drank, not the bearded face of the King of England was in his mind's eye, but the slightly vulpine features of the present duc de Guise.

"Quite the right thing to do," said Mr. Leslie to Lady Dorothy. "Quite right to drink the king's health. I thought the boy was going to propose Emily and myself, and I didn't know how I'd get through if he did. He's a good lad. Heart in the right place. None of this bolshevism."

"I always cry when the king's health is drunk," said Lady Emily. "Martin, you were splendid. It was just the right thing to do. I remember when your father—what is it, Gudgeon.?"

"Beg pardon, my lady, but as Mr. Martin's glass is one of the special ones, I thought you might be relieved to know that it is not broke. It merely rolled under the table."

"Thank you, Gudgeon."

If it were possible to turn pale when one had drunk far more champagne and port than one is used to, Martin would have done so. Were the omens against the house of Bourbon? He had succeeded in drinking their health. and making all the guests and servants drink it. He had flung the glass from him that no less worthy toast might profane it. And now the glass had been picked up by Gudgeon, would be washed by Walter, and put away for future use. For the first time that day he felt depressed. But realizing that he would disappoint his grandparents if he didn't play up, he made a manful effort to be himself, and was rewarded by feeling much happier.

CHAPTER XIII

THE FALL OF THE LILIES

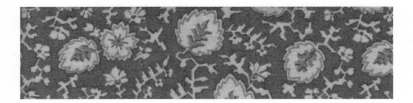

HALF AN HOUR LATER LADY EMILY, magnificent in blue velvet, sapphires and lace, was receiving her guests in the drawing-room, supported by Martin. The folding doors between the drawing-room and the morning-room had been opened and the band was put on a platform at one end. So hot and windless was the night that the french windows on to the terrace were all open.

The vicarage party were among the early arrivals. Madame Boulle was astounding in dark red lace, Ursule looked far more prepossessing in virginal pale blue and was clinging as usual to Miss Stevenson, who carried off a rather daring affair in black satin with considerable success.

Madame Boulle was loud in her appreciation of the room, the lights, the toilettes, the guests. She said it reminded her of the balls which her grandmother the countess used to give, balls which were frequented by the highest members of the nobility. The French, she added, were famous through the whole world for the gaiety and entraînement of their balls, but there was nevertheless, in an English ball, a certain solid comfort which was not always found in France.

"Mais, écoute que je to dice, Martine," she continued, "there is one thing that is extremely English, namely your habit of celebrating the day of birth rather than the day of your saint. In France, Martine, your feast day would be the eleventh of November, the day of St. Martin."

But before she could expatiate fully on this subject, she was swept onwards by the rest of her family, Jean Claude, who came last, saying in an audible aside to Martin:

"We shall all be here till la Saint-Martin if maman goes on talking."

His mother, overhearing, turned a baleful eye on him.

"Have I to reproach you in public for insolence to your mother, Jean Claude?" she asked rhetorically. "And it seems to me that you have not yet wished many happy returns of the day to your comrade, Martine. You are wanting in heart, Jean Claude. Congratulate Martine at once."

"Many happy returns of The Day," said Jean Claude, looking at Martin significantly. "Do you notice anything about me?"

"You do look a bit blown out," said Martin. "Anything wrong?"

"No, it is The Flag which is wound about me, under. my waistcoat," said Jean Claude.

"Why didn't you leave it in the cloak-room?"

"The flag-bearer lives and dies with the flag," said Jean Claude, simply and nobly.

Martin could have wished that Jean Claude looked less peculiar, his grey satin waistcoat, obvious relic of Professor Boulle's young days, distended by the lilies of France, but it was too late to make any comment.

Programmes were now rapidly being filled up. David brought Mary a programme in which his own name was written across numbers eight to twelve. The rest of her evening was quickly divided among Martin, Pierre, and various neighbours. John, coming a little late, found her almost booked up and was forced to be content with number seven and a possible extra at the end.

Pierre Boulle, faultlessly elegant, with a white carnation in his buttonhole, approached Agnes with a beating heart and asked for a dance.

"But you must have more than one," said Agnes, pulling on her long white gloves. "Are you quite all right after getting so wet when you saved Emmy? You know it is astonishing that she didn't catch cold, but ever since she had her tonsils out she has hardly caught cold at all. Before that she used to have terrible colds every winter. I can give you ten and eleven and twelve. It is so much nicer to go on dancing with one person, because if you dance with people for long you seem to get more used to them. And I must introduce you to my cousins, Hermione and Rose Bingham. You were kind enough to give them some tea, I think, so you know each other. That is all right."

She laid her gloved hand on Pierre's arm and led him to the Binghams. Pierre went through the form of asking the twins to dance, but his whole being was in turmoil at Agnes's touch. Somehow he must live till the tenth dance. It would be difficult to live through such an eternity, but it should be done. Goddess of moonlight, of pearl, of snow, white Madonna, tour d'ivoire, said Pierre to himself.

"I say, Mary," said Jean Claude, catching at Mary as she went past.

"What?"

"Remember that at twelve o'clock precisely you ask the band to stop. And then we shall all play our parts. No harm can come to you," he added fiercely. "It will not be the first time Pierre and I have had an affair with the flies."

"With who?"

"The police."

"But there aren't any police here, Jean Claude. Don't worry about that. Aren't you dancing?"

"I do not dance," said Jean Claude, who had forsworn that exercise for much the same reasons as Miss Stevenson.

But here he spoke too soon, for Lady Dorothy Bingham, merciless to what she called "ballroom skulkers," saw him standing about, ordered John to introduce him to her, and became his patroness. Not till he had miserably danced twice with her and once with each of the twins did he have the brilliant idea of introducing her to his mother. The master minds met, and recognized each other, and for the greater part of the evening they discussed the care and subjugation of a family. Lady Dorothy, who had three sons in the army, was for a time ahead, but Madame Boulle had a living husband, visible witness to her power, and scored heavily on this, as Mr. Bingham had died meekly and miserably many years earlier.

"What are you doing, Professor, eh?" said Mr. Leslie to Professor Boulle. "Not a dancing man?"

"No, I only look on."

"Play bridge?"

The professor's face lighted up. Bridge was his secret passion, discouraged by his wife, who, because she did not play, considered it waste of time.

"Contract?" inquired Mr. Leslie suspiciously, feeling that foreigners would probably not have got beyond beggar-my-neighbour, or some peculiar game of their own which would end with knives and pistols.

"But naturally. What else could one play?"

Mr. Leslie hurried away, collected Mr. Macpherson and a fourth man, and took them off to the library.

"Quite safe here," he said. "Have some supper brought in here, if you like. Let the young people amuse themselves. What do you play, Professor? Half a crown a hundred? By the way, I suppose you play cards in English?"

"Oh, yes. I have played a good deal with English friends."

"That's all right. I mean, you have some queer names on the Continent. What's No Trumps in French, Professor?"

"Sans atout."

"Oh, yes," said Mr. Leslie reflectively. "Doesn't sound natural, you know, though."

Mary soon found Miss Stevenson with Ursule, and asked her to come and meet Mr. Holt. As they went across the drawing-room she looked furtively at Miss Stevenson's bag. It was of black satin with an initial on it in brilliants.

"What a pretty bag," she hazarded.

"I had it made to go with this dress," said Miss Stevenson. "Yours is pretty, too. David gave me one like that, but it wasn't in my style, so I gave it to my friend, Lionel Harvest. He embroiders divinely and he is going to copy it."

Mary hardly knew whether to be angry or jubilant. It was like that Miss Stevenson's cheek to give away David's bag to someone called Harvest. On the other hand, what a richly merited snub for David if only he knew. Mr. Holt was found and the introduction effected.

Mr. Holt, flattered at being approached by a representative of Broadcasting House, exerted himself to be pleasant. Miss Stevenson, who had just enough superficial knowledge of gardening to make a good show, made herself as agreeable as possible. Ursule giggled appreciatively.

Mr. Holt suggested that they should all three go to the schoolroom, where Lady Emily kept some of her valuable old gardening books, and there talk over the matter quietly. After the mortification of finding himself unnoticed in a large party, an attractive audience of two women was balm to his wounded spirit.

Miss Stevenson was obviously clever, and the French girl was at least French.

"And then," he added, "we can go in to supper early, say about half-past eleven, and secure a table for ourselves before the crowd."

The dance was now in full swing. Lady Emily, sitting on a sofa, watched the dancers and held a court. John made himself agreeable to any girls who looked deserted or shy, and occasionally came over to see his mother. When he went to claim Mary for their dance, he found her looking happy and excited.

I'm having a lovely evening," she said. "Everyone dances so

well. Martin is very good. Pierre is a wonderful dancer, almost as good as you are. And after this I have five dances with David. John, I do like the Leslies."

"I think the Leslies like you."

"Do you really? Your father has been very kind to me. And Aunt Agnes looks so lovely, and Aunt Emily too."

"Now, stop chattering," said John, "and dance."

They danced in silence and perfect accord. When the band finally stopped they went out onto the terrace. Moonlight lay on the world.

"I wonder," said Mary presently, "what the summerhouse looks like by moonlight."

"Would you like to go and see?"

"Yes, do let's. Oh, but there wouldn't be time. I have the next dance with David and I mustn't miss him."

John took her back to the drawing-room and they waited by the window. The dance began, but no David came. Mary's talk became nervous and disjointed, and her eyes wandered restlessly about the room. John, who was sorry for her, suggested dancing till David came, but Mary's feet behaved foolishly and she was ashamed of herself. John, who was by now feeling annoyed with David, took Mary to the supper-room and asked her what she would like. She asked for champagne, and drank it quickly and angrily.

"Shall we stay here for a bit?" said John. "It is quiet and we can see David if he passes the door. I expect he has made a muddle of his programme, silly ass."

"But he wrote his name down himself," said Mary, showing John the programme.

"Well, if he doesn't turn up I shall cross his name right off your programme and put my own instead."

"Oh, not yet, not yet, please. Oh, there he is."

John got up and went into the ballroom.

"Look here, David," he said, "Mary has been waiting half this dance and all the last one for you. It isn't good enough.

Come along, and don't try to cut any more dances. What were you doing?"

"My dear chap," said David, taking John's arm, "for the Lord's sake don't come the heavy brother over me. I got stuck with the twins somehow. I never know if it's Hermione or Rose, and I didn't notice which dance it was. I say, Mary, I am sorry and sorry and ten thousand times sorry. May I go down on my knees and ask forgiveness?"

He knelt down in supplication.

"Get up, David, and don't be an ass," said John unsympathetically. "Take Mary into the ballroom and don't walk on her feet."

David seized Mary and whirled her away. John watched them as they danced, Mary's face upturned to David's, oblivious of everything but the moment. There were no deserted girls standing about, so he slipped out onto the terrace and walked down to the bottom of the garden, where he sat on the brick wall, watching the moonlight on the stream, hearing the noises of restless birds and little animals, trying to choke down his anger against David, an anger which he was forced to recognize miserably as jealousy. To be jealous of one's own younger brother was something at which one's pride revolted, something which one must conquer at any cost. It was unreasonable to expect that Mary should think of him if David was about. Mary had enjoyed her one dance with him, he knew that without being told. But as soon as she thought of David her feather-light feet had dragged, her face had changed to uncertain expectancy, her talk had been abrupt, she had hardly heard or seen him. Well, good luck to David and good luck with all one's heart—only he wasn't quite good enough for Mary. He would always be the same charming, perfectly unreliable creature, delightfully selfish, quite heartless, if to have a heart meant pain for himself. Mary must surely see what he was like. Again and again he had let her down. The lunch, the strawberries, the dances to-night, all such little things, all to be such big things after a year of marriage.

He thought of Mary as she had been that morning in the summer-house when no thought of David's presence was near them. How nearly he had told her that he loved her. Well, thank heaven, he hadn't. If David meant the world to her, so it must be. But I must speak to her at once, he said to himself; she can only say no. So he sat on in the moonlight, seeing no way to his own happiness, afraid for Mary's happiness, and in the distance the lights shone and the music sounded.

People were beginning to settle seriously to the business of supper when Mr. Holt and his companions came into the dining-room. Mr. Holt, an old campaigner, marked down the most secluded and comfortable table, made straight for it, pushed aside Lady Dorothy Bingham, who was moving in the same direction, apologized to her with fulsome courtesy while keeping him self well between her and the table, and finally established himself with Miss Stevenson and Ursule.

"Now," said Mr. Holt, picking up a menu, "what shall we have? Soup? Lobster salad? Chicken?"

"Just a little lobster salad for me," said Miss Stevenson abstractedly.

"Everything, please," said Ursule. "It is a very good supper and we should enjoy it."

"I applaud your decision, Miss Ursula," said Mr. Holt. "I also shall begin with soup and proceed with the other courses."

"Well, so will I," said Miss Stevenson. "It is probably mere exhibitionism when I refuse food. One must check that in oneself. And what is more, we'll have champagne."

Ursule giggled. "I shall eat everything," she announced, "but I shall not drink champagne. Maman would be furious."

"Alas, champagne is forbidden to me," said Mr. Holt. "A small whisky and soda is all I dare to take."

"Well, frankly, champagne doesn't do me much good either," said Miss Stevenson. "Lemonade, please."

Supper was a great success. Mr. Holt, still delighted with

his audience, was able to tell many of his anecdotes of the
nobility and gentry which had once been so fresh. Ursule
liked hearing all these noble names, and was thoroughly
enjoying her large supper. Miss Stevenson observed Mr. Holt
seriously and intently. She had decided that he would be just
the person to broadcast for her, and had obtained his not
reluctant promise to come and see her at her office.

Suddenly Lady Dorothy Bingham was seen sweeping
down upon them. Mr. Holt looked anxious, fearing that she
might bear malice for his capture of her table, but such was
not the case.

"I'm coming to sit with you people," she said in her hunt-
ing voice. "I want to talk to Mr. Holt."

"How delightful," fluted Mr. Holt. "And pray, Lady
Dorothy, allow me to introduce Miss Stevenson and Miss
Boulle."

"I think Lionel Harvest is a nephew of yours," said Miss
Stevenson. "He is under me at Broadcasting House."

"Is he? Queer boy, Lionel. I'd let my girls go out with him,
but I don't know that I'd let my boys." Here Lady Dorothy
laughed the laugh before which every fox in her division of
the county quailed. "He'll come into four thousand a year
though when old General Harvest dies."

Miss Stevenson registered this statement with her well-
trained brain.

"Now, Mr. Holt," continued Lady Dorothy, "I want you to
come and see my garden. Emily doesn't want you. She as good
as told me so. You come with me and the girls to-morrow and
we'll have an afternoon with my rock-garden, and then I'll
send you on wherever you want to go. Here, Gudgeon, tell
somebody to bring me some chicken and champagne."

Mr. Holt struggled between pride and mortification. It
was appalling to be told before his audience that his hostess
didn't want him. On the other hand,. Lady Dorothy's robust
flattery, her ardent desire to carry him off, a prize, from under

Lady Emily's nose, was like a breath of old days. True, she had
bullied him cruelly that afternoon, and for that matter was
bullying him now, but it was sweet to be wanted once more,
to feel that one's advice was sought. Besides, Lady Dorothy's
father was a duke, and Lady Emily's merely an earl.

"My dear lady," he said, "nothing would give me greater
pleasure than to obey your behest, to see your garden, to give
any poor advice that it is in my power to give, but I must first
be assured that in going with you I should be guilty of no sort
of discourtesy towards my present hostess."

'Well, you won't," said Lady Dorothy, to whom, as a matter of fact, her cousin had said, "Oh, Dodo, that Mr. Holt has
invited himself for two nights and Henry will be furious." To
this she had replied, "Don't worry, Emily, I'll, take him off
your hands."

"Nine-thirty sharp to-morrow morning we leave. Good
champagne Henry has."

"The whole supper is excellent," said Ursule.

"Can you tell me the time, Mr. Holt?" said Miss
Stevenson.

"Oh, dear, oh, dear, it is almost half-past twelve. I should
have been in bed an hour ere now," said Mr. Holt anxiously.

"Well, you can't get up and go to bed and leave me here
alone," said Lady Dorothy, "for I don't count these girls.
Where are all the men? I don't see Rose and Hermione shav-
ing supper with a man old enough to be their grandfather.'

Miss Stevenson was only restrained from being rude to
Lady Dorothy by remembering that she was Lionel Harvest's
aunt.

"I am going back to the vicarage now," she said. "I don't
dance, and I have had a most interesting talk with Mr. Holt.
I shall write to you, Mr. Holt, as soon as I get to town. Come
along, Ursule, you're not dancing, and the walk will do you
good after all that supper.

"I suppose one may take the sweets that are on the table?" said Ursule doubtfully.

"Of course, child," said Lady Dorothy. "Put them all in your bag."

Ursule did as she was told, and she and Miss Stevenson went away.

Pierre had passed a delirious half-hour dancing with the lovely Mrs. Graham, who moved as exquisitely as she spoke. Agnes much enjoyed dancing with so accomplished a cavalier as that nice Monsieur Boulle who had so kindly rescued Emmy. After the second dance she said she would like to go on the terrace.

"But first will you get me my shawl?" she said. "It a white silk embroidered shawl on mamma's sofa."

Pierre fetched it. They stepped out onto the terrace where, with infinite tenderness, he put the shawl upon her lovely shoulders.

"Thank you so much," said Agnes. "One always feel warmer with a shawl on. Let us go and sit on the grass I do hope Gudgeon has remembered to have the chair dusted. Nothing is more annoying than to get one's frock dirty on a garden chair."

Pierre thought of taking off his coat for her to sit on but not only do shirt sleeves with a white waistcoat look far from romantic, but he felt his coat was an unworthy, and possibly uncomfortable, seat for her.

"Wait a moment," he said, "I will get some cushions."

In an instant he ran up the terrace steps, entered the ball-room, seized some cushions, and was back with Agnes.

"Oh, thank you," she said, fully sinking into the chair. "That is so nice. I love dancing but if one dances
    too much, one gets tired."

"It is my fault," cried Pierre, self-reproachfully. "I made you dance too long. Why did you not stop me?"

"No, it was very nice. I enjoyed it. But do sit down. Isn't there a chair here?"

"May I sit at your feet?" said Pierre in a low, husky voice. "My heart is already there."

"How nice of you. My husband had a Spanish friend who used to say such charming things. I have quite forgotten his name."

Pierre was seized by violent jealousy of all Spaniards.

"Ah, do not think of your Spanish friend: think of me for a little, Mrs. Graham."

"Is it damp on the grass then?" asked Agnes. "It can't be very damp, for it hasn't rained for a week, but Brown may have been using the sprinkler. If it is damp, do get a cushion."

"No, it isn't damp. But you are so cold."

"No, really I'm not. I am deliciously warm now you have got my shawl. But I dare say you are cold. You know, I am afraid you got cold when you saved Emmy from the pond. You were quite wet. Do get a cushion, Monsieur Boulle."

Pierre sat in unhappy silence.

"I am very unhappy," said Agnes plaintively.

A thousand swords sprang from their scabbards in Pierre's heart.

"If I can be of any help, command me," he said.

"I am afraid Robert will be quite annoyed when he hears," continued the lovely complainer.

"I have the greatest respect for Colonel Graham, both as your husband and as a soldier," said Pierre, "but if by word or deed—"

"You see, I told him I didn't want Peter in the house, but he would encourage him, and now I don't know what to do. If he came in I simply couldn't resist him."

Ha! So the fool of a soldier husband had encouraged the visits of this Peter, probably a handsome, rich young guardsman, so different from a poor young professor, and Mrs. Graham had yielded. She said she could not resist. Ah, how could she, poor angel, all gentleness, all affection? If he could kill Peter, or kill Colonel Graham, he would gladly suffer the extreme penalty of the law for her sake.

"And so of course he got overfed in the house, and now my head housemaid writes to say he is dead. Robert will be quite annoyed. And the children will be quite unhappy too. Don't you think we ought to go in now? I believe it is going to rain."

Indeed, clouds were massing up over the garden and the moonlight only shone fitfully.

"Stay a little longer," pleaded Pierre. "This moment alone with you is so precious. I only ask to kiss your gloved hand, to be near you in silence for an instant. I may never be with you again, and never again shall I see a woman so beautiful as you are."

As Agnes appeared to be thinking about something else, Pierre, with deep reverence, took her gloved hand, laid it palm uppermost on his own, and dropped the lightest kiss into the little hole where it buttoned up.

"How' charming of you," said Agnes. "Robert had an Austrian friend who used to kiss one's hand so charmingly whenever he came to call."

Pierre was instantly consumed with burning hatred of all Austrians.

"And now we really must go in," said Agnes. "Do give me your arm, Monsieur Boulle. I am quite buried in this chair."

Pierre sprang to his feet and offered his arm. As Agnes rose, her hair brushed his face.

"Oh, the perfume of your hair," murmured the unhappy young man.

A deep bell sounded through the night as they ascended the terrace.

"The stable dock," said Agnes. "What time was it? Half-past eleven?"

"No," said Pierre, looking at his watch, "half-past twelve."

"I had no idea it was so late. Darling Clarissa is fast asleep, and so are Emmy and James. I do so hope, Monsieur Boulle, that you didn't catch cold when you so kindly saved Emmy. Wet trousers must be so very uncomfortable. Martin, are you ready for our dance? That is delicious. I feel quite rested now, Monsieur Boulle."

Pierre who, in the hope that Agnes would dance again with him, had not booked any more dances, was preparing. to go when he remembered his manners and his hostess. He went up to Lady Emily's sofa, and bending over her hand bade her good night and thanked her for inviting him.

"I think your mother and your brother have gone home," said Lady Emily, "and Miss Stevenson and Ursule went too. I think your father is playing bridge with my husband. Don't you want to stay for him?"

Pierre made his excuses and left. He would willingly have walked for miles on the hills to commune with his soul and with nature, but dancing-shoes are hard on the feet, so he crept into the vicarage and under cover of his mother's voice, which was roundly scolding someone in the drawing-room, got safely to his room. Here he intended to keep vigil all night. But habit asserting itself, he undressed without noticing what he was doing, and then thought he might as well go to bed.

It was no good being angry with David. Mary, stung by his neglect, had meant to be cold, capricious, treat his heart as a football, pay him out in his own coin; but it couldn't be done. David only had to look at one, to speak to one, and one was again his eager trembling slave. They finished that dance and the next.

"Come in the garden a bit now," said David. "Or shall we have supper? We have two more dances together. Or, I'll tell you what. I'll collect some food and we'll have a picnic in the garden."

He went into the dining-room, collected a trayful of food and a bottle of champagne.

"Here, Mary, you take the bottle and two glasses and I'll

take the vittles. We can get out this way without going through the ballroom."

They went out by a side door into the garden and David led the way round the house, down to the garden wall. The summer-house struck him as a good place for a picnic, and he made his way towards it.

"Blast those gardeners," he said amiably, "they've taken all the chairs away for the dance. You'll have to sit on the steps, Mary. Here, you can have my handkerchief to sit on."

He spread his handkerchief on the brick steps and Mary sat down. Both young people fell on the food with a hearty appetite.

"Of course I would break the top off the cork," said David, after wrestling with it in vain, "and my knife has only got one of those things to get the stones out of horses' hoofs or stick pigs with. Well, I am not the first gentleman that has knocked the top off a bottle. Hold the glasses ready so that I won't waste it. Oh, drat that moon; why does it have to go in just when I want some light?"

With considerable skill he knocked the head off the bottle and filled the glasses.

"I shall only give you one glass," he said. "You are not one of the hard-headed sort."

At this instance of his solicitude, Mary nearly fainted. The supper was proceeding charmingly when Mary suddenly gave a small shriek and asked David the time.

"What on earth does time matter? My dear Mary, this is a dance, not an Institution."

'Well, certainly time doesn't matter much to you when you keep a person waiting for a dance and a half," said Mary, pot-valiant with her one glass of cham-pagne, and a victim to her sex's peculiar passion for provoking unnecessary quarrels.

"Oh, come, Mary, you didn't mind that, did you? It was only the twins, and you have no idea how funny they are."

'Well, I did mind. And please tell me the time."

"The minster clock is just going to strike twelve and yonder is the moon. But why this insistence?"

"Oh, David, I'm sorry, but I must go. I have got to be in the ballroom before twelve."

"Curious Cinderella complex you have. What can be so important?"

"I can't tell you, David. Something frightfully important that I promised Martin."

"Martin? My dear girl, you are mad. Either these dances are mine, or they are not. Of course if you want to punish me by cutting the rest of my dances—" said David, assuming a beaten air. He got up and leaned over the river wall.

"Oh, no, David, it isn't that. But Martin and Jean Claude will be so disappointed."

"Jean Claude too," said David in a sepulchral voice, without turning round. "Am I to be slighted for a spotted Frenchman, a plum-pudding dog?"

"No, no, not slighted. David, let me go. I'll be back in a few moments."

"I am not keeping you," said David.

The stable clock sounded twelve.

"Oh, I am too late," cried Mary.

"Splendid. Now you can stay here and be sensible. Or if you really want to go, do go. It doesn't matter about me."

"But it does, David. It matters about you more than anything in the world."

"Say that again," said David, turning round with much interest. 'Do I really count? Wasn't it just a pretext to leave me, because I bore or annoy you?"

"How can you say that," cried Mary, on the brink of tears, "when you know—" She stopped.

"What do I know?" asked David, putting both his hands on her shoulders. "You precious goose, what do I know?"

He drew Mary to him and with the ease born of long practice, settled her head comfortably under his chin. Mary, drowning in the bliss of feeling David's shirt front against her cheek, said nothing, thankful, so far as her scattered senses allowed her to think at all, that she had not actually made the unmaidenly remark which was on her lips.

The stage was set. The moon came out from behind the clouds and shone on beloved and lover. John, pacing back along the grass by the wall, saw his brother and his crystal-voiced love, and turned back under the dark trees.

"Well, that's that," said David, releasing Mary, "and very nice too, Miss Preston. And now do you want to know the time?"

"No. It's too late and anyway it doesn't matter. Oh, David, did you see—"

"I saw the lovely top of your head. Now, we'd better collect the remains, or Brown will think burglars have been carousing here. Come on, Mary."

Mary, her head swimming, helped David to gather up the scraps of their supper, which they carried back to the house.

"Lovely dances they were," said David. "Have you lots of partners now?" He looked at her programme. "Heaps. That's right. So have I. And after that wigging you gave me, I'm not going to cut any more dances."

The duc de Guise must have tossed uneasily on his couch that night. Some spirit, hovering pallid over his slumbers, must have whispered to him, at that hour when faith and hope are lowest, that of the five loyal young hearts who had sworn to unsheathe the sword in his cause, but two remained faithful. Of the remaining three, two had been seduced by love, one by food. Let us hope that the majesty of France could make allowances for both.

A little before midnight Martin and Jean Claude met in the hall. But no other member of the devoted band was present at the assignation.

"I can't see Pierre anywhere," said Jean Claude, "and I've looked everywhere for Ursule. I nearly got caught again by that terrible mégere your Aunt Bingham when I went into the supper-room, so I fled quickly. Where is Mary?"

"I can't find her," Martin said gloomily. "I could have sworn she wouldn't let us down, but you can't trust women. What shall we do?"

"What time is it?" asked Jean Claude.

Martin drew his watch from his waistcoat pocket and pressed the spring. In a delicate voice it sounded twelve times and then played two lines of "The Last Rose of Summer."

"Ventre saint gris!" said Jean Claude, who affected this Bourbon manner of speech when not in hearing of his parent. "Make it sound again."

Martin obligingly did so.

"But really, what are we to do?" he asked, putting the watch back into his pocket.

"We shall make a demonstration alone," said Jean Claude. "True courage rises higher in the face of misfortune. To a true Frenchman the hour of discouragement is also the hour of supreme effort. My ancestors, the Florets—"

"Oh, that's enough gas about your old ancestors," said Martin. "Get the flag out."

"It will make a better effect if I unfurl it suddenly in the ballroom," objected Jean Claude.

"All right. Have it your own way. The dance is just over. Come on. I'll say 'Vive le roi,' and then you wave the flag and say Vive le dauphin."

The dance had, in fact, finished. The dancers were going in to supper or out into the garden as the two representatives of a lost cause advanced up the room. Halting before the sofa where his grandmother was sitting, Martin cried in a resolute voice, "Vive le roi."

"What, darling?" said his grandmother.

"Say your bit, can't you," he hissed to Jean Claude. "Je ne peux pas," said Jean Claude. "Ce maudit drapeau —debarrassez-moi de ça, Martin."

"You great ass," said Martin, pulling at the end of the flag which was sticking out of Jean Claude's grey satin waistcoat. "Why didn't you get it out in the hall, as I told you?"

With considerable difficulty the two boys extricated the flag from its hiding-place.

"Vive le dauphin," said Jean Claude, waving it about in a half-hearted way.

"What have you boys got?" asked Lady Emily. "Come and sit here with me. What a charming flag. Is this the surprise?"

Martin kicked Jean Claude.

"Well the surprise hasn't quite come off, gran," he said, "because the others were to be in it and they forgot. But Ursule made this flag—it's the French royal standard."

"How beautifully she sews," said Lady Emily, examining it. "It is a lovely piece of work. May I really keep it? I shall show it to Conque. You must tell Ursule how much I admire her skill. Have you boys had plenty of supper?"

"Not yet, gran."

"Then you can take me in and give me a little, and then I shall go to bed."

Martin helped his grandmother to rise and gave her his arm to the dining-room. Jean Claude followed in sulky confusion, remonstrating with Martin under his breath.

"You great ass," Martin whispered back, as they crossed 'the hall. "It was as much your fault as anybody's," and he handed his grandmother into the dining-room.

"*Merde!*" said Jean Claude, very loudly and defiantly, which was a mistake, for at that moment his mother, dressed for departure, came out of the ladies' cloak-room and fell upon him.

"*Mais, voyons, Jean Claude, c'est infame ce que to dis là. Ou as-tu done appris de telles saletés?*" she cried. "Come back with me at once and go straight to your bed. I am covered with confusion at your behaviour. "

Without listening to his attempts at explanation she

dragged him off and was still giving him what she called une verte semonce when Pierre got home.

Rain was beginning to fall in heavy drops and the dancers were all coming in from the garden. Martin ate an enormous supper and danced with much enjoyment till the last guests had gone.

"It's been a ripping evening," he announced to such of his family as were still up. `The best birthday I've ever had. Thank you all most awfully for everything. You look rotten, Uncle John. Well, good night, everybody."

He reeled sleepily up to bed, and after gloating for a few moments on a motor cycle catalogue and making his repeater chime several times, he fell into a deep, blissful sleep.

But alas for the lilies of France! In his Belgian château the duc de Guise moaned in his sleep. A dream, unnamable, chilling the blood of royalty, stood beside his couch,, telling him in mournful accents that all was over. Of those two gallant young hearts, last hope of his cause on Albion's shore, one had let the lilies fall and turned his thoughts to motor bicycles. The other, his own namesake, had been taken home in disgrace by his mother. The omen of the unbroken glass had been fulfilled. The tricolore still flew over the Elysee.

CHAPTER XIV
GUDGEON'S HOUR

THE RAIN WHICH HAD BEGUN in the early hours of the morning continued steadily all night. The household at Rushwater woke to find the world shrouded in water, torrents pouring across the lawn, dripping from the eaves. The storm had brought no coolness to the air. Wet heat, added to the natural reaction from the night before, created an atmosphere of depression and lassitude. Martin, postponing the evil moment of getting up as long as possible, thought vaguely that he had nearly made a fool of himself last night and how jolly lucky it was on the whole that their plans had fallen through. It was all very well for French people to be royalists, but, hang it all, a man of seventeen couldn't be expected to keep up that sort of thing. And there was a bicycle in that catalogue which looked like the bicycle of his dreams. He could easily pay the deposit now and trust to luck for the monthly payments. He then made his watch chime ten several times and got up.

There was no one but John in the dining-room when he got downstairs. A disordered place at the table showed that Mr. Leslie had breakfasted at his usual time and gone out. Martin began to tell his uncle about the glories of the bicycle, but Uncle John was for once quite unsympathetic and told his nephew not to gabble so much, as he had a headache. David strolled in presently with the news that all the ladies were having breakfast in bed.

"Quite the most sensible thing to do too," he said. "I met trays of delicious food going up to them. Haddock? Oh, my God, no, not on a muggy morning like this."

He rang the bell.

"Gudgeon, is there any cold ham? Bring it along, and tell Walter to pack my things. I may be going up to town this morning."

"Oh, David," said Martin, "you can't go so soon."

"Sorry, Martin, but I've an idea about my novel and I want to see a man before he goes to America."

"But surely you aren't going to-day?" said John with such surprise in his voice that David stared at him.

"Why not? I've heaps of things to do in town."

"But you can't rush off like this," said John, almost angrily, as Gudgeon came in with the ham. "Oh, damn it, I can't discuss things with half the world listening. David, I've got to see you before you go, so let me know before you leave. I'll be in the library or the school room."

He threw his table napkin on to the floor and went out of the room.

"What's bitten Uncle John?" said Martin.

"He does look upset," said David in real concern. "I haven't seen him look so worked up for years. Well, thank goodness Dodo and the twins have gone and taken that toadstool Holt with them. Shirts and things all right, Martin?"

"Yes, rather, David, they are stupendous."

"Oh, Martin, I rather want to see Joan before I go. Are you going down to the vicarage to-day?"

"No, thank goodness. It's a day off. But I can ring them up if you like."

"No, don't bother. I'll do something about it later. Perhaps I won't go till the afternoon."

As he spoke, three mackintoshed figures passed along the terrace and knocked at the french window. Martin jumped up and opened it a little way.

"I say, you'll make the place in an awful mess if you come in this way," he remarked hospitably. "Better go round to the front door."

Miss Stevenson, Ursule and Jean Claude resumed their journey, and shortly appeared in the dining-room. "Come and have some breakfast," said Martin. "We had ours ages ago," said Miss Stevenson, sitting down.

"Yes, please, Martin," said Ursule. "Haddock, how lovely. And hot scones."

She collected a substantial meal round her and sat down with a satisfied expression.

"Can we talk alone?" said Jean Claude to Martin.

"Well, yes, if you really want to," said Martin, not relishing the prospect of fresh royalist activities, or recriminations about last night's unfortunate débâche. "Come along to the schoolroom."

"Well, Joan," said David, "it was nice of you to come up this morning, or I'd have had to come down to you. I wanted to talk to you particularly."

"So did I, David."

"What about Ursule?" asked David in a low voice.

"Oh, she's all right," said Miss Stevenson, gazing with some pride at her protégée's appetite. "Besides, all I have to say is for anyone to hear. I don't believe in concealments and secrecy. A girl should have the chance of knowing everything. An intelligent discussion of our present relationship will probably be of great value to Ursule."

David was not a little alarmed by this portentous opening. He found Joan extremely attractive, and what was more she might still be very useful, but the word relationship had a sinister sound.

"Well, I wanted to talk to you, Joan, about this broadcasting work. I shall probably be dramatizing my novel as a radio play, and I want to get into touch with the right people. I count on you to help me. We'll be seeing a lot of each other this autumn I expect."

"If you approach me as a friend, David, I will do what I can. Officially, of course, my hands are tied. You let me down over that poetry reading, and I had a lot of trouble about it."

"Oh, I say, Joan, I'm frightfully sorry. I'd no idea," said David, taking her hand. "Forgive me."

"Honey, please," said Ursule. David shoved it across to her with his disengaged hand.

"It is curious," said Miss Stevenson, "how much pleasure bne can get from a man holding one's hand, or even putting his arm round one, when any further intimacy would be, frankly, repellent."

For perhaps the first time in his life David was entirely at a loss. Miss Stevenson made no effort to withdraw her hand; he could not quite tell whether her remark was an invitation to him to put his arm round her waist; to remove his hand after what she had said would be almost discourteous. So he sat in some embarrassment. Joan certainly looked her best in the morning. Lots of girls looked washed out the morning after a dance, but Joan was fresh and neat in her silk frock, and if it were a question of putting one's arm round people, why, it would be as much pleasure to him as it would be to her. So he did it.

"Thank you, David," said Miss Stevenson, pleased but apparently unmoved. "You are really the perfect friend. I thought at one time that you might be more, but I decided against it. We are not the type for harmonious relationships. So it is hopeless for you to try."

"But I never asked you," expostulated David, in the voice of a cross child, and withdrawing his arm from Miss Stevenson's waist. "Really, Joan, you are preposterous."

"Not at all. Marriage may or may not have been in your mind, that is indifferent to me, but it was inevitable that you should ask me to live with you, so I am sparing you pain by telling you at once that I could never consider it. It would be a great mistake for both of us."

"But, good Lord, Joan, I don't go about living with people."

"It is that or marriage for you," said Miss Stevenson, looking at him with scientific detachment. "However, that is nothing to do with me. Now we have settled that subject we will return to our own affairs. If you really keen on radio plays, you had better go and see Lionel."

"Lionel Harvest?"

"Precisely. Lionel is now in that department and will go far. As a matter of fact, I came to tell you that Lionel and I are going to enter into a companionate marriage."

"Can I have a peach?" asked Ursule.

"Help yourself, Ursule, they are on the sideboard," said Miss Stevenson kindly. "I know that my ideas are very old-fashioned in some ways, but I still cling to the belief that companionate marriage is in many ways the best solution of our problem. It will, of course, be a legal companionate marriage."

"Legal?" said David, his world rocking about him. "I don't understand."

"Broadcasting House have certain prejudices which, as loyal employees, we are bound to respect. So we shall be married at a registrar's office quite soon. I shall invite you. But the marriage will be, in its essence, purely cornpanionate. Lionel and I have been thinking it over all this summer, and I had some news by chance yesterday which decided me definitely."

Miss Stevenson coloured slightly and becomingly.

"Well," said David, recovering his poise, "all the best of luck, and I'm delighted. I'll look Lionel up as soon as I get back to town. But I may be going to South America. I don't know."

"Well, good-bye, my dear," said Miss Stevenson, clasping David's hand. "And I may say now that as a mere question of emotion, there are, frankly, many men that I would care less to live with than you, but our types would make it impossible. Come along, Ursule."

"And take some biscuits in case you are hungry on the way home," said David, pressing a plateful on Ursule.

"Thank you," said she, putting them into her coat pocket.

David let the ladies out by the french window and went off to find John. He was really anxious about his brother's haggard appearance, and also wanted to let off steam to him. It was intensely mortifying to be turned down by a girl to whom you would never have had the faintest idea of proposing, honourably or otherwise. Also, from his knowledge of Joan and her world, he thought it more than probable that she would tell all her friends exactly what she had done, and everyone would laugh at him. The idea of being laughed at by Lionel Harvest was peculiarly repulsive, and David felt a strong urge to go straight up to town and kick Lionel, without telling him why. But as for marrying Joan, why, one would as soon think of marrying Mary, dear little thing.

He tried the schoolroom, but only found Martin and Jean Claude, having a delightful talk about motor bicycles. To Martin's great relief, Jean Claude had come to tell him that the royalists were disbanded. Professor Boulle, having suspected a little of what was going on, had spoken to Pierre and Jean Claude on the subject of keeping one's ideal in one's heart and not making it too cheap. Pierre, revelling in the pangs of unrecognized love, had shut himself up with his books, and Ursule was only interested in her food and Miss Stevenson. Jean Claude, still in the depths of disgrace with his mother, had come to seek refuge with Martin, and was delighted to find his comrade as ready as he was to ignore the scene of the preceding night.

"Seen John anywhere?" asked David.

"No. I say, David, do look at this Rover model."

"Sorry, Martin, I'm busy. I'll look at it another time."

"You must bring your auto bicycle to France next Easter," said Jean Claude, "and we will make excursions. I shall sit behind and you will conduct. The French roads are much better than the English roads for going fast. The French roads are, in fact, recognized as the best roads—"

David shut the door and went to the library. Here he found John sitting hunched up in a chair, looking at the unlighted fire.

"I say, you do look rotten," said David. "What's up?"

"Nothing. David, don't go to town to-day. I'm clearing out myself."

"Just as you like, but I don't know if I'm going or not. I want to see father first. I think I shall do as he wants and take on that job at Buenos Aires for a bit."

"Buenos Aires?"

"Yes, you know, that land father wanted me to look after. It wouldn't be bad fun for a year or so."

"This is all very sudden," said John perplexed. If David was going to marry Mary, why go to South America? Or perhaps it would be their honeymoon.

"You may well say so. I only made up my mind about five minutes ago."

"I suppose you'll get married before you go," said John, Carefully keeping his voice steady.

"Married? But why? Does one have to get married to go to the Argentine? But I didn't know how near being married I was. You know Joan Stevenson."

John looked up, surprised.

David poured into his brother's half-incredulous ears his account of Miss Stevenson's visit, her calm assumption of his passion, her cool rejection of a suit which it had never occurred to him to press, and final mortification, that he was sure she would make a story that everyone would laugh over for weeks.

"So I think I'll clear out for the present," said David. "I can work on my novel on the boat. If I weren't an English gentle-man, John, I'd say a few hearty words about Joan. Marry her. Why, I'd as soon think of marrying Mary."

"Look here, David, this is serious. Don't joke. Haven't you asked Mary to marry you?"

"Good Lord, no. She's a dear girl and a splendid walker, but not a girl I'd ask to marry me. That's a thing I'd be serious about."

"But," said John, getting up and going over to the window, "I was in the garden last night."

"Were you? So was I, but I don't see what that has to do with it."

"Look here, David," said his brother, still with his back to him, "you and Mary were near the summerhouse about mid-night. I was walking about and I saw you. So I went away at once. I've been waiting to congratulate you."

"My dear old ass," said David, flinging his arm round his brother's shoulders, "did you think we were taking things seriously?"

"I damn well did."

"Don't tell me you minded," said David, on whom the true state of things was just beginning to dawn.

"Of course I did," said John, prowling up and down the room, "but I wasn't going to stand in your way."

"You great footling ass," said David affectionately, "I suppose you want to marry Mary yourself."

"Of course I do."

"Well, why not then? Father and Macpherson will be delighted, and mother and Agnes will cry. It's all perfect. Come along and let's find her."

"Wait a moment, David. Are you sure she doesn't care for you?"

"Oh, do stop being quixotic, John. Whether she cares for me or not, I'm not going to marry the girl, and that's flat. As for last night—bless your innocent heart, that wasn't a rapturous embrace. It was only a small moonlight madness. They all get it. Come on."

Full of enthusiasm at this fresh turn of affairs, David dragged his brother from the room.

A quarter of an hour earlier Mary and Agnes were in the nursery playing with the children, while Nannie and Ivy were busy in the night nursery. Agnes looked lovely and placid as ever in spite of her late night, but Mary was a washed-out wreck. Ashamed, frightened, exultant, remorseful by turns, she had not slept at all. David's embrace had been a pinnacle of rapture, but what were the consequences to be? It was a question that she dared not ask herself. In vain did she try to read aloud to Emniy. The most drivelling adventures of Hobo-Gobo and the fairy Joybell were unable to hold her attention. Her voice quavered and she began to cry.

"What is the matter, Mary dear?" asked Agnes.

"Come and take Clarissa on your lap and tell me all about it."

Mary obediently picked Clarissa up from the rug where she was playing and sat down near Agnes. The feeling of a fat Clarissa in her arms was certainly comforting, but it did not stem the flood of her tears.

"Now, what is it, darling?" asked Agnes again. "Is it about anybody?"

To this leading question Mary only replied by begging her aunt to promise not to tell anyone, ever, because it was so awful.

"Of course not. We won't tell anyone, will we, darling Clarissa?"

Mary then poured out an incoherent jumble of words from which her Aunt Agnes gathered that David was so wonderful, but he was so unkind, and John was so kind and always made one feel safe and comfortable. And she had been in the garden with David last night and he had kissed her on the top of her head, and did Aunt Agnes think this meant they were engaged. Because if it did she would die, because though she adored David and had thought of him a great deal and really had been quite foolish about him and still thought him frightfully good-looking, she couldn't possibly be engaged to him, it would be too awful. And she couldn't bear to think that John, who had always been such a dear to her, should think badly of her.

"But why should he?"

"Because he saw me last night. He came out from the trees onto the grass and saw us, and then he went away again."

"I wish Robert were here," said Agnes. "He would know exactly what to do. I think we had better tell John. That is much the simplest."

"Oh, Aunt Agnes, I couldn't."

"But why not? It is always much better to get things straight, and a man can always arrange things. We will come downstairs and ask him.'

"But what will he say? And what will David say? Oh dear, oh dear. Oh, how I wish Uncle Robert were here."

Agnes delivered her offspring to Ivy and took Mary to her bedroom, where she let her dabble about with some very expensive skin tonic and some special face powder, which cheered Mary up a good deal.

"And now we will go and find John and everything will be quite all right," said Agnes comfortably.

As she and Mary came into the hall, they met John and David.

"We were just looking for you, John dear," said Agnes. "Mary has been so unhappy and we thought you could help."

"I was just bringing John along to find Mary," said David. "He has been in no end of a stew and all about nothing."

There was a pause. As the principal persons in this scene remained obstinately mute, and indeed showed symptoms of backing away from their seconds, Agnes took the matter into her own hands.

"Now we will all sit down and explain," she said. "David, you were very annoying last night, and Mary is quite unhappy. She thought you wanted to marry her, and of course that upset her very much, because she didn't want to."

"My dear Agnes," said David, "I don't want to boast, but this is the second lady who has thought I wanted, to marry her this morning. I simply couldn't bear to marry anyone, so tell your client so."

"Well, you have been too naughty and unkind," said Agnes, "and Mary is quite annoyed."

At these words from the gentle Agnes, Mary was overcome with remorse.

"Don't be angry, David," she said. "It is only that I was afraid we might be engaged, which would have been dreadful. But you have been very kind really, like giving me that lovely bag and the basket of wild strawberries."

"If that's all," said David, "I shall now unmask. John was trying to do Enoch Arden this morning, and I shall now be David Garrick. Those wild strawberries, Mary, were not my thought. It was John who told me to send them."

"Oh, David, but you said—"

"I know I did. I had quite forgotten. As a matter of fact, John rang me up that day we had lunch together and said you were unhappy because I had forgotten to give you strawberries, and suggested that I should bring some down to you. So I did. The one noble action of my life was prompted by another. So there."

Mary gazed at him in silence.

"So, Agnes," he continued, "having done my best on your client's behalf, I shall now withdraw, and I think you'd better come too, as John appears to have creeping paralysis at present."

Agnes got up.

"There, Mary," she said, "I told you the best plan was to tell John."

"You and I," said David to his sister as they left the hall, "will now go up to the gallery and look over the edge at the young people. I don't intend to go to South America till I have seen this thing through.

"Are you going to South America, David? That will be very nice, because you will see Robert."

"I certainly shall, if he hasn't left before I arrive."

"If he has left you could always send him a wireless when your ships get near each other. It is so nice to get a wireless when one is on a ship. Of course Emmy and darling Clarissa will be bridesmaids and James can be a page. But David, you must be best man. You can't go to South America without being best man. Robert's best man was a very charming man in his regiment, whose name I can't remember."

"Martin can do that," said David, as they reached the gallery and leaned over the balustrade.

"So he could. And now John needn't let the Chelsea house. It will do nicely for him and Mary, so that is all very delightful. I hope Robert will be home in time for the wedding."

"Now leave Robert alone for a minute and try to concentrate, Agnes. Look at them."

John and Mary, left to themselves, became a prey to silent embarrassment. At last John, speaking with considerable difficulty, asked Mary if she could ever forgive him.

"For what?"

"For thinking what I thought last night."

"If what you thought last night is what I think it is, I expect it did look rather like that. But truly, John, it wasn't really being kissed. It was only David's chin on the top of my head. I nearly died of misery when I saw you. I wanted to explain, and I was afraid, and I never slept all night with misery."

"My poor lamb," said John. And sitting down by her on the sofa, he gathered her into a most satisfactory embrace, to the intense interest of his brother and sister in the gallery above.

Just then, Gudgeon, crossing the hall, was for once taken aback by what he saw, and uttered an exclamation.

John looked up.

"It's all right, Gudgeon," he said cheerfully. "You can carry on. Miss Preston and I are engaged.'

"I am very happy to hear it, sir," said Gudgeon. "If I may say so, Mr. John, nothing could give more satisfaction in the Room and. the Hall."

"Thanks awfully, Gudgeon. And now you might go away again like a good fellow."

But Gudgeon's hour and power were upon him. Stepping over to the gong, he took the gong-stick from its rest, gave it a few preliminary twirls, and executed such a nuptial fanfare upon his favourite instrument that the whole house rang. Mary, startled, tried to get up, but John held her firmly in her proper place. David and Agnes from above were laughing, and, in Agnes's case, crying. Mr. Leslie came out of the library.

"What the devil are you up to, Gudgeon?" he asked. At the same moment Lady Emily limped out of the morning-room.

"Is that the gong, Gudgeon?" she inquired.

"No, my lady," said Gudgeon, waving his gong-stick towards the sofa, "it is the wedding bells—in anticipation, of course, my lady."

COLOPHON

This book is being reissued as part of Moyer Bell's Angela Thirkell Series. If you are interested in Angela Thirkell, contact the Angela Thirkell Society, P.O. Box 7798, San Diego, CA 92167 or e-mail: JOINATS@aol.com

The text of this book was set in Caslon, a typeface designed by William Caslon I (1692-1766). This face designed in 1725 has gone through many incarnations. It was the mainstay of British printers for over one hundred years and remains very popular today. The version used here is Adobe Caslon. The display faces are Adobe Caslon Outline, Calligraphic 421, and Adobe Caslon.

Composed by Rhode Island Book Composition, Kingston, Rhode Island. *Wild Strawberries* was printed by Versa Press, East Peoria, Illinois on acid-free paper.